PRINCE ALI

AN ARABIAN HORSE NOVEL
WONDER HORSE BOOK ONE

VICTORIA HARDESTY
AND NANCY PEREZ

PUBLICATION
CONSULTANTS
We Believe In The Power Of Authors
PO Box 221974 Anchorage, Alaska 99522-1974
books@publicationconsultants.com—www.publicationconsultants.com

ISBN 978-1-63747-071-8
ebook ISBN 978-1-63747-072-5

Library of Congress Catalog Card Number: 2017933157

ACKNOWLEDGEMENTS

Nobody writes a book in a vacuum. There are lots of people who help. We'd like to take a minute to thank some of the people who helped us with this story.

Rebecca Gordon, Lynn Votaw, Bob Von Boeckmann and Sharon Zarogoza read several versions of this manuscript offering suggestions, questions and pointing out rough spots.

Retired Deputy Sheriff Robert Johnson of the San Bernardino County Sheriff's office helped us figure out what the Sheriff's Department would most likely do in a high profile criminal case like this.

Chris Kramer, our first reader, sent us in the opposite direction of where we were headed. We are so thankful she did. Her observations laid the foundation for this book and several more in the same category.

Our husbands, Michael Naquin and Ray Perez, supported us and held back the myriad of interruptions that occur daily in the average household.

Rebecca Goodrich suggested a publishing company for us with an excellent recommendation. She also provided tough love and guidance when we could no longer see the forest for the trees.

Lastly, our friends and families who put up with the "crazy writer" in their midst and encouraged us to keep at it.

CHAPTER ONE

C aroline Howard knocked softly on her daughter's bedroom door at 1:05 a.m. "Becky, it's time. The baby is coming."

Eight-year-old Becky threw her covers off in a flash. Fully dressed in a sweatshirt, pants, and socks, Becky's heart pounded with excitement as she swung her legs off the bed and into her boots. She reached for her jacket at the foot of the bed, pulling her jacket over one arm. She rushed to the door pulling the other sleeve of her jacket on. She threw the door open and charged out, making a right turn down the hallway toward the kitchen, nearly running into her Dad.

"Hey, slow your roll, young lady," Walter Howard laughed. "We have plenty of time."

Walter had been through this many times. Walter and Caroline bred Arabian horses for years. Most of them were textbook deliveries. Spirit, their best mare, had two foals before this one.

Becky had been too young to go to the barn for those foals. This one, however, was different. Becky decided this foal was hers right from the start. She wanted a horse of her own. She went to the breeding farm with her parents when they picked Spirit up after the vet confirmed she was pregnant. Becky knew Spirit well. She was the first horse Becky rode, but Spirit was her mom's horse. Walter and Caroline showed Becky the stallion who fathered Spirit's foal. Becky fell in love with him at first sight. He was gorgeous to look at, but he was also sweet and kind. He took treats from Becky's tiny hand with a gentleness not often seen in stallions.

Becky spent most of Spirit's pregnancy trying out names for "her" horse. She finally settled on Prince Ali. When her parents reminded her the foal could be female, she told them she knew better. Spirit's foal was a boy! She was adamant about that. Prince Ali was his name. And he was going to be as handsome as his father, and just as nice too!

Becky went to bed every night for two weeks wearing her clothes so she could get to the barn quickly when Fernando, the Howard's barn manager, let them know the birth was imminent. Now Becky was so filled with excitement to see her new horse, she nearly vibrated.

Walter and Caroline laughed to themselves as they tried to calm their daughter down before heading to the barn. "You will have to be very quiet when we get there. You don't want to disturb Spirit, you know. We can all watch through the window between the feed room and the foaling stall until she delivers her baby."

Frustrated with the pace of her parents, Becky turned around and faced them. "I know, Mom and Dad. I won't disturb Spirit. I want to get there, so I don't miss anything. I want to be the first one to see my Prince Ali."

"Come on, kiddo," Caroline said as she slipped her arm around her daughter's shoulder. "Let's go see if you've been right all along. I don't want to name a poor little filly Prince Ali."

"Mom, I told you. He's a boy. Wait and see!"

Walter and Caroline grinned at each other over Becky's head as they marched through the kitchen, mudroom, back patio, and into the barn area. Inside the barn, a dim light glowed from the feed room and guided the trio. First, Fernando pushed the folding cot he'd been using for the past several nights into a corner to allow more room at the window between the feed room and the foaling stall. Next, he flipped a bucket upside down for Becky to stand on so she could see through the window.

Fernando told Walter, "She started pacing about 11:30 tonight. I kept an eye on her, and she broke her water just before I came to get you. She is down now and in labor. The baby will be here soon."

"Thank you, Fernando, for keeping watch for us. When this is over, I want you to go home and sleep for a while. Take tomorrow off."

"Señor Walter, I sleep pretty good on the cot. But, my wife will appreciate you. I haven't been home much for the past couple of weeks."

"I see feet! Mom, Dad, I see feet! Prince Ali is coming," Becky whispered a little too loud in her excitement.

"Sshhh, let's not make too much noise," her mother cautioned. "Keep your eyes on that. Pretty soon, you will see the nose."

Becky concentrated on what the mare was doing in the stall beyond the window. She held her breath as the mare had a sudden, violent contraction. Then, as the mare relaxed, Becky was almost vibrating again. "Mom, Dad, isn't that the head I see?"

"Yes, kiddo, that's the baby's head. Keep watching. It won't be long now," Caroline whispered. "Stand still on that bucket, or you're going to fall off." She giggled under her breath.

Spirit had two more strong contractions in a row as she strained to push her new baby into the world. The foal's shoulders finally passed through the birth canal, and the mare heaved a groan of relief. She relaxed her head and shoulders and lay still in the straw bedding that filled the stall. She inhaled deeply. The hard part was over. The baby slid into the straw behind its mother. Fernando slipped quietly into the foaling stall and removed the membrane over the foal's face. The baby lifted its head and took a deep breath. Fernando removed the rest of the membrane covering the baby. The foal flopped its head around, struggling to turn over on its stomach.

The new baby was dark in color from the tips of its ears to its feet. Short curly hair tumbled down the back of its neck and between its ears. Yet, in the soft light, it looked more black than anything. The only feature that differed was the four-pointed star of white hairs centered on its forehead above its eyes.

While Spirit relaxed for a few minutes, Walter, Caroline, and Becky slipped into the foaling stall and sat in the straw with their backs to the wall. They all pulled their knees up and wrapped them with their arms while they laid their chins on their knees and watched the new baby.

"What color is he, Mom?" Becky finally whispered.

"I'm not sure yet," Caroline said. "If he's bay, he should have beige-colored legs from the knee down to his hooves. This baby has black legs. We might not know for sure until he dries off. We can check his eyelids. If he has white hairs there, he'll be gray like his father."

"Are gray babies all born dark like this one?" Becky wanted to know.

"Not all, but most of them," Caroline whispered back. "Some are born red, like the chestnut mare we have. When they turn gray, they almost look pink for a while when they still have red hairs mixed with the white ones."

"Really? Mom, we can't have a pink boy! That would be dumb," Becky whispered.

"Well, I've seen one or two. I've also seen blue ones. If they are born black, sometimes they grow up with black hairs mixed with white, so they look blue."

"Well, he looks black right now. We don't want a pink baby, but a blue one wouldn't be bad since it is a boy," she said thoughtfully.

"Let's let this one dry out a bit and let his mother get to know him. We'll know for sure if it's a boy or a girl in a few minutes," Caroline said.

The trio sat back and watched. Spirit rested briefly, then turned herself around toward her new baby. She began bathing it with her tongue. She licked the little face and cleaned its ears. The mare finally stood up to reach all of the baby and continued with her tongue bath. She finished her initial washing and laid down next to her baby for a rest.

Fernando and Walter crawled on hands and knees through the straw to the newborn and looked him over. Walter looked under the tail and grinned at his wife. "She's right! It's a boy."

He then looked closely at the baby's eyelids. "I see gray hairs. He'll be gray when he grows up," he announced.

Becky was beside herself. "Prince Ali! Prince Ali! See, I told you so! And, he's mine!" She was squirming with joy. "My Prince Ali! I knew it! I knew it all along!"

Caroline threw her arm around Becky's shoulders. "Okay, I'll give it to you this time. You were right. But wishing doesn't always make it happen. I'm glad it did this time. He's a pretty baby. He's going to grow up to be a handsome horse. Let's hope he gets his father's disposition."

"When do I get to ride him?" Becky pleaded.

Caroline shook her head. "He hasn't even stood up yet, silly girl. He has to be three years old before you ride him, you know. You are eight years old right now. When you are eleven years old, he will be three years old. That's the soonest you can ride him. Okay?"

Under her breath, Becky gasped, "Three years! That's a long time to wait. I hope Prince Ali is worth waiting that long."

Caroline stifled a laugh. "Three years will go by faster than you think."

Fernando and Walter completed the initial examination of the new baby. Ali was squirming around in the straw, trying to figure out what to do with those long legs sticking out in front of him. The two men gently dipped the end of his umbilical cord in antiseptic solution to prevent infection and sat down to watch him try to get to his feet. Ali got his hind feet under his body and struggled to get up on legs that resembled stilts. He tumbled over in the straw but kept trying. His mother stood up beside him and encouraged him. He looked at her legs and tried to imitate them with more success. He finally stood without wobbling too much and squealed with delight. Becky squealed and laughed at him.

"Mom, doesn't he sound like a little pig? That squeal is adorable," she said.

Walter smiled over Becky's head at Caroline. "Actually, I think he sounds just like you," he said.

"Oh, Daddy, I'm not a little pig either!" Becky retorted. "I don't ever think I looked as cute as he does."

Walter held his daughter close with one arm around her shoulders. "Well, you never saw yourself at this age. I thought you were the most beautiful, cutest, sweetest little thing I'd ever seen in my life. I fell in love with you right then and there, even though you were all wrinkly and red and crying as loud as you could."

"Oh, Daddy," Becky spat, never taking her eyes off the baby horse in front of her. She giggled. "Was I really all red and wrinkly?"

"Scouts Honor," Walter said as he hugged her close. "But, I thought you were the most beautiful thing I'd ever seen, next to your mother, of course."

Suddenly, Ali tried to take a step forward. He was looking intently at Becky. He fell right over on his nose. He snorted and got to his feet again. He took another step forward before falling over sideways this time. He flopped himself around and got up again. He took two steps toward Becky before stumbling and falling. Something was glinting in the low light that fascinated him. He had to see what that was. He struggled until he was standing right in front of Becky. He stared at her then stretched his neck in her direction. He grabbed a piece of whatever was glinting in the light and tugged on it. It was Becky's long blonde hair. The baby's actions surprised her, and the tug on her hair hurt a little. She squealed.

Prince Ali was startled by the sound and fell over again. Whatever that was he put his mouth on tasted funny. Ali wasn't sure he liked it. All of a sudden, Ali wanted something but didn't know what or where to get it. He got back to his feet and walked toward his mother. She stood still as Ali searched her side, beginning at her neck. He wasn't finding what he sought. He was starting to get frustrated. Walter's eyes met Fernando's, and the two men got to their feet to give the colt a hand. With one on each side of Prince Ali, the two men helped him find Spirit's milk bag. He latched on immediately and began nursing. He made little squealing sounds between slurps of his mother's milk. The humans in the barn were having a hard time not laughing. Ali nursed until his hunger was satisfied. Finally, he looked straight at Becky and flopped down in the straw, closed his eyes, and went to sleep.

"That poor little one is tired. So am I. I think it's time to call it a night," Walter said. "I'll have the vet out in the morning to look him over. We should get some sleep ourselves."

Becky got up slowly and reluctantly. It was the middle of the night, and she was tired. But she could have sat there watching the new baby for hours. He'd completely stolen her heart. She loved him. She knew he would be her best friend forever.

CHAPTER TWO

C aroline Howard had no trouble finding her daughter from the night of Ali's birth. Then, if she needed Becky for any reason, all she had to do was check in the barn. Becky spent every waking minute with her new horse. On weekdays, she rushed to the barn in her pajamas to say "Good Morning" to him, and ran back to say "Goodbye" before Esperanza, her Nanny, took her to school. She stopped in the barn first thing on arriving home from school and spent the balance of the afternoon in the barn after she changed out of her school clothes. Then, Caroline had to retrieve her from the barn for dinner and once again at bedtime.

Becky and Ali developed a special greeting for each other. Becky always wrapped her arms around his neck and gave him a hug the minute she stepped into his stall. It became easier as Ali grew. He used his neck to press her body close to him. He held her, and reached for her pony tail with his mouth. He didn't chew on it, he simply held it in his mouth. There were times, if she'd interruped his mealtime, that he slobbered green goo in her hair. Sometimes he added bits of hay at the same time. She laughed as she pulled bits of hay out of her hair, but it was a special greeting they reserved only for each other.

Becky insisted she would teach Prince Ali how to lead. When Fernando walked Spirit to the turnout for exercise, Becky haltered

Ali and led him out behind his mother. She haltered and led him back to the barn when Fernando brought the mare back inside for dinner.

Walter and Caroline Howard evaluated their new foal a day after his birth. They were impressed with the baby, from the tip of his nose to the end of his tail. They thought Prince Ali might be the best Arabian foal they'd ever seen. However, they knew many owners felt the same way about their foals, so they kept their opinion to themselves. Becky thought he was the most beautiful horse on the planet, but she would have thought that if he was a "plug nag" because he was "her horse."

The Howards took several photos of the baby and sent them to the owners of the stallion. They were impressed with the foal as well. They drove from Paso Robles to San Juan Capistrano to see Prince Ali a week later. Walter and Caroline were surprised. It was 270 miles and took close to five hours each way.

When they arrived, Prince Ali was in the turnout with his mother. The two couples stood side by side at the rail, watching the baby run around and play.

"He's the best baby our stallion has produced," the wife told Walter and Caroline. "I can't wait to see him grow up. If he looks as good as I think he will, you have a National Champion on your hands."

"You think so?" Caroline mused. "I rode his mother to my first national title. We hoped for a good baby from that breeding."

"He's pretty young, but look at his conformation. I can't find any flaws. He's also got one other characteristic I'm surprised to see in one so young."

"What are you talking about?" Caroline asked, perplexed.

"Open your eyes and take a good look at that baby. He has charisma. He has charm. He has that "Look At Me" attitude. He catches you with his eyes. He makes you want to look at him! Believe me, if he keeps that attitude, the judges won't miss him. They'll all be looking at him!"

"You think so?" Caroline asked in surprise.

"Yes, I know so," the stallion owner said. "This is the best baby our stallion has sired, and he's been breeding mares for ten years now. Your mare and our stallion are perfect together. We need to do this again."

The Breeder's wife explained, "He's got that "X" factor that will push him right to the top. You're going to need a good trainer, one that won't be harsh with him. You want to let that "X" factor shine."

Walter and Caroline talked about the Breeder's visit later that evening. Since Prince Ali was born at the end of January, they wouldn't need a trainer for him for most of the year. They decided to put off any decisions until September. If Prince Ali still looked this good then, they would take videos of him. Caroline would put together a list of potential trainers they could send a copy of the video. They would make a decision later that year. In the meantime, Becky could have her best friend at home to play with as he grew.

Becky lived and breathed Prince Ali. At school, all she talked about was her new horse. At home, she spent every waking minute she could with him. She informed her mother that Prince Ali was her "very best-est friend."

Walter mentioned his missing daughter one evening. Caroline told him she was in the barn with her horse. Walter asked, "How long is this going to go on?"

Caroline shook her head, "I remember my first horse. I was crazy for that gelding. I spent as much time as I could with him, at first. Then the newness wore off a little. I spent more time on my homework assignments and watched a little TV before bedtime. This is just a phase. It will wear off. Give it time."

Two months later, the newness still hadn't worn off for Becky. Prince Ali hated the days she went to school. He was obedient and easy to handle, but the sparkle left his eyes when she was missing. Caroline and Fernando both noticed. When Espi, what everyone called the nanny Esperanza, brought Becky home from school, they both swore the horse could hear the sound of Espi's car a block away. Ali's ears pricked up, and he stood eagerly at the fence, waiting for her to get out of the car.

When school let out for the year, Becky still spent every day she could with Ali. He was weaned by that time, so Becky taught him about baths and taking trail walks on the bridle path behind the Howard's property. She pointed out the squirrels, rabbits, lizards, and birds they saw on the trail. Other riders used the trail, so Becky taught him trail courtesy by stepping back to allow riders to pass them.

Fernando replaced some old fencing along the back of the property. Becky begged him for a couple of fence posts she could use to teach Ali to jump in the arena. Fernando made sure to pull all the nails out first. Becky led Ali to the posts lying in the dirt and hopped over them first. Ali followed her. That sent Becky into gales of giggles as she exclaimed they were already jumping together.

Caroline began to spend more time on the patio watching Becky and Ali playing together. It was like having two children who enjoyed each other. She also noticed that Prince Ali, even though he was a baby and much younger than Becky, outweighed her but was very careful not to hurt Becky. She saw him fall over to avoid crashing into Becky and thought it was just a single event until she saw him do it a second time. She realized Prince Ali knew he was bigger than Becky and could hurt her, but would do anything he could to avoid that, even if it meant getting hurt himself.

Caroline bought a large ball so Becky could teach him how to play soccer, horse style, as well. After that, Becky's only time in the house was for breakfast, lunch, and dinner. She ate quickly, so she didn't miss a single minute with her Ali. Caroline had to retrieve her from the barn when it was time for bed.

On Becky's first day back at school in September, Walter and Caroline looked Prince Ali over carefully. He'd grown a lot. He was beginning to gray out, and the gray color suited him. They took new pictures of him and sent them to the Breeder, along with a short video of him trotting around the arena. Caroline got a call back from them that evening.

"Get him ready for Scottsdale in February! He's going to blow their socks off!" the Breeder said enthusiastically. "That colt has the moves to go with everything. He's going to win you a National Championship!"

They talked about possible trainers for Prince Ali. One that was on the shortlist for the Breeder was also on Caroline's list. Chris O'Neal took over the training business his father and mother started. He went to school in California, at Cal Poly in Pomona, with Caroline and Walter, and married Sharon, a woman Caroline showed with as a teenager. His training barn was doing very well at the local, regional, and national levels. Chris was also known for his kindness with his training horses.

Walter and Caroline talked about it after Becky went to bed that night. "I remember Chris and his wife, Sharon. If I was going to pick a trainer for Prince Ali, that's who I'd pick. The only problem with him is his location. He took over his Dad's business, and they live outside of Boulder, Colorado. Becky will have a fit if she can't see her horse every day. How will she react when we tell her that her horse will be several states away from her? That's a conversation I'm dreading," Caroline admitted.

"I want the best trainer we can get. I want someone who will be kind to our horse and still get the most out of him. The location will be a problem, but that's probably the best for the horse. It's something that will not make our daughter happy. Why don't we get a professional out to do a short video? We can send it to Chris and see what he thinks. Then, depending on what he has to say, we can cross that bridge when we get there," Walter suggested.

CHAPTER THREE

C aroline had a short video of Prince Ali made that week and requested several copies of it. She sent one to Chris and Sharon O'Neal in Colorado with a brief note enclosed. Sharon O'Neal found it in the mail three days later. She read the message and set the disc aside for Chris to see when he got a chance. Chris put it on the coffee table in the living room and forgot about it for several days. Sharon reminded him.

After dinner that night, Chris picked up the disc and plugged it into the DVD player, and sat back to watch it from the couch. The first thing he saw was Prince Ali staring right at him as if he were in the same room with him. That caught his undivided attention. Then Prince Ali spun around and trotted down the white rail fencing of the Howard's arena. Chris caught his breath. He watched the balance of the video; fortunately, it was a short one, without breathing at all. He reran the video, and again, and again. Finally, he called Sharon into the living room, and they watched the video together one final time. When the video started, Chris said, "Look at that! He's looking right at the person holding the camera. If horses could smile, he's doing it. It looks like he's looking right at me!" The video changed to the shots of Prince Ali trotting down the rail in the arena. "Now, look at that trot! His foreleg is above level! Notice how he's still watching the cameraman. It looks like he's watching us! I've never seen a horse draw you in like that. He has charisma by the bucketful. He likes to be watched, and he's showing off!" Chris and Sharon watched the video to the end, and Chris reluctantly shut the DVD player off.

"Can you get me a plane ticket to Orange County, California by the weekend?" he asked his wife. "I'll need a rental car while you're at it. But, first, I'd better call the Howards and see if they are going to be home."

Chris dashed off to their home office and looked up the phone number. He dialed the phone and impatiently waited for someone to answer it.

Caroline was walking down the hallway with her arms loaded. She'd been shopping for more new school clothes for Becky. She was on her way to Becky's room when she heard the phone ring. She stopped in her office, dropped the packages in a chair, moved around the desk, and picked up the phone a little out of breath.

"Hello," she answered

"Hello. Caroline? Caroline Howard?"

"Yes, that's me."

"Caroline, this is Chris O'Neal."

"Oh, Hi, Chris. You wouldn't be calling about the video I sent you, would you?"

"I sure am. Are you going to be home this weekend? I'd love to fly over and see your Prince Ali in person."

Caroline's eyebrows climbed a bit on her forehead. "Really? You want to come here to see him?"

"Absolutely. That is if it's okay with you and Walter. I can fly over on the first flight Saturday morning from Denver."

"As far as I know, we don't have any plans, or at least nothing I can't put off to another time. We'd love to see you and let you see our boy."

"Perfect. Then it's a date. I'll have Sharon call you with the details. I'll rent a car, so I'll need directions to your place from the airport. Can you recommend a good hotel nearby? I may have to stay over until Sunday."

"Chris, if you are flying in to see our boy, you don't need a hotel. We'd love you to stay here as our guest," Caroline said.

"That will be great! I haven't seen you two in quite a while. It will be fun catching up," Chris told her. He finally began calming himself down. He was afraid they'd already decided to take Prince Ali to another trainer. He wasn't getting that impression from this phone call. He breathed a sigh of relief as he hung up the phone.

Chris caught up with Sharon as she walked toward the kitchen to clean up the dishes. He hugged her, picked her up, and swung her around. "I can't believe it!" he said. "This could be our ticket! They haven't put him with a trainer yet. He might just be the one! He might be my "one-in-a-lifetime horse!" He could be the one that makes our training program famous! Keep your fingers crossed. Please call Caroline and tell her when my flight arrives and get directions to their place for me? Please rent me a car too. This is going to be a long week just waiting for Saturday."

Saturday did finally come. Chris got up at 2:00 a.m. to pack for the weekend. Sharon made the two-hour drive to the Denver airport to drop him off. He was early but couldn't sit still. He paced up and down the concourse waiting for his flight to board. He was too excited to nap during the flight. After landing, he rushed to the car rental counter and picked up his rental car. Traffic was light early Saturday morning, so he arrived at the Howard's home before 10:00 a.m.

Earlier that morning, Caroline told Becky a trainer would be at their house that Saturday to see Prince Ali. Becky took it on herself to get him bathed and groomed right after he finished his breakfast. She walked him on the bridle trail until he was completely dry, then put him back in his stall so he wouldn't lay down and roll in the arena and get himself all dirty again before the trainer arrived.

Becky was in Prince Ali's stall, chatting away when Chris O'Neal arrived. Caroline met him at the front door and showed him to the barn. Before getting to Prince Ali's stall, she showed Ali's mother, Spirit, to Chris and Spirit's two previous babies.

Caroline looked in the stall. "Becky, can you bring Ali out here? This is Chris O'Neal. He wants to take a look at him."

Becky jumped up, dusted the bedding off her jeans, and quickly put Ali's halter on him. Then, she pushed the stall door open and walked Ali into the breezeway aisle. Next, she picked up the body brush and dusted Ali off again with the brush.

"Why don't you take him outside to your arena? I'd love to see how he moves," Chris suggested.

Prince Ali knew there was something different about this man. He didn't know what it was; it was just different. He looked at him differently, but he seemed kind, so Ali was not disturbed by him at all. When Becky took his halter off in the arena, Ali was ready for some exercise. He also had someone new watching him, so he put on a show. He trotted his biggest trot, threw his head around, snorted and blew like a stallion. His tail flipped completely over his back, and his knees were pulled above level in his excitement to show off for a stranger.

Chris took it all in with his eyes wide open, not missing a single thing. Ali finally wound down and stopped in the center of the arena. He looked straight at Chris as if he dared him to look away. Chris couldn't take his eyes off Prince Ali! He watched in wonder. It took him a few minutes before he could open his mouth.

Chris finally looked at Caroline. "He is spectacular! If he looks this good at home, where he is relaxed and comfortable, I can hardly wait to see him in a showring. Let's talk about Scottsdale tonight. I want to play with him a little while I'm here and see how he takes to some simple training if you don't mind."

"Can I stay and watch?" Becky asked.

"Becky, maybe we should let Chris get to know Ali by himself. Why don't you and I go clean out your closet? I got you new clothes, and you have too many in your closet already. Some of those we can give to the Salvation Army or the church's clothing drive," Caroline said.

"Aww, Mom. Please let me stay with Chris and Ali," Becky pleaded. "I want to watch."

"Caroline, it would be alright with me if Becky stays to help me out. I can teach her a few things too. You never know, she might make a good amateur handler for Prince Ali," Chris suggested.

"If you're sure it's okay with you," Caroline relented. "If Becky gets in your way, we've always got a closet that needs some attention."

Becky stayed in the barn area working with Chris until her mother called them in for lunch. Esperanza made a special lunch for "company" that day. Chris was impressed. He loved food with the Mexican flavors, and Esperanza's dishes checked off all his boxes. After lunch, Walter came home from his office and joined Caroline and Chris on the patio for a discussion.

"I'm impressed with Prince Ali," Chris began. "His conformation is very correct, he is easy to work with, and he has the show attitude that will get him to the top. I'd love to be his trainer. I want to be his trainer. I'm excited you are thinking of me as his trainer!"

"What would you do with him? How would you plan his future if we decide to put him with you?" Walter asked.

"My first thought would be Scottsdale next year in February. As a yearling, I'm convinced he will do well in the showring. He has a "want to please you" attitude, so he's easy to work with. Ali's also a show-off. He likes the attention. In the past, the babies I've worked with go through their "ugly" period between four and nine months of age. He's seven months old now, right? If this is his "ugly period, I don't see that at all.

"What do you mean by the "ugly" period?" Caroline asked.

"When foals are in their rapid growth period during their first year, some of them get gangly looking, with their butt higher than their withers or their withers higher than their butt, their neck looks too short, their legs too long. They don't look like they're put together correctly for a while," Chris chuckled. "Your Ali is in that period right now, but I don't see "ugly" anywhere on him. On the contrary, I think he's spectacular from every angle."

"Do you think there's a chance he could go through the "uglies" later? Walter asked

"No. If he hasn't by now, he's only going to get better. We have plenty of time to get him ready for Scottsdale. The rest depends on how he does there. If he does as well as I think he will, we could end the year at the Nationals in the Futurity and maybe get some of your money back," Chris chuckled again.

"I'd like to get my laptop and go over the financial arrangements if you don't mind," Walter suggested. He got up and walked inside to the office for it and returned. "I'm the finance man here, so let's go over the details."

The Howards and Chris O'Neal went over estimated costs for training and showing the young colt for the next hour. Walter created a spreadsheet with the numbers. He totaled everything up. "Wow, that's quite a bit for a yearling's first year," Walter commented when he saw the numbers.

"Remember, much of what we talked about is going to depend on how he shows at Scottsdale. We can pick and choose between some of the other shows we talked about. I wouldn't want to drag that poor horse to every show in the country as a baby. We can finalize the plan after the show in Arizona."

"That sounds sensible to me," Walter admitted. "We know how Ali is here at home, but we don't know how he'll be in a strange place with a lot of strangers around."

"When do you need us to get him to your facility if we plan on Scottsdale?" Caroline asked. "Taking him that far is going to be rough for Becky. She's attached at the hip to that horse, you know."

"Yes, I saw that before lunch," Chris admitted. "He doesn't need a lot of time to get ready for a halter class in February. If you plan to bring him yourselves, why don't we plan for the week after Christmas? Then, you can stay with us a few days before you head back to California. I know Sharon would love that, and my son, Todd, can keep Becky company. He's nine this year, so they're only a few months apart in age."

Walter sat and sipped his iced tea, thinking for a few minutes. Finally, he looked at his wife and nodded. "I think we should do this. I believe it is the right thing for the horse. I know it's going to be rough on Becky, but she'll get over it. We'll all go to Scottsdale to see Ali again. That's only a month and a half. We can decide more after we see how he does in Arizona. Are you with me on this?"

Caroline nodded in agreement. Walter reached his right hand out to Chris and said, "You are officially our trainer." Chris took the hand and let his breath out. He didn't realize he'd been holding it. "I'm pleased as heck to be Prince Ali's trainer!"

With the business settled, the adults sat on the patio and chatted. They swapped stories about their time in college and their lives since. Chris told the Howards about the passing of his parents and taking over the facility he helped them build. Espi brought out a fresh pitcher of iced tea and some nibbly snacks. Caroline introduced her to Chris as Becky's nanny before lunch. He finally asked about her. "You call her the nanny, but she made the most incredible lunch today, and now these snacks too. I can smell something wonderful every time your kitchen door opens. Do nanny's cook too?"

Caroline laughed. "Espi is much more than a nanny. We hired her when Becky was two days old. My parents were gone by then, and Walter's parents lived in Florida. I had a full-time job with an attorney's office at the time, and Walter worked for an architectural firm in Orange County. So we needed a nanny, and I needed someone to show me how to care for my baby before going back to work. We hired Espi. She's a widow with no family of her own, except for siblings that live close. She's part of our family now. She took over the housekeeping, cooking and takes care of Becky for us. I can't imagine how we'd get along without her. I quit my job when Becky was four. Walter started his own firm a year earlier, and it took off. But Walter and I have gotten very involved with our community here in San Juan Capistrano. I volunteer a lot for the Women's Groups and the J. F. Shea Therapeutic Riding Center. Walter has his business and is involved with the Rotary Club and City and County politics. When we built this home, we included a private suite for her. That way, Espi can always live with us."

"I bet Sharon would love to find someone like Espi. She takes care of the books for our business, helps train some of the horses, and manages the horse shows besides getting Todd to and from school. She's a busy woman. I'll suggest that to her when I get home," Chris said. "Maybe Espi has a clone in Colorado?"

Sunday morning, Chris had coffee on the back patio with Walter and Caroline. They continued their conversation about Prince Ali. "I need to get back home. If I stay here much longer, I won't fit in my show clothes," Chris laughed. "I can't thank you enough for your hospitality. Espi's cooking is terrific, but I overate again last night."

After coffee, Chris went to the barn and haltered Prince Ali. He brought him into the barn aisle and went over the few things they worked on the previous day. Chris was pleased Ali remembered and did what he asked. He stroked the young colt and praised him. "You are going to be a Champion, Ali. Remember that. I'll see you in December." Then, Chris left for the airport and spent the entire flight thinking about the handsome young colt in San Juan Capistrano. He knew, without a doubt, everyone in America would learn about him and remember him.

CHAPTER FOUR

The Sunday morning Chris left California was busy for the Howards. Caroline had several projects for the Parade Committee she worked on, and Walter went back to his office for several projects he needed to finish. Becky spent the day with Prince Ali. Over dinner that night, she asked her parents about Chris O'Neal. "Is he going to be Ali's trainer?" she wanted to know.

"Yes, dear. We've decided to put Ali in training with Chris so he can show him at the Scottsdale Show next February," Caroline explained.

"Oh, that's exciting! I can hardly wait," Becky exclaimed. Then she thought about it for a few minutes, and her heart sank. "Does that mean Ali has to go to Chris's house?"

"Yes, it does," Caroline answered. "We will all take him there the week after Christmas. That's several months away."

"Can I still see him every day?" Becky's heart pounded.

Walter looked at his daughter. He could see the tears forming in her eyes. He wanted to be as gentle with the news as possible. "No, Becky. You won't be able to see him every day. Chris needs time with him alone to get him ready, and Chris lives too far away for you to see Ali every day like you do now."

"Daddy, he's my best friend! What am I going to do without him?" The tears overflowed and streamed down Becky's cheeks.

Caroline's eyes met Walter's. She looked at Becky. "Honey, he will be here until after Christmas. That's still a long time. Why don't you enjoy him and stop worrying for right now."

"But, Mom, Ali is my best friend!" Becky choked out.

"Honey, we know that. But Ali needs to go to school sort of like you do. He needs to learn how to be a showhorse. Ali can't learn that here at home. But we promise you that we'll take you to every show he goes to so you can spend time with him there.

Becky excused herself from the table and rushed off to her room. She threw herself on the bed and cried herself to sleep.

For the next couple of months, Becky tried to ignore the fact Ali would be leaving home after Christmas. She spent as much time with him as her parents allowed. Finally, she asked her mom to show her where Chris lived on a map. Caroline pulled an Atlas out and showed Becky Boulder, Colorado, on the map.

"That doesn't look so far, Mom," Becky said as she studied the map. "We could practically walk there."

Caroline chuckled under her breath. "Not really, Honey. We have to cross California, then Utah, then most of Colorado to get there. It will take us 14 to 16 hours to drive there with Ali in the trailer. I don't think we can walk him over to Chris's house."

"Are we going to drive him there and leave?" Becky asked as tears formed again.

"No, Honey. We will get up early and drive him there, and then we will spend a couple of days in Colorado at Chris's house. Chris has a son about your age. You can get to know Todd while we're there."

"Mom, Todd's a boy! I don't like boys. I'd rather be with girls. Are you and Dad going to stick me with a boy I don't even know for a couple of days?" Becky asked with a grim expression.

"Well, I heard from Chris that Todd likes horses the same way you like horses, so you have something in common right off. I also heard from Chris that Todd is an excellent gamer. You are too. So you have two things in common. Why don't you give him a chance? You might like him."

Becky rolled her eyes. "If I have to… ."

Caroline had a hard time suppressing her laugh. "Well, you do!"

Weeks flew by. Becky put off thinking about leaving Ali so far from home until the first day of December. Her dread grew as Christmas came closer and closer. Christmas gifts that year included new snow clothes for the trip to Colorado. Caroline kept in touch with Sharon O'Neal, so she knew there was plenty of snow at the ranch that year. Becky was puzzled by the new waterproof jacket, gloves, pants, and sweaters among her gifts at first. When she mentioned it, her mom explained, "There's plenty of snow at Clearwater Creek Ranch this year. You're going to need them, or you'll freeze to death in Colorado."

Becky remembered they were leaving with Ali in the morning. It brought fresh tears to her eyes. She didn't want her parents thinking she didn't like her gifts, so she wiped them away quickly. Then, she concentrated on the excitement of the trip. She finished her packing by 2:00 p.m. that afternoon. She spent the balance of the day in the barn with Prince Ali.

"Mom, are you sure Ali will be okay in the trailer by himself?" Becky asked as Walter pulled out of their driveway at 5:00 a.m. the following day.

"Yes, I'm sure. Remember, we've taken Ali on several rides in the trailer to get him used to the idea. He'll be fine. We'll stop to check his feed and water. We're going to cross a lot of desert in California and Nevada before we get to the Rocky Mountains in Colorado. We need to stop to eat too, and we'll need gas for the truck. You can check in on him every time we stop, okay?"

Becky snuggled down on the back seat of the truck and fell asleep for a couple of hours. She woke at the first rest stop Walter pulled into. Becky hopped out of the truck and hurried to the escape door on the side of the trailer. She pulled it open and hopped in. Prince Ali whinnied at her. She checked his water bucket, which was still nearly full, and his haynet, which was almost empty. "Mom, Dad, we need some more hay in here," she shouted.

Walter brought another flake of hay from the truck bed and helped Becky re-fill the haynet. Then, all three of them had a short restroom break before resuming the trip.

Walter exited the highway and drove the truck through the gate at Clearwater Creek Ranch at 8:30 p.m. that night. It was freezing cold and snowing. Caroline called Sharon from the highway so she and Chris could show Walter where to park the rig near the barn to offload Prince Ali. Chris used a flashlight to point Walter in the right direction. Once Walter switched off the engine, Becky hopped out of the truck and back into the trailer through the escape door. She hugged her horse and told him he was at his new school. Chris O'Neal would be his teacher. She told him she wanted him to learn a lot to show in Scottsdale in a month and a half. She promised him she would be there to see him then.

Walter and Chris opened the rear door of the trailer and stepped inside. "Wow, he's grown quite a bit since September!" Chris remarked. "He sure looks good. Let's get him out of here. I have a heavier blanket ready for him. He'll need it in this weather."

Becky stood back and watched the two men unload Prince Ali and walk him into the barn aisle where Sharon stood holding the heavier blanket. She and Chris pulled it on Ali over the lighter-weight blanket he wore at home in San Juan Capistrano. Chris then walked Ali to a fresh stall in the barn and latched the door when he came out, holding Ali's halter and lead rope in his hand.

"How did he do on the trip? Did he eat and drink well?" Chris asked.

"Yes, he did great with the trip. He ate and drank water all the way here," Walter told him. "He was good in the trailer."

"Well, let's get you inside, then," Chris said. "We'll help with your bags. Sharon has two guest rooms all ready for you. Are you hungry?"

"No, we stopped for dinner before we got to Denver. We're good, just tired. I'm looking forward to sleeping," Walter laughed.

The six of them grabbed the bags from the trailer's tack room, where Walter stashed them in Grand Junction. Caroline told him about the snow forecast, so they moved the luggage out of the truck bed then. The snowfall at Clearwater Creek Ranch was light, with an accumulation of only six inches. Everyone took off their shoes and boots in the mud-room before hauling the baggage into the O'Neal's home.

Chris lead the way through the expansive kitchen/dining room and the great room to the stairway along the far wall. "Your rooms are up here," he said as he hoisted one bag on his shoulder and began the climb. He turned left down a corridor on the second floor and stopped at the first door. "This room is for Becky," he said as he opened the door. The charming room had a dormer window facing east and an attached bathroom, double bed, and dresser. Todd set down one of Becky's suitcases. "My room is next door. Just knock if you need anything," he told Becky as the rest of the group moved further down the corridor. Chris opened the door of the second guest room and set the bag he was carrying down inside. "This is your room for the next couple of days," he told Walter and Caroline. "The bathroom is that first door," he pointed, "and the second door is the closet. Make yourselves at home. Sharon usually has the coffee ready by 6:30 in the morning. But you can sleep in after that drive if you want. I have to get things started in the barn by 7:00 a.m. Goodnight." Chris stepped out of the room, pulling the door shut behind him. He walked back to the kitchen with Sharon. "How about something cold to drink?" he asked her. While Sharon put ice in two tall glasses, he asked her, "What did you think of Prince Ali?"

"I didn't get to see much of him, but what I did see, I liked," she answered. "He's got size on his side, he has a beautiful face, long and shapely neck, and his legs look great from what I could see below the blankets. I see what you mean about his charm. He does catch you with his eyes, doesn't he?"

"Yeah, he does. Let's hope that still works at Scottsdale. If it does, the judges won't be able to take their eyes off him!"

The next morning, Todd wandered down to the barn before breakfast. He'd knocked on Becky's door. She didn't answer, so he assumed she was still asleep. He walked over to Prince Ali's stall. The feed crew was still at the other end of the barn feeding horses. He didn't see Ali over the half wall either. He peeked in the stall. He saw Prince Ali lying on his side, fast asleep. Becky was beside him, also fast asleep. He was surprised. He whispered loudly, "Becky, wake up! You shouldn't be doing that."

Prince Ali startled at the sound. His eyes flew open, and he lifted his neck to look around. He nudged Becky with his nose to wake her. Then, he nickered softly to her. Becky's eyes flew open, and she sat upright, embarrassed to be caught sleeping in the stall.

"You shouldn't do that, you know," Todd said again. "You could get hurt if someone startles your horse."

"What do you know?" Becky snapped back. "I've been napping with my horse since he was born."

"Yeah, but he's not so little anymore! My Dad would have a cow if he caught you in that stall sleeping with your horse."

"You aren't going to tell him, are you?" Becky pleaded.

"Nope. Just be careful and don't do that if he can catch you," Todd suggested. "I'm not a tattle-tale!"

Becky stood up and dusted herself off, pulling stray pieces of wood shavings out of her hair. She opened the stall door and walked into the aisle next to Todd. "He's my best friend, you know. I don't know how I will get along at home without him. Would you please keep an eye on him for me? Maybe you could call me after school every day and let me know how he's doing?" The tears were forming in her eyes again. Todd was a little embarrassed by her show of emotion, but he understood it.

"Maybe, if my phone works in his stall, I can video call you so he can see you and you can see him. Would that help?"

Becky sniffled and wiped her eyes dry. "Todd, would you really do that for me? Yes, that would be wonderful. I can't tell you how much it would mean to me. Thank you so much!"

"Yeah," Todd said. It was such a little thing. He just had to figure out when she got home from school and what time it was in Colorado so they could get the timing right. "Easy Peasy," he thought. "How about we get back to the house. My mom is making breakfast, and I'm starving!"

Becky's hunger pangs started right then. She felt hungry too. As they walked back to the house, she looked at Todd sideways so he wouldn't know she was looking at him. He wasn't a bad-looking boy, she thought. He seemed nice too. He'd impressed her with his offer to call her from Ali's stall. Maybe these next few days wouldn't be so bad after all, even if he was a boy.

CHAPTER FIVE

L ater that afternoon, Todd asked her if she wanted to play computer games with him. It was freezing outside, so the idea sounded good to her. Todd's playroom adjoined the Great Room in the O'Neal house. Sharon and Chris had sense enough to close it off from the Great Room with glass so they could keep an eye on Todd and his friends when they played, but it reduced the racket in the rest of the house.

Becky and her parents had time to look around the house that morning. The Great Room faced the Eastern slopes of the Rocky Mountains, separated by acres of pastures and arenas for working and turning horses out. The view was spectacular through the 24 foot high windows in that room. The house was, per Becky, a log cabin on steroids. The front of the house had a large covered driveway so Sharon could unload her groceries and not get soaked with rain or snow. Massive 12 foot high double doors stood at the front entrance. They were custom built with elk, deer, mountain lions, and bears in a mountain scene carved in them. The flagstone paved foyer led to the Great Room with its huge windows and a lovely patio area on the outside. The Great Room showed exposed beams and cross beams. Two large chandeliers of elk antlers hung high above the seating space. A gigantic rock fireplace occupied one wall, with the staircase to the second floor tucking behind it. The second floor had dormer windows from every room, including the Master Suite, that looked to the east and caught the first rays of the sun each morning. The furnishings in the home were Western Rustic in nature, with a few western antiques thrown in here and there. It was comfortable and casual.

The kitchen and dining room of the house were open to the Great Room as well. Sharon explained they'd redone the kitchen a few years ago and knocked down the walls that separated it and the dining room. The dining table was large enough to seat at least 12 people for dinner. Chris's Dad had it made from trees he cut down to open up the western pastures.

Besides the Western-style artwork on the walls, Chris and Sharon hung their favorite photos of horses Chris trained. Their Win-Photos lined the hallways. On the ground floor, underneath the upstairs bedrooms, was a complete second apartment with two bedrooms. When they first got married, Chris and Sharon lived there and moved back to Colorado to help Chris's Dad and Mom. It was furnished but empty at the moment.

After Becky and Caroline took their tour of the house, Becky told her mom, "I'd love to live in a house like this someday. This house is neat."

"Don't you like our home?" Caroline asked. She loved their more formal Spanish Colonial home in San Juan Capistrano.

"Yes, sure. But we can't watch TV in the living room. That's just for company. We have to go to our bedrooms or the family room to do that. I like this "everyone" room best."

Todd led Becky to his game room. It had six gamer chairs sitting around a large screen. He pulled out a box of games and asked Becky to pick one. She shuffled through the chest and didn't find a single game she had ever played before. She told Todd that.

"Well, be prepared then," Todd said. "My Dad loves to play with my friends and me. He taught me the strategy for each game so that I could beat my friends. Be prepared to lose!" he laughed.

"I guess you don't know my Dad also taught me. He also likes to win. I wouldn't be so sure I'd win if I were you. I'm wicked good," Becky laughed.

Becky selected a game and handed it to Todd. He plugged it into the machine, sat down in one of the chairs, and picked the game control unit up. He showed her some of the steps needed to score, and the two competitors were off and running. Todd was surprised at how quickly Becky picked up on the game and how fast she accumulated points. In the end, Todd only bested her by two lousy points. He was shocked. It was the first time she played the game, and she was that close to winning it.

He picked another game, one he usually won. Becky stuck right with him and nearly beat him again. Then it really became fun! The competition was closely matched. Both of them had the skills to win. Todd had to work extra hard to stay ahead of Becky. He developed serious new respect for her. When she beat him on the very next game, Todd was surprised and tried to tell himself he let her win, but finally conceded she won the game fair and square. He went all in and beat Becky in the next three games in a row, barely. She was on his heels the entire time. He had to concentrate hard to get ahead of her and stay there. But, the harder he worked to beat her, the better he liked her. She was always a good sport about losing. "Next time, I'll get you!" was her stock answer. She didn't get mad as one of his friends did. She didn't accuse him of cheating like another friend usually did. Instead, she conceded the loss and promised to give him a run for his money the next time. And, she didn't puff up about it when she won. She began winning the games as often as he did, and the two kids laughed and laughed. They had the time of their lives.

Beck and Todd stopped playing games when Sharon called them to the table for dinner that night. After dinner, Todd got up and began clearing the table. Becky jumped up and helped him. Both of them were a little short to stand at the kitchen sink and wash pots and pans, but they scraped plates and loaded them in the dishwasher for Sharon.

Becky wanted to go back to the barn to say goodnight to Prince Ali, so Todd took her into the mudroom, where they tugged jackets, boots, and gloves on before walking outside. Once they got halfway to the barn, Becky stopped in her tracks and looked around. There was a little light on over the mudroom door. There were lights on the sign for Clearwater Creek Ranch by the highway. There was a light on over the barn entrance. Other than those, there were no lights within view except overhead. The storm the Howards arrived in blew off to the east. So the sky above the two kids was clear and filled with millions of stars.

Becky was amazed. She stared at the stars, unable to speak for a few minutes. "Is it always like this here?" she asked Todd.

"Lots of times it is," Todd answered as he stared at the night sky. "The only time we don't see stars like this is when the clouds cover them up, and it rains or snows or gets ready to. Don't you have stars in California?"

Becky, her head still tipped back for the best view, muttered, "Yes, we have stars, but not like this. This is amazing!"

"I've been with Dad and Mom at lots of horse shows in lots of places. There's one other thing here, besides the stars, that you only get here. Close your eyes and take a deep breath. Tell me what you smell."

Becky closed her eyes and sucked in a lungful of air, letting it out slowly. "Wow! I see what you mean. I smell cold. I smell clean. I smell the woodsmoke from the fireplace. I smell snow. I smell pine trees. It all smells wonderful! The pine smell reminds me of Christmas!"

"It's funny, but you don't smell anything like this in Boulder or Denver. So I think you have to get way out of town to smell this and see the stars like tonight," Todd said.

"I could stand right here and look at the stars and smell this wonderful place, but my feet are getting cold," Becky finally said. "Maybe we should get into the barn and get out of the snow for a few minutes."

The two kids hurried inside the barn and walked down the aisle to Prince Ali's stall. Ali nickered at them as they opened his stall door and stepped inside. Becky threw her arms around Ali's neck and squeezed him. He was covered in blankets and a hood, so she couldn't scratch his withers for him. She stole a carrot from the refrigerator in the house and offered him a nibble of that. He happily crunched on it while he pushed his nose into the front of her jacket.

Becky looked down at her jacket. "Oh, you big silly!" she exclaimed. "You have to keep your carrot slobber to yourself," she laughed as she brushed it off her jacket front.

"My dad sure thinks a lot of your horse," Todd told her. "He was pretty excited when he came back from your house in September. Your horse sure is a pretty one."

"I think he is handsome. Only girls are pretty. Boys are handsome but thank you for telling me that. Did you happen to bring your phone with you? Maybe we could check to see if you get enough signal to call me?"

"I was one step ahead of you," Todd answered as he pulled his cell phone from his jacket pocket. "I need to get your cell number plugged in here too," he said. He switched the phone on and looked at the signal. "We got enough signal for the calls. We won't know if we have enough for video until we try it, but at least we know I can call you."

While Becky hugged her horse and fed him carrot bits, Todd programmed Becky's home and cell numbers into his phone. When he finished, he said, "Guess we should be heading back to the house. It's getting late, and the days start early here on the ranch."

The following two days included horseback rides on the property with Todd's and Becky's fathers going along. The youngsters rode Chris's "dead-broke" lesson horses to get them out of the barn for a while. Todd and Becky also spent time playing games in Todd's game room until Becky won at least half the time. Caroline helped Sharon fix breakfast, lunch, and dinner and had time to catch up since their days of showing horses together. Finally, Todd and Becky dragged their Dads outside to the large patio beyond the great room for snowman building and a snowball fight to top that off. Todd and Becky also spent a lot of time in Prince Ali's stall with him at Becky's request.

At the end of the final day, Becky couldn't sleep well, despite being physically tired from all the activities. She knew she and her parents were leaving Colorado the following day, and she wouldn't be able to see her horse for a month and a half. She cried herself to sleep.

Becky got up before first light and packed her bags for the trip home. When she finished and set her bags beside the door, she slipped out of her room and quietly down the stairs. Becky walked in stocking feet to the mudroom, pulled on her parka, boots, and gloves before slipping out the back door. She walked across the covered patio to the walkway to the barn. As she stepped down onto the walkway, the first rays of dawn peeked over the eastern side of the ranch.

The barn sat north of the house. When Becky took her second step, she glanced around. She caught her breath. Dawn colored the mountains to the west in a pallet of pastels ranging from pale blue-gray to rosy pink and golden orange. A few puffy clouds floated above the mountain tops and shared the delightful palette with the snow-capped peaks. Becky stared in wonder at this early morning display. She shut her eyes to seal the image in her brain. As she did, she breathed deeply of the cold air. She noticed the spice of pine and wood smoke she enjoyed before, although it was different at this time of day. She opened her eyes again and realized she could see her breath in the cold morning air. She giggled to herself. "I sure hope we get to come back here," she said before striding on toward the barn.

Becky slipped into Ali's stall and threw her arms around his neck. Tears flowed. She could no longer speak. When she finally got herself under control, Ali's hood was soaked with her tears. He nickered softly at her. She sat along the wall and told him how much she would miss seeing him every day. Ali laid down beside her and stretched out on his side. She laid down along his neck and back, put her head on his neck. She hugged him and fell asleep again.

Todd found her 45 minutes later. "Psst, Becky! Wake up! Dad's coming to the barn to check on the feed crew. You can't let him find you sleeping in here with Ali."

Becky sat upright, tears threatening again. Todd reached out his hand and helped her to her feet. When Ali was sure Becky and Todd were clear of him, he stood up and shook the bedding off his blanket. Becky brushed her jacket down and pulled bits of shavings out of her hair too. "Thanks for getting here first," she told Todd. "I don't want to get your Dad upset with me. I'm going to miss Ali so much. I had to have just one more visit with him."

"Your parents are getting packed. My mom is making breakfast before you leave. Let's get back to the house. I promise I will call you from Ali's stall every day if I can." Todd said as he opened the stall door and stepped into the barn aisle. Becky followed him and closed the stall door behind herself.

"Oh, there you are!" Chris said as he walked into the barn. "I think your mom is looking for you," he told Becky. "I think you two are needed to set the table for breakfast," he told Todd. Then, Chris walked to the back of the barn to check on the feed crew.

"Wow," Todd said. "That was close!"

"Yeah, Thanks," Becky mumbled as the two walked back to the house.

Becky went through the motions over breakfast, picked at her food, and didn't eat much. She also didn't have much to say to anyone. When the time came to load the luggage up and leave for home, she made one final dash into the barn to say goodbye to Prince Ali. She climbed in the back seat of the truck holding tears back until the truck reached the highway. Becky pulled blankets up to her chin before laying down and crying herself to sleep. She slept much of the way home.

CHAPTER SIX

B ecky spent most of the first week home from Colorado in her bedroom. She didn't go to the barn one time. She attended school but didn't participate much at all. She didn't interact with her school friends either. When Espi brought her home from school, she waited in her room for "the call."

Todd, as promised, took his cell phone to the barn and called Becky every day from inside Prince Ali's stall. When the weather was clear enough, he turned on the video option so Becky could see her horse and talk to Todd at the same time.

Prince Ali heard Becky's voice over the phone and whinnied back to her, brushing the phone's back with his nose while Todd desperately tried to keep from dropping it. "My Mom is going to kill me if your horse makes me drop this and crack the screen again," he complained to Becky. "Mom and Dad had to get me a new phone for Christmas because my old one was so cracked I could hardly use it anymore."

Becky immediately chided Ali, "Now don't you make him drop his phone. I don't want you to get in trouble while you are there."

"Aw, he's not in trouble. My Dad really likes him. He says he's doing better than any of his yearlings have ever done in training. Dad thinks he's going to kill it in Scottsdale!"

"Are you going to Scottsdale?"

"Oh, ya!" Todd grinned. "My parents are both going, and they can't leave me at home alone, you know. Besides, I'm trying to learn from my Dad. I plan to be there to see how Prince Ali does in the showring. You're coming too, aren't you?"

"Of course!" Becky said. "I want to see my horse. He's my best friend, you know. I miss him." Becky's voice cracked, and tears formed in her eyes.

"Don't you go crying on me," Todd chided Becky. "Wait until you see how beautiful he looks in Dad's new show halter. He got it just for him. Ali is turning gray early, so Dad got one with a lot of silver on it. It looks wonderful on him."

"Can you show me?" Becky asked.

"No. My Dad will scalp me if I mess around in his show tack. That's off-limits, but I can tell you that you will love it when you see it."

Becky and Todd spent nearly an hour together every day on the phone. At first, they only talked about Prince Ali, but they began talking about school, other games they wanted to play, and people in their circle of friends. Within a couple of weeks, they began to look forward to the phone calls and became good friends.

The month and a half flew by. Becky came home from school the day before their departure for Arizona, quaking with excitement. She ran to her room and began packing her bag for the week's stay in Scottsdale. She was going to spend nine days with her horse and her other best friend, Todd.

Becky came to the dinner table that night buzzing with excitement. "I talked to Todd. He and his parents got to Scottsdale yesterday. Todd says it is cold at night but not as cold as where they live. He says most of the stalls are decorated and pretty now. The big trainers have their top horses there for this show. Several of them have seen Ali. Todd says they think he's great! His Dad says he's going to do well at this show.

I can't wait to see him. It will be so nice to have him back home."

"What do you mean by that?" Caroline asked her daughter.

"You told me he was going to be in training until Scottsdale. I figure we get to bring him home now, don't we?" Becky said with dread in her heart. She got through the days knowing her horse would be home after the big show in Arizona. From her mom's look, now she wasn't so sure.

Walter furrowed his brow before speaking. "You're right. We never said anything about what happens after Scottsdale. I know it is a big deal to you to have Prince Ali home so you can see him every day. But, Becky, if he does well, we want to continue showing him this year. If we do that, he'll have to stay with Chris O'Neal in Colorado. You want him to do well, don't you?"

Becky sat at the table, stunned. She hadn't considered what would happen next with her horse. She assumed he would come home. Her eyes filled with tears again. "Yes, I want him to do well," she choked out. "But, I miss him."

"I will make you a promise. If Prince Ali does well this time and your Mother and I decide to leave him with Chris in Colorado for a while, you will go to every show he does. We will take you, even if we have to fly, so you can see him and spend time with him."

The tears finally escaped Becky's eyelids and rolled silently down her cheeks. She nodded her head in agreement with her father and sat quietly with her hands in her lap for a few minutes.

"I'm not very hungry, Mom. Can I be excused?" Becky finally asked.

"Sure, I'll come and talk to you in a minute," Caroline said to her daughter as she looked questioningly at her husband.

As soon as Walter and Caroline heard Becky's bedroom door shut, Caroline looked at Walter. "I guess we should have prepared her for that. I didn't think to."

"Neither did I," Walter said. "But, Caroline, he's a horse. We spent a pretty penny buying his mother in the first place, not to mention what we spent to get her in foal. Becky is just going to have to understand."

"I know," Caroline said. "I remember getting attached to a gelding my parents bred one time. He was my best friend too. I showed him in the junior classes and had a lot of fun with him. I referred to him as my horse, just like Becky refers to Ali as hers. But my parents sold him one day. Someone offered a good price, and they took it. I was devastated. It was their business, and they sold an asset. I didn't understand. I do now. I don't want her to feel the way I did when that happened."

"We're not selling him. He has potential as a breeding stallion. We need to show him to make that a possibility for us." Walter said.

"Sure, I know, but I think Becky is a little too young to understand that. Ali is too young for that as well. I don't want to sell that horse out from under our daughter. I'll talk to her tonight," Caroline said. "In the meantime, I need to get our things packed. Didn't you want to get on the road early in the morning?"

The Howards arrived at the Scottsdale Show Grounds the afternoon before the show officially started. When Becky and her parents arrived at Coldwater Creek Ranch's stalls, Prince Ali squealed with delight when he spotted Becky. She rushed to him and threw her arms around his neck. He grabbed her ponytail in his mouth and held it as she hugged him.

People packed the vendor booths looking at all things "horse" available at the show. The food booths offered everything from deep-fried candy bars to smoked turkey legs. Becky insisted on an enormous bag of Kettle Corn. She and Todd walked around the barns looking at the beautiful decorations and the gorgeous horses there for the show.

"Are you sure my Ali is going show well against all that competition?" Becky asked him.

"Wait until you see him when my Dad and Mom get through with him. You won't ask that question again. He's a good solid yearling. I've seen a couple of others here. He's better than they are." Todd told her.

The morning of Prince Ali's first class, Becky insisted she be at the showgrounds with him as Chris got him ready. Becky helped bathe Ali and walked him back to the barn so Chris and Sharon could finish grooming him. Ali was calm during all the preparations. Becky was a nervous wreck. Sharon suggested Todd and Becky get some breakfast at one of the food vendors to get them out of the way while she and Chris worked with Ali. Becky and Todd walked back to their stalls just as Chris led Prince Ali out of the grooming stall. Ali didn't notice the kids at first. He was paying attention to Chris as Chris asked him to stand up and show himself in preparation for what he would do in the showring. Prince Ali stepped into the proper pose. He stood with his front feet side by side, one back foot slightly behind the other, lifted his tail slightly, elevated his neck, and pointed his eyes and ears directly at Chris.

Becky caught her breath. She'd never seen Ali look that way. His grooming was show perfect, down to the hoof polish on his hooves. Chris's new show halter on him gleamed in the early morning light and emphasized the silver hairs in his coat. He didn't look like a foal any longer. He wasn't a baby horse at all. And he was beautiful!

Chris was pleased! Ali looked like everything he thought he would. He lowered the lead so Ali could relax and walked over to pet him and stroke his neck. An older woman who happened to be walking past the barns as Chris was asking Ali to stand up for him stopped to watch. She stepped closer, her eyes never left Prince Ali, as she asked, "Who is this magnificent colt?"

Becky heard the woman. Before Chris could answer, she said, "This is Prince Ali, and he is my best friend."

Chris stepped toward the woman and stretched out his right hand. "Hi, I'm Chris O'Neal, Ali's trainer. I'm showing him in the Yearling Colts class in a few minutes."

The woman took Chris's hand in her's. Caroline and Walter Howard heard her introduce herself to Chris before they could walk over to where they stood with Ali. She was one of the movers and shakers in the Arabian breed and had been an important influence for more than 50 years. The Howards were stunned. They introduced themselves to the woman as Prince Ali's breeder/owners.

The woman stepped back. "I'd better get over and find a seat. This is one class I don't want to miss. I've not seen a better yearling colt in years and years."

Chris was just as excited as the Howards as they watched the woman hurry to the grandstand. "Wow! Did you hear that?" Chris whistled. "I think he's going to show well today. Keep your fingers crossed! We might have a winner here!"

Everyone at Clearwater Creek Ranch's barn hurried to the grandstands to find seats for the class. Chris patted Ali's shoulder.

"You're looking good, youngster. Let's go show them how this is done, shall we?" Chris lead Prince Ali toward the ingate to the arena. He stood waiting for the class to open. He stroked Ali's neck to reassure him as he struggled to get his own emotions under control. What if Ali refuses to stand for the judges? What if Ali refuses to trot around the arena? What if the judges don't like him? What if…..? Chris finally closed his eyes and did what his father taught him to do years ago. Chris envisioned winning. He heard the announcer call Prince Ali's number as the winner of the class. He saw himself taking Prince Ali on his victory pass at Ali's high floating trot while the spectators clapped and cheered.

When he opened his eyes again, Chris found his confidence was back. He stroked Ali's neck and told him, "We're going to win this one, my little buddy. You are going to be famous!"

The ingate opened. Chris stood in place as two young colts ahead of them entered the arena at the trot. Chris stroked Ali's neck again. "This is it! Let's give them a real show!" Chris started trotting beside Ali into the arena.

Prince Ali looked at the grandstands that surrounded the arena. People packed the seats. This was his big chance to show off for a real audience. He pushed himself into his high floating trot. Chris had to run to keep up with him. Prince Ali looked into the crowd and caught the eyes of people as he passed by. He snorted and flipped his head, holding his tail upright, so his tail streamed behind him like a flag. Ali did put on a show. And he loved every minute of it!

When his turn came to stand for the three judges, his attention was entirely on Chris. He stood like a statue. When the three judges finished walking around him to evaluate his confirmation, they asked Chris to trot his horse toward the wall, directly away from them. They watched the smoothness and balance Ali displayed in his movements, then Ali turned it up again to his high floating trot to finish his turn and get back in the lineup of yearling colts. The crowd clapped, cheered, and screamed their appreciation of Prince Ali. Ali soaked it all in and trotted bigger and higher than ever. He was thoroughly enjoying himself.

Todd and Becky were sitting in the stands by themselves. Becky's parents and Todd's mother were on the other side of the arena. When Ali came charging in, Becky's heart was in her throat. On one hand, she wanted Ali to win. On the other hand, she wanted him to lose so they could take him home. Her desire for the win overcame the other side before he was halfway around the arena. She was screaming and clapping for him as loud as the other spectators and Todd.

After reviewing all the yearling colts in the class, the three judges conferred in the center of the arena before turning in their judging cards. The staff reviewed the cards and added up the points for each horse. Then they turned in the results to the announcer. Prince Ali had scored first on all three judge's cards! The announcer called out Prince Ali's unanimous win first. Pandemonium broke out in the stands with that announcement. Everyone there agreed with the three judges and let them know that.

Chris took Prince Ali to the center of the arena for the first place presentation and winning photo. Chris helped the show staff put the rose ribbon garland around his neck and put his Championship Ribbon on his halter for the pictures. Halfway to the out-gate, Prince Ali saw Becky standing waiting for him and tugged on the lead. Ali wanted to share his win with his best friend. Chris went along and ran beside him. Becky threw her arms around her best friend and hugged him for dear life. She told him what a good boy he was and how much fun it was to watch him win. It helped make it more worthwhile for Prince Ali. He knew, without doubt, he'd made Becky proud and happy.

"Don't get too carried away," Chris told Becky. "We have to go right back in the arena in a few minutes."

Becky looked dumbfounded.

Chris explained. "Prince Ali just won the Yearling Colt class. The next class in the arena is the 2-year-old Colt class. After the judges decide in that class, the first and second place horses from the Yearling class and the 2-year-old Colt class have to go back in the arena to judge the Junior Champion Colt class. Ali has a good shot at that too!"

"Are you serious?" Becky asked. "How can a Yearling go up against a 2-year-old? Aren't they much bigger?"

"Size isn't everything," Chris explained. "Size does matter, but Ali is almost the same size as those 2-year-olds in the arena right now. He's also got something most of them don't have. He loves what he's doing, and the spectators and judges all can see that."

"How does that help Prince Ali?" Becky asked.

"Becky, Ali has something extra most horses, and most people, don't have. He has what the French call "joyeau de vive," which means "joy of life." It's hard to define, but you know it when you see it. He's a happy horse. He loves what he's doing. He's a natural show-off but in the nicest way possible. He likes the attention in a good way. I've never had a horse in training like him before. He is one of a kind. Does that help explain it?"

Becky looked puzzled. "I guess so. I know some show-offs at school. Most of us don't like them. They are the ones with the answers to the teachers' questions. They make the rest of us feel stupid because they know the answer, and we don't. That doesn't make me happy to be around them at all. Ali is different. I'm happy when I'm with him. How does that work?"

Chris smiled at her. "Becky, you got part of the answer right there. You are happy when you are with him. He helps make you feel that way. Even when he shows off, he's there to make you happy, not show you how dumb you are. See the difference? Ali makes people feel good, not bad. That's because he feels good too, and he's excited about that! It is hard to be unhappy around an animal or a person like that."

Chris took Prince Ali back into the show ring for the Junior Championship class. In a highly unusual move, all three judges agreed unanimously that Prince Ali was the Junior Champion Colt for the year, with the first place colt from the 2-year-old Colt class placed as the Reserve Champion.

The year began with red roses and blue ribbons. It was a great start.

CHAPTER SEVEN

Becky talked with her parents after the show in Scottsdale. "I know you want to show Prince Ali some more this year, so he'll stay in Colorado with Mr. O'Neal, his trainer. But, I want to spend time with him too. Todd asked me to come to Colorado for Spring Break and maybe part of Summer Break. Can you let me do that, besides going to all Ali's shows this year?"

That was a tricky question for Caroline Howard. Her daughter never spent more than one night away from home on a sleepover with one of her friends. She'd never thought about her daughter being gone for a whole week before, much less part of the summer break from school. That could be an entire month or more.

"Your Dad and I will talk about it, and I'll talk to the O'Neals. Then I will let you know. Remember, we promised you that you would be there for every show we take Ali to."

"I know, Mom." Becky began. "But I don't get to spend much time with Ali at the show. He's always in his stall keeping clean or out with Chris getting worked or bathed or groomed, or he's in a class where everyone there is watching him. He and I don't get much time together that way. I miss him."

Caroline called Sharon O'Neal later that afternoon and talked to her about Becky spending time with them in Colorado. Sharon was all for the idea. "Becky is great! I like your little girl. So, by the way, does Todd. He says she's the best gamer he knows, and he enjoys her company, even "if she's just a girl." You know kids of that age. I thought Todd would rather be roughhousing with his friends, but he insists Becky is a close friend. If you can part with her, I promise to treat her like I treat my son. They will both have chores if they want privileges."

After Becky went to bed that same night, Caroline had a conversation with Walter. He agreed with Becky. "Maybe we should let her go and spend time in Colorado. She'll learn something she can't learn here. Sharon and Chris are great parents. Look at their son. He does his chores and cleans his room without being reminded, from what I could see. They are both great riding coaches too. If Becky gets lessons from Chris, maybe she'll be able to ride Prince Ali in the shows when that time comes. Besides, it will give you some extra time off this summer so you can do things you want to do without worrying about our kid. Why don't we let her go for Spring Break and see how that works before we talk about Summer Break?"

"If we say yes to Spring Break in Colorado, how are we going to get her there? I don't want to drive her there and drive back a week later to pick her up." Caroline mused.

"I have plenty of mileage points on my American Express card. We buy three round-trip tickets to Denver. You can fly over with her, hand her off to Sharon, then fly back home. At the end of the week, you fly to Denver and pick her up and fly home with her. I think she's a little too young to fly that far by herself."

Caroline slept on it that night. She told Walter the following day she would make the arrangements. She called Sharon O'Neal and let her know as well. Over breakfast, she talked to Becky. "You can spend Spring Break with the O'Neals in Colorado. But I need you to make me a promise. You mind Sharon and Chris the same way you mind me, your Dad, and Espi, or you won't be allowed to go again. Do you understand?"

Becky jumped up from the table and rushed to her mother, throwing her arms around Caroline's neck. "Oh, thank you, Mom. I promise! I will not disappoint you or Dad. Thank you! Thank you! Thank you!!"

Spring Break in California coincided with a horse show Chris wanted to take Ali to in Denver, Colorado. Becky got to see everything from an insider's perspective. She and Todd pitched in to help load gear, horse feed, baggage, and all the other things needed for a three-day horse show. Chris and Sharon planned to stay in a local hotel, but Todd and Becky planned to sleep over on cots in the Ready Room at the fairgrounds. Becky knew that way she would have a lot more time to spend with Prince Ali. Becky thought it might be like camping out, which was something she'd never done before. One of Chris's grooms also stayed at the fairgrounds with Todd and Becky.

Chris had two horses to show the first morning. He had Prince Ali in the Yearling Colts class and a mare in the 3-Year-Old Mares class. Todd, Becky, and the groom got up early, took Ali and the mare to the wash area, and bathed them just as the sun came up that morning. They took them back to the groom rooms, dried them, and covered them in clean day sheets before Chris and Sharon arrived.

Chris and Sharon had enough extra time that morning to enjoy a cup of coffee with a donut before the classes began for the day. They decided they liked the idea of Becky spending her school vacation time with them. They set it up with Walter and Caroline to have Becky stay with them for the summer.

Several people who attended the show in Scottsdale were exhibiting in Denver that weekend. When they saw Prince Ali's name in the show program, they talked to their friends about what they saw in Scottsdale. It passed from person to person. People flocked to the seats in the grandstands before the Yearling Colt class began, hoping for a good look at the extraordinary colt from California.

Prince Ali was on his "A" game again. He didn't disappoint anyone. He gave them all a show they would remember. He won his Yearling Colt class, and the judge named him the Junior Champion Colt for the show.

During his first year of showing, Ali never placed lower than first in local and regional shows. He qualified easily for the US National Show in October. Prince Ali also won there. He won his age group class and futurity class, giving Walter and Caroline a check to put back in the bank for his next showing year. Caroline also had additional beautiful trophies to add to her trophy case.

CHAPTER EIGHT

Prince Ali began his second year of showing the same way he ended his first year – winning! Every time he put his hoof in the show ring, he came out with roses and blue ribbons.

It began where the previous year did in Scottsdale. The only difference was Ali was a year older, a bit taller, and his coat grayed out even more.

In late March, Sharon O'Neal received a large envelope in the mail. She didn't recognize the foreign address, so she set it aside and rediscovered it a week later. When she opened the mail and read through the letter enclosed, her breath caught in her throat. She dropped the letter to her desk as she flew out of the barn office looking for Chris.

Chris was in the barn aisle taking the saddle off a horse he finished working. She rushed up to him and said, "Chris, I have a letter on my desk you need to see immediately!"

Chris looked at her speculatively. "Is this good news or bad news?" he asked.

"Great!" was all she could muster in reply.

Chris called one of the grooms over to finish his horse and followed Sharon back to the barn office. She picked up the letter and packet that came with it and handed it to Chris. He got through the first two lines before he had to drop in a chair in front of her desk.

He continued reading and flipped through the packet of information before making any comments.

"Do you realize what this is?" he asked his wife.

"Yes, I think I do," Sharon answered. "What are we going to do about it?"

"We don't have much time. I'm not sure this is doable. Should we look into it before we call the Howards, or should we call them first? What do you think?"

"Let's talk to Caroline. This would be expensive, and we have to move fast. If they are interested in pursuing this, it will help if Caroline pitches in with all the paperwork and arrangements we need to make," Sharon suggested.

"Okay. Give her a call. If you put it on speakerphone, we can both talk to her about it," Chris suggested.

Sharon closed the office door before picking up the phone and dialing the Howard's number. When Caroline Howard answered the phone, Sharon told her she was putting the phone on speaker so she and Chris could both talk to her. Caroline's eyebrows climbed a bit on her forehead as she waited.

"Caroline, we got something in the mail today you need to know about. Prince Ali received an invitation to the Arabian World Championship Show in June. We don't have a lot of time to make the necessary arrangements to get him there. We want you and Walter to think about this and decide if you wish to pursue it. This show only invites 25 of the best 2-year-olds in the world to the competition. The event is at the Salon de Cheval in Paris. The prestige of winning a class at that show is beyond my comprehension. It is a celebrated international event and would give you international acclaim if your horse does well. But, we only have four days to decide whether to accept the invitation or not. They want 25 horses. If you don't want to go, they will cross Prince Ali off the list and call the next horse down on their list. If you're going to go, it must be a definite yes." Chris couldn't think of much else to say. He crossed his fingers.

Caroline didn't say a word for 30 seconds. "Whoa! That's a surprise! You say we have to give them an answer in four days? Do you have any idea how much it costs to get a horse to Paris? I'm assuming you mean Paris, France? What about passports, flights, etc.? Who goes with him? How long does he have to be out of the country? Wow! I have more questions than answers. How do we go about planning for this?" Caroline finally wound down and stopped.

Sharon spoke up, "I have a couple of friends that work for the Arabian Horse Association in Denver. I'll give them a call and call you right back. They may have suggestions for us about everything you just asked and more. Will you be home for a while?"

Caroline nodded her head as she answered, "Yes, I'll be here. I may give Walter a call just to give him a heads up on this, but we can't make a decision until we have more information. That would be his answer right at the moment," she chuckled. Caroline thought about something else that popped up in her head. "You know if we decide to send Ali and Chris to Paris, Becky is going to want to go. We did promise her she could attend all his shows, even those we had to fly her to. I will cross that bridge when I get there. Since Todd and Becky talk all the time, can I ask that you not let him know about this until we decide? Becky would be on this like white on rice and unfit to live with if we said no."

Sharon couldn't help but laugh out loud. "Yes, we'll keep this to ourselves until we get information for you. Heck, if you let Becky go, Todd will be all over it on this end to go as well. Holy Toledo! I think we have enough pressure worrying about the horse. This way Todd isn't going to bug us daily about it in the first place. Oh, the joys of parenting pre-teens!"

Sharon made her calls to Denver and got a lot of information from her friends there. She also called their vet and talked to him about it. He gave her some additional information and promised to check on any vaccination requirements he may have missed. Sharon called her travel agent about flights for Chris. Fortunately, it was early enough to take advantage of early bookings for the flights and hotel.

Chris found out how long Prince Ali had to stay in the quarantine facility before moving to the Salon de Cheval. He decided to take his best groom along. That way, one of them could stay with Ali at all times. It added costs for the trip but provided better security for Prince Ali while they were out of the country. Chris also had one more brilliant idea he discussed with his vet. If he arranged for the groom to fly with Prince Ali on the flight, it cut down the cost a bit and might help Ali because he would be traveling with someone he knew.

Chris and Sharon talked with Walter and Caroline later that evening and went over all the information they found that day. Walter wanted to sleep on it one night. The following day, he asked Caroline to call the O'Neals back and set it in motion. Prince Ali would go the Paris. He didn't want to bring Becky into the plans yet.

Sharon made up a detailed list of things to do and dates for completion. She sent a copy of Caroline. They went over it by phone and divided the tasks up. Some had to be done in Colorado because Prince Ali was there. Caroline paid for the trip for Prince Ali, Chris, and his head groom, Roberto Vega. Chris selected Roberto because he was from Canada. His mother was French-Canadian, and his father was born in Spain. He spoke English, French, and Spanish, so Chris thought he'd be the perfect one to take along and help translate for him.

In the meantime, the ranch was busy. Sharon kept track of the horses coming and going, hiring outside transporters when needed. Chris was the only trainer that worked with Prince Ali. He did the training work on all the horses but turned several over to his assistant trainers when he felt they could show the horse as well as he could. That freed him up to train additional horses or attend shows further away from their ranch.

Sharon found a transporter for Prince Ali's trip to Paris. The plane could pick Ali up at Denver's International Airport. The boxes the horses flew in were bedded deeply in shavings to protect the horses, with padded sides and thickly padded floors with drains. Several veterinarians flew with the horses in case of any emergency during the flight. She arranged for Roberto Vega to fly with Prince Ali, so he had a companion he knew instead of a stranger. Roberto was excited about it. He looked forward to flying in a plane full of horses, and he was especially fond of Prince Ali.

The O'Neals and the Howards finally told Becky and Todd. Becky was thrilled and expected to attend the show in Paris. She was disappointed when her parents told her that wouldn't happen this time. There wasn't time to plan a vacation to France. Chris was the only one going on the trip. Becky pouted a little about it, but that soon disappeared when she talked to Todd. Todd told her his Dad would be staying in a hotel close to the Salon de Cheval. Between Roberto and Chris, they split up the time. One of them would always be with Prince Ali while the other took a turn sleeping in the hotel. It didn't sound like much fun at all.

Becky was in Colorado with the O'Neals when the day came for Prince Ali to fly to Paris. She rode with Chris and Todd to the airport to send her horse off on his big adventure. Becky hugged him and told him to do well at the show. She told him she would be waiting for him when he got back. Chris, Todd, and Becky watched as Roberto walked Prince Ali up the long ramp to the loading door of the plane. Ali looked back at Becky over his shoulder before entering. Becky held her tears back until they were in the truck on their way back to Clearwater Creek Ranch.

Chris left the following morning. His flight went to New York before he changed to an international flight to Paris. When Chris arrived in Paris, he passed through customs and took a cab to the holding facility for animals. He asked the taxi to wait a few minutes for him. He struggled to make himself understood until Roberto happened to hear him and told the man at the gate who he was. The man smiled and opened the gate for Chris.

Roberto told Chris someone found him a cot to sleep on. He put it outside Ali's stall door and spent a comfortable night. He said the staff at the facility were helpful. Chris looked in on Ali and left to check-in at the hotel. Chris found one of the staff at the holding center spoke broken English. They managed to understand each other. Chris told him why he and the horse were in Paris. The guy was impressed and took another look at Prince Ali. He whistled in appreciation. Three days later, the quarantine hold on Ali lifted. A transporter arrived to pick Prince Ali up and take him to the Salon de Cheval. He and Roberto said goodbye to the staff members who were so helpful to them, climbed into the truck, and disappeared into Parisian traffic for several miles.

While Roberto stayed with Prince Ali in the horse van, Chris dashed into the building to check in and found out where their stalls were.

Neither Roberto nor Chris saw a pair of brown eyes that followed Ali through the maze of stalls to their assigned ones. One bedded stall was for Prince Ali, and the other one was the grooming room. Chris hauled all his gear into that one after checking Ali's stall and putting him in it. Roberto carried in a fresh bucket of water and put some of the feed Chris brought from home in Ali's feeder while Chris arranged his gear.

A gentleman in Arab dress appeared at the door of the grooming room. "Excuse me," the man said in English. "I would like to speak to the owner of the horse in the next stall. Would that be you?"

"No, I'm not the owner, but I am his trainer, and I can speak for the owner. What can we do to help you?" Chris looked puzzled.

The man handed Chris a business card. "My employer asked me to give this to you. He is interested in the horse."

Chris smiled and took the card from the man. He handed the man a card of his own. "I'm Chris O'Neal, the owner of Coldwater Creek Ranch in Colorado, USA."

The Arab gentleman asked, "Would you mind if my employer came over to see this young stallion of yours in about two hours?"

"I'd be honored to show Prince Ali to your employer," Chris told him. The gentleman gave a slight bow and thanked him for his time. He disappeared into the crowd of people in the barn area. Chris looked at the business card the man gave him. His employer's name was HRH, followed by a five-word name Chris couldn't figure out how to pronounce. Then it struck him. HRH?? Would that be His Royal Highness? Was the employer he referred to a Prince or a King?

Good heavens! He was dumbstruck. He didn't know what to say. He showed the card to Roberto. Roberto came to the same conclusion he had. They were expecting a visit by a member of a royal family from somewhere in the Middle East. Were they supposed to bow? He had no idea. His first thought was to make sure Prince Ali looked presentable. He grabbed brushes and combs and began working on Ali.

Two hours later, a young man stepped out of the crowd and walked toward Ali's stall. He was wearing jeans, running shoes and a polo shirt. He looked like everyone else in the barn area taking care of the horses for the show.

When he arrived at Ali's stall, he said, "Excuse me. I'd like to speak with Mr. Chris O'Neal."

Chris looked up, smiling. "I'm Chris. What can I do for you?"

"I came to see your young stallion," the man said. "One of my grooms came to see you earlier. I saw the horse when you brought him in and wanted to take a closer look. My friends call me Sameer."

"It's nice to meet you, Sameer. Why don't you come in the stall with us? You can get a closer look at Prince Ali," Chris suggested.

Sameer came into the stall and approached Prince Ali. Ali nickered to him and watched him as he looked carefully at Ali. He walked closer and stroked Ali's neck, then walked completely around him, looking at every part of him.

"He truly is magnificent!" Sameer said. "I have a colt in this competition, but I believe yours is the better of the two. Tomorrow night's competition will be exciting. How does this one move?" While he spoke, his brown eyes never left Ali.

"Beautifully!" was the only thing Chris could think of.

"Ahh, then it will be a real contest," Sameer said with a smile. "I think my colt does too. We look forward to the contest tomorrow evening."

Chris carefully prepared Ali for his class the following day. He took him out for exercise in the morning and scrubbed him within an inch of his life afterward. When Ali was completely dry, he took him back to his stall and groomed him for his class. When Ali was prepared, Chris took time to put on his clothes for the class, including the shirt and tie, polished shoes, and belt. Roberto looked him over, whisked a few light hairs off his pants, and told Chris they were both as ready as they could be.

Chris walked Ali toward the ingate to the arena and held him back as other young stallions entered the arena. He knew Ali would make an entrance, and he wanted it to have the most impact on the judges and the spectators. Chris closed his eyes and thought about their entrance and asked for some Divine Guidance and help. When the last one of 24 colts entered the arena ahead of them, he asked Ali to move forward.

Ali was excited. He'd heard the spectators around the arena, and he wanted to give them something to cheer about. He was pumped up and ready to show! The minute his hoof landed in the arena, Ali began to fly with his high floating trot. Chris had to run as fast as he could to keep up with him. Ali looked at the spectators, catching eye after eye as he flew by them. Ali knew they were looking at him, and it made his movements even more pronounced. He looked like he never touched the ground as he made the complete circuit of the arena. Spectators couldn't believe what they were seeing and began screaming and cheering him on.

When they reached the starting point and the end of the lineup of 25 colts, Ali settled down and paid attention to Chris. He also turned his head from time to time, catching the eye of spectators all around the arena. One by one, the handlers presented their colts to the judges. Some of the colts were excited and almost refused to stand still so the judging panel could walk around them. When Prince Ali's turn came, he stood as still as a statue, focused entirely on Chris, as the judges walked their circuit around him. When the judges finished evaluating Prince Ali, one of them asked Chris to trot his horse away from them toward the rail, then trot him back into his place in line. Ali exploded! It was as if he'd been holding his breath while they looked him over, and he wanted to move out. He did in his best and strongest trot back to his place in line. The arena erupted once again. Spectators shouted, screamed, and cheered him on, and the louder they became, the higher Ali trotted.

The purpose of this class was to thin the entries down from 25 to 12 for the finals in two days. Chris and Ali knew they'd done their best and relaxed a little while the judges compared notes and turned in their cards to the officials. Staff members added up the points. A list of finalists landed on the announcer's table.

After a brief pause, the announcer started calling the numbers of the colts invited to return to the final competition, where they would select the finest 2-year-old stallion in the world.

Chris held his breath as the announcer called the finalists numbers over the loudspeaker. He closed his eyes again, hoping that Ali's number would make that final call. Ali's number was the last one announced! Chris was delighted! Prince Ali made it into the finals. He couldn't wait to make the phone call home and let his wife and the Howard's know the good news. He turned Ali toward the outgate and began fighting his way back to their stalls. Crowds of spectators blocked his path. Everyone, it seemed, wanted to get a close-up look at Prince Ali. Ali was delighted. He whinnied at people and allowed anyone who wanted to pet him to do just that. It took almost an hour to get back to their stalls. Chris was exhausted by the time they got there. He pulled the halter off Ali in his stall and let him relax and eat a few nibbles Roberto put in his feeder. Chris left the stall and sat on the bench outside with a cold canned soft drink. Roberto joined him.

"That was a spectacular show Ali put on," Roberto said. "We've taken him to shows before, but I've never seen him do it like that."

"It felt good to me too," Chris said. "I'm glad we made the finals. It sure feels good to get to this point with an American-bred horse. Do you know what the odds against that are? Some of the finest Arabian breeders in the world here in Europe and the Middle East are showing against us. Some of them have more money than I can even imagine. They have the best mares and stallions in the world available to them. Do you realize they would consider Caroline and Walter Howard as "back-yard" breeders compared to them? Don't get me wrong, Caroline and Walter are thoughtful breeders, and they only breed for one or two foals per year. They struck gold with this one!"

Chris shrugged his shoulders and leaned back against the stall wall. His mind was traveling in a thousand directions at once. He closed his eyes and tried to empty his mind. He was elated and exhausted at the same time.

"Mr. Chris," the man with brown eyes stood in front of him as he spoke. Chris opened his eyes to see the man who visited Prince Ali two days ago. He wore traditional Arab clothing this time, including a jewel-encrusted dagger in his belt and the usual headgear on his head.

Chris jumped to his feet. "Your Highness, it is nice to see you again," Chris said to him.

"Please, Chris, call me Sameer. I was in the stands watching the class. I was happy my colt made the finals. But, I must have Prince Ali! I could not believe what I saw. He is magnificent in every way. I must have him. Name your price."

Chris was stunned and didn't know what to say. He stumbled for words. "Sameer, I don't think he is for sale. I'm his trainer, not his owner. His owner is a 10-year-old girl in California. I'd have to talk to her parents. I know how she feels about her horse. He is her best friend."

"Ahh, I see how that could be a problem. But my offer stands. If they name a price, I will pay it even if I ask my father for help. If they do not consider selling him, ask if they plan to syndicate him. I will buy shares!"

"I have to call them to let them know Prince Ali is in the finals. I will mention you and your offer to them. I can let you know later today," Chris said.

"Good. I am holding a celebration dinner here at the Salon de Cheval this evening. I will love to have you as my guest if you do not already have plans. It will be in the banquet hall in the next building at 7:00 pm. Are you free?"

Chris was surprised again. "Sure, I was going to bring something in from the café across the street. I'd be delighted to have dinner with you."

"Good," Sameer said. "I have many people to introduce to you. I also wanted to tell you I admire the way you handled your horse today. He was relaxed and easy with you, but when you asked him to show for you, he did. It was clear to me he likes and respects you. It is also clear to me that you like and respect him. It is the perfect relationship between trainer and horse."

Chris smiled and nodded. "Sameer, I can't take all the credit for that. Prince Ali is that kind of horse. I must also admit that little 10-year-old girl raised him well. I just showed him what I wanted him to do, and he does it."

Sameer chuckled. "I have a 10-year-old daughter myself. I must get her to the barn and see what she can teach me. I'll take my leave now. I will see you this evening." The man and one who appeared to be his bodyguard turned and melted into the crowd.

CHAPTER NINE

At dinner that night, Sameer introduced Chris to the movers and shakers of the Arabian Horse world in Europe and the Middle East. He met breeders from France, Germany, Poland, Spain, Belgium, Sweden, Great Britain, Australia, and so many members of royal families in the Middle East, his head spun. He had a pocket full of business cards from them, and he gave out nearly all the business cards he brought with him. He had no idea Prince Ali caused such a stir.

During the two hours he spent in the banquet hall, he received additional offers to purchase Prince Ali, several with spoken prices that blew him away. He also received five different offers for jobs in Europe and the Middle East. The salaries quoted were unimaginable. Everyone attending the dinner was in the stands during the semi-finals and saw Prince Ali in action. Many did pedigree research on their own and knew who his sire and dam were and their parents, grandparents, and great-grandparents. Everyone at the dinner planned to be in the stands for the finals. Most of them were betting on Prince Ali to take the prize. Chris refused to bet on that. He'd seen it before. A horse might do well in the preliminary round and fall apart in the final one. It was like a horse race. The horse everyone bet on to win could stumble at the gate and come in last place.

Chris's anxiety level increased with every minute closer the finals became. He was a nervous wreck that morning. When Chris dumped an entire bucket of freshwater into Ali's stall that morning, missing Ali's water bucket entirely, Roberto stepped in.

"Chris, you need to take a walk and get yourself together. I will get Ali ready. This is just a horse show, not an execution. Take a walk outside. Go across the street and have a pastry and a cup of coffee. Settle down and get a grip. When you get back, we'll get you into your tuxedo and get you and Ali to the arena in time."

Chris saw the wisdom. He'd never let himself get befuddled before a class at any horse show before. He needed the talking to as much as he needed some fresh air. He walked across the street and ordered a pastry and a cup of coffee. He sat at a little table outside and enjoyed the sights for 30 minutes. Chris relaxed. He knew Prince Ali would do what he was meant to do. He walked back across the street to the Salon de Cheval with a new air of confidence.

Roberto had Prince Ali groomed and ready. He helped Chris get into his tuxedo and checked him over, brushing off loose pieces of bedding and light-colored horse hairs. Roberto walked Ali out of his stall and handed the show lead to Chris. "Knock 'em dead!" he told Chris.

This time, the audience was decked out in more fur than Chris thought came from the entire state of Alaska. Diamonds and other jewels reflected off womens' necks and arms, and fingers. The shimmer and sheen from their gowns were nearly blinding. Every man dressed in formal wear. The Middle Eastern contingent wore their traditional robes and head coverings. Every horse handler in the arena wore a tuxedo, as did the judges and officials.

Prince Ali put on a show as he did in the preliminary round, with the rousing support of the audience. After the judging panel reviewed the 12 horses, time stopped for a few minutes. The judges added up the points and compared notes before turning their scores in. A few minutes of silence hovered around the arena before the loudspeaker announced the placings, starting with the 12th place horse. Chris was surprised. The call was backward. When the announcer called the number of the fourth-place horse, and it wasn't Prince Ali's number, Chris stopped breathing. That meant Ali placed third, second, or first.

The announcer called the number of the third-place horse for the Bronze Medal. It wasn't Ali. That meant he was second or first. Chris's heart stopped beating. The announcer called the number of the second-place horse for the Silver Medal. It wasn't Ali. That meant Ali had to be First! The announcer confirmed that. Prince Ali was the First Place Gold Medal winner. Chris's knees buckled, and he nearly dropped. Prince Ali seemed to understand what was happening and tugged on the lead, pulling Chris back to the "here and now." Ali wanted his prize. Chris shook his head and ran beside him as Ali trotted to the center of the arena for his ribbon. The cheering nearly deafened them both.

Chris stood beside Ali while the photographer took their win pictures before giving Prince Ali a bear-hug and wither scratch. Prince Ali looked pleased in the photographs. He did not look arrogant. He looked like he'd won and knew he deserved it and was happy with it. Chris looked elated.

As soon as Chris got Ali back to his stall, he called home and asked Sharon to put the call on speakerphone so Todd and Becky could hear. "You can tell Caroline she will have to enlarge her trophy case," he said. "Prince Ali is the best 2-Year-Old Colt in the world. He won the Gold Medal." Chris couldn't hear another thing from his wife. Becky and Todd were screaming too loud.

CHAPTER TEN

P rince Ali went on to win the National Championships in Canada and the United States in the 2-Year-Old Colt Halter classes. He took home prize money in the Futurity Class again. He also won several Junior Champion Colt classes at smaller shows in Texas, North Carolina, and Michigan.

Chris called his vet out to x-ray Ali's legs at the end of September that year. "When do you think we can start his saddle training, Doc?" Chris wanted to know.

"Looking at this," The vet pointed to the knee, hock, and fetlock joints in the x-rays, "I'd say you need to give him until October 15th before you put the weight of a saddle on him. You can use the training surcingle and long lines to start his groundwork anytime. Give him until December first before you try weight on his back at the walk. You should be able to trot and canter him by his birthday in January. His legs look good. He's healthy. You know what you're doing. I know you never push a horse too early. If you want to get him into the showring under saddle, I'd shoot for March or April."

Right after the US National Championship show, Chris began long-lining Prince Ali. He taught Ali how to wear a bridle and a smooth, broken bit in his mouth. Chris taught Ali about wearing the training surcingle around his midsection behind his withers. He tightened the cinch around his heart girth, where he would wear the cinch for a saddle in the future. Chris attached the long lines to each side of the bit. He threaded them through the eyes on each side of the surcingle so the reins were approximately where a rider's hands would hold them while riding. Chris pulled on the reins gently so Ali could feel the tug on each side of the bit in his mouth.

Prince Ali was a quick study of the whole procedure. He learned that a pull on the right rein meant a turn to the right, a pull on both reins evenly meant halt, etc. Ali loved the long-lining. He enjoyed a different kind of work and excelled with it in a few short days. As Ali got better at long-lining, Chris took him out of the arena and began walking around the ranch, using the lines to direct him where Chris wanted him to go. They began taking short trail walks along the perimeter of the ranch.

One day in early December, they took a long walk off the ranch. As they headed back, it began to snow. When Chris and Ali got back to the barn, Chris hugged him. "Buddy, you are going to have to start wearing a saddle soon. That wasn't bad on the way out, but the walk back in the snow was tough. You're going to have to start packing me home on your back."

The very next day, Chris pulled his work saddle and pad from the tack room and put them on Ali's back. It felt strange to Ali, and the added weight felt weird to him. It wasn't uncomfortable, just different. Chris took him into the covered arena and worked him on a lounge line to get Ali used to the feel of the saddle and the stirrups moving on his sides. Chris stopped Ali in the center of the arena. He put his weight on the saddle. Ali didn't flinch a bit, so he swung himself up into the saddle and sat still. Ali turned his head from side to side, looking up at Chris. That was strange. Chris was suddenly taller than he was. The extra weight on his back felt weird too, but not uncomfortable.

Chris used the reins to turn Ali. Ali took two steps to the right. He kept looking back at Chris. Suddenly, Ali understood. He'd seen other people on horseback before. This was the first time for him. He liked it. Chris asked him to walk the perimeter of the arena. Ali was proud to carry him. He was so excited he began to jig a little. Chris pulled him back to a walk. "Buddy, we have to teach you to walk with a rider before you get to trot," he laughed.

Chris and Ali worked on walking, turning left and right, stopping, and backing up at the walk for the next month. Ali enjoyed the work and appreciated it when Chris let him know he was happy with his progress. The extra carrot pieces didn't hurt one bit.

Several days before Ali's third birthday, Chris finally let him move out under saddle. He kept Ali slow, more like a Western jog-trot for a few laps around the arena. He also tried the left and right turns, halts, and backing up. Ali did so well he thought it was time to move him on up into his more intense trot. The next day Chris put his saddle-seat saddle on him. He asked Sharon to watch and tell him what she thought.

Chris walked Ali into the arena and waited until Sharon got to the center so she could watch him all the way around. He cued Ali to trot. Ali started at the slow jog he'd done the previous days. Chris squeezed him with his legs and clicked to encourage him to speed up. That was all the encouragement Ali needed. He struck out at his high floating trot. Chris adjusted to the new speed and started posting. Ali began to enjoy himself. Sharon told Chris later it looked like Ali was grinning from ear to ear. Ali found his pace and began to fly. Ali let out a yell of pure joy. He was having the time of his life, and so was Chris. Chris rode two complete circuits of the arena before pulling Ali back to the walk. He walked Ali to where Sharon stood.

"What did you think of that?" Chris asked her.

"I think you have an English horse there, and I think he likes it a lot," Sharon said. "If he throws his front legs out a little further, you almost have a Park Horse on your hands. I'll make you a bet that Ali would look great in a Native Costume. That would be the fun class to show him in."

Chris was almost panting from the excitement. So was Ali. Ali wanted to go again. Chris thought better of that. Ali was using muscles differently with the weight of a rider on his back. There was no way Chris would take chances with Ali. He walked him out then walked him to the barn to remove the tack. Roberto was waiting to take Ali to the wash rack.

Sharon called a woman she knew in Temecula, California, not far from San Juan Capistrano, where the Howards lived. She made custom-designed and fitted Arabian Native costumes. They discussed colors and design ideas. The woman told Sharon what measurements she needed for the horse and rider. Sharon called Caroline Howard about it. Caroline had some pictures as well. Between Sharon and Caroline, they helped the costume maker create the perfect costume for Prince Ali. It was two-toned teal with silver trim, silver tassels and set with Swarovski crystals. The blanket was scalloped along the bottom and over the horse's rear. A silver thread embroidered geometric pattern on dark teal followed the edges of the blanket and the edges of the rider's aba, or cape. The rest of the blanket, headpiece for the horse, breast collar, and aba were lighter teal with a floral pattern set in crystals.

When the designer finished the costume, Caroline picked it up and showed it to Becky before shipping it to Colorado. Sharon showed it to Chris. "We'd better try this on Ali. I need to walk him around in it a few times so he doesn't have a problem with all this swinging around him. When is the next show with a costume class in it?" he asked her.

"That would be the March show in California," Sharon said.

"Great, we'll be ready by then," Chris told her.

Chris set up an evening to assemble all of his staff and many clients. During a costume class, the spectators stomp their feet in the grandstands and yell an old Beduin war cry as the horses enter the arena at a hand gallop. He wanted to be sure Ali was ready for that commotion as well as all the tassels flipping around. Chris knew many show committees scheduled that class in the evening, so the bright arena lights highlighted all the glitter on the costumes. He thought it could be a distraction for a younger horse. Ali was young. Chris didn't want to leave any margin for error. He wanted Ali prepared in advance. He didn't need to worry. That evening everyone stood around the outside of the arena. Chris walked Ali out of the barn in his costume. He cued Ali to a hand gallop, and they charged into the arena. Everyone outside the arena hooted, hollered, yelled, and clapped as loud as they could. Prince Ali gave them a show! He loved it. He was ready for the big time.

CHAPTER ELEVEN

During Prince Ali's third year, Chris added more shows to his schedule. He included shows in different parts of the country. Chris felt that would increase Prince Ali's appeal as a breeding stallion when the Howards decided it was time for that.

As promised, Becky attended every show so she could spend time with her horse. In addition to that, Becky spent her Spring Break and Summer Vacation with the O'Neals in Colorado. She had a bedroom in their home and began leaving some of her things there, so she didn't have to pack quite so much. Becky and Todd were close as siblings, and they liked each other. Sharon and Chris O'Neal treated Becky as though she was their child during her visits. House rules for Todd applied equally to her. She had assigned chores the same as Todd. Becky soon dropped the Mr. and Mrs. O'Neal when she talked to them. She began to call them Mom and Dad the way Todd did. That was only a little complicated when the Howard family came to Colorado to stay the week between Christmas and New Year's Day. Becky had two of each.

Prince Ali continued his winning ways. Every time he put a hoof in the show ring, he won. By the time the March show in California came around, Prince Ali was going so well under saddle he won his first English Pleasure and Native Costume classes in addition to his Halter classes. Ali's winning in the under saddle classes proved to many people that he wasn't just a pretty face. Ali could do so much more, and very well indeed. He always had tough competition from some famous and well-bred competitors with many wins of their own.

After his triple Championships in Canada, Chris brought Ali home, hoping for a month or two off between that show and the US National Championship show. By that time, Ali filled Caroline Howard's trophy case, and she purchased another one.

Becky still had a couple of weeks in Colorado before flying back to California for school. Caroline took the rotation this time and decided to fly to Colorado to pick Becky up but added a couple of days to her schedule. She wanted to stay a few days in Colorado herself. Walter was at one of his conferences on the East Coast and not home anyway.

Caroline was at the kitchen table having a glass of iced tea with Sharon when the phone rang. Sharon answered. She listened for a few seconds with a curious expression on her face. "He's on one of his training horses right now. Can I ask him to call you back?" She listened and took down a phone number. "Sure, I'll have him call you as soon as he can."

"That was a strange call," she told Caroline. "That was the woman who rides Lightning, the Colorado Mavericks mascot, during their home games. She wants to talk to Chris about his gray horse. I can't imagine who that might be unless she's referring to Prince Ali."

Caroline's eyebrows climbed up her forehead. "Maybe we should get this message to him right away so we can find out what her call is all about? It sounds interesting!"

Sharon took the note, and the two women walked to the barn. Chris was handing the horse off to Roberto for a rinse. "Hey, Chris, you got an interesting phone call. Why don't you call this woman back from my office in the barn? Caroline and I are curious what her interest is in your gray horse."

"My gray horse?" Chris said, puzzled. "I don't own a gray horse. Was she talking about Prince Ali?"

"She didn't say. We're dying of curiosity. Would you please call her? We want to know what this is all about," Sharon told him.

Chris picked up the phone and dialed. "Hi, This is Chris O'Neal. I understand you want to talk to me." He listened. "Where are you right now?" He listened. "Can you come over here and ride him? He's comfortable here, so that might be a good idea. You can get a feel for him that way." He listened. "Okay, we'll see you in a couple of hours." He listened. "See you then."

"Well, that is a surprise." Chris began. "That was the trainer for Lightning. Lightning has a slight injury and can't perform in the next two home games for the Colorado Mavericks. She's looking for a substitute to fill in. She wants to see if Prince Ali can do that."

"Wow! Just WOW!" Caroline said. "That's quite an honor."

"Let's not get our hopes up," Chris suggested. "She's on her way here from Denver. I'm going to let her ride him here and see what she thinks. If she likes him and thinks he'll do what she needs, maybe we can celebrate then."

"Caroline, come with me. I need to get something out for dinner," Sharon said. "We can talk in the kitchen. I don't want to tell the kids until we know for sure. There's no need to get their hopes up. Our family has been Mavericks fans for as long as I can remember. Having a horse from here sub in for Lightning would be a real honor, not to mention a lot of fun!"

"I agree with you. I can call Walter later on this evening if things look good," Caroline said. "I sure won't tell Becky until we know."

Nan Jacobs arrived at the ranch almost two hours later. She walked directly to the barn looking for Chris. He had a horse in cross-ties, pulling the tack off so Roberto could rinse him down.

"Chris?" she asked.

"Nan Jacobs, I'd know you anywhere," Chris said. "My family watches all the Mavericks games at home."

"Well, Chris, I've seen you in the showring with that gray horse. I saw him as a yearling, a two-year-old, and recently a three-year-old under saddle. I'm impressed. You've done a great job with him. What is he like to work with?"

"Oh, Nan, you have no idea. He's the best horse I've ever worked with. He is so willing to work with me, and he wants to please. He gives me 110% every time. He is as good as gold on the ground too. He eats and drinks well at shows like it doesn't bother him. He has enthusiasm for working. He has a special something that makes you want to watch him. He loves life. And he's affectionate, not a biter or kicker ever."

"Well, he sounds about perfect. Let's go see him."

Chris showed Nan the way to Prince Ali's stall and opened the door. The two walked in. Ali nickered at Chris and looked curiously at Nan. Nan walked over and stroked his silky neck down to his withers. Her fingers found the itchy spot and gave it a good scratch. Ali turned his neck around to look at her and chuffed his enjoyment.

"Boy, for a three-year-old stallion, he sure is calm," Nan said.

"Yeah, he's as cool as a cucumber. We had a storm here last year. The rain came down in buckets, and the lightning sounded like it was right over our heads. Several horses in the barn were flipping out over it. I checked on Ali. He didn't pull his head out of his feeder. He just kept on munching as if he'd been through lightning storms every day."

"Those are all good points," Nan said. "How do you think he would react to riding into a stadium with 70,000 screaming fans?"

"One thing I can say about Prince Ali is that he's a ham with a capital H. He loves the crowd. He looks into the crowd and makes eye contact with them. The more they scream and cheer, the higher he flies, but he is completely under control at all times. I've never seen or felt anything like it."

"Dang, that sounds perfect! Can I ride him?" she asked.

"Sure, Here's his halter and lead. I'll go get his tack out. Can you walk him down to the cross ties?"

Chris rode Ali in the arena while Nan watched closely. Chris told her what he was doing as he passed her on the rail at all gaits. After a few passes, he pulled Ali to a halt at the gate. "Your turn," he said. "Remember to click for the trot and double click for the strong trot."

Nan mounted and adjusted the stirrups. She walked Ali down the rail while she got a feel for him. Then she asked him to trot. After a complete round at the trot, she asked him to canter. When she finished an entire round at the canter, she pulled Ali back to a walk.

She walked him around, turning left and right, then asked him to halt. She walked Ali back to the arena gate and dismounted.

"WOW! That was like driving a million-dollar Lamgorgini!" she told Chris. "I've never ridden a horse like that. I love Lightning, and I'm used to him, but this was an experience I'll never forget. What do you think about asking the owners' permission to use him?"

"A couple of things first," Chris said. "We need to check the schedule to make sure there isn't a show conflict. Then, we should probably get him to Denver and let him ride around the field to get accustomed to the area. This will not be like his usual show. How did you get Lightning used to the crowds, loudspeakers, players on the field, and all that stuff?"

"I have a plan," Nan said. "The team is home practicing every day. I can make arrangements for everything. If we get the okay, I can do that to get him to Denver as soon as tomorrow. Does he rear? If not, I can teach him, but I'll need to keep him at my ranch for a couple of days. I'll sign whatever release the owners need. I think we can make your Prince Ali a football star! Both home games will be televised."

The two walked Ali back to the barn and handed him over to Roberto. Nan, being a trainer, had a pocketful of horse goodies. She handed a couple to Prince Ali and gave him another scratch on the withers before walking back to the house with Chris.

Sharon checked the schedule. The two dates for Mavericks games were open. Ali wasn't en route to or from a show or showing those days. Caroline, Walter, and Becky gave their enthusiastic approval. Nan talked to the team's manager. He promised tickets to both games and all travel expenses for the weekend for the Howards and the O'Neals.

Chris talked with Nan. He had several horses he needed to work with and get ready for shows. They decided Chris would bring Prince Ali to Nan's ranch the day after Becky and Caroline left for California. Chris would pick Nan up and drive to Maverick Field to walk Prince Ali around and get him used to the location. Then he would drop Ali off at Nan's ranch before going home. Nan planned to work with Ali to teach him to rear on command, then bring Prince

Ali back to Clearwater Creek Ranch. She and Chris would set up the schedules for the game weekends then.

Nan showed Chris how to get to the private area she used for Lightning on game days. It was screened from public view and had guards on duty when Lightning was there. The stall was large and bedded deeply. The automatic waterer was clean and in good working order. Nan stored feed, grooming supplies, and game day costumes for her and the horse in the locked tack room next to the stall. A small grass paddock surrounded the stall so Lightning could relax in comfort before and after game appearances. Nan and Chris used the hitching post inside the paddock fence to tack Prince Ali for a ride. Chris mounted, and Nan led them to the tunnel entrance.

The tunnel went completely under the stadium. The team covered the concrete floor with 2" thick rubber mats so a horse wouldn't slip walking through it. The tunnel ran straight through to the ground level of the field. A staircase down from the players' dressing room was about halfway between the entrances of the tunnel. The tunnel had bright ceiling lights so the players or horses wouldn't be blinded by daylight when they stepped out on the field.

Nan walked beside Chris and Ali through the tunnel to the packed dirt area that surrounded the grass field. When they stepped out, the players were practicing. Some ran plays, practiced throwing and kicking the ball, and the coaches called plays. Nan used a walky-talky to speak with someone in the control room. The loudspeakers turned on and blasted the sound of 70,000 people in the stands during a game. The players froze in confusion. Prince Ali came to an abrupt halt. One of the coaches ran over to see what the commotion was all about.

Nan explained. They needed Prince Ali to hear the noise he would hear on game day. The players practicing was all part of that too. He needed to see the ball thrown or kicked, and the players tackle each other, the sounds of so many people in the space, etc. She introduced him to Prince Ali as Lightning's stand-in. He ran back on the field and spread the word to the other coaches and players. They continued their workouts.

"Chris, when the Mavericks score a touchdown, that's when Lightning streaks out of this tunnel. He races down the corridor behind the player's bench to the other end of the field and back. I fly the flag as we go. I did spend some time with Ali and the flag at my ranch. Some horses get upset with something flying and flapping above their head and ears. Ali was wonderful. He didn't flinch a bit. Why don't you take a gallop down and back and let me know what you think? See if you can get Ali to ignore the commotion on the field."

Chris cued Prince Ali. Just as they came out of the tunnel, the canned crowd noise changed. The recording caught a significant play on the field that day, and the crowd screamed and cheered. Ali thought they were cheering for him. That pumped him up. He was excited. He stepped into his high floating trot, looking around for the people. The only people he could see were players on the grass. They noticed him and stopped what they were doing to watch him. He charged down to the opposite end of the field and spun around before striking out for the entrance tunnel. Chris stopped him a few feet inside the tunnel. "How was that?" he asked Nan.

"I usually gallop Lightning down the sideline, but I think Ali's trot is even better and showier. That's what I'm going to do on game day. Did you notice how excited he got? It looked like he thought the crowd was cheering him. What a difference that made. I can't wait. You're right. He is a ham with a capital H." she laughed. "Now, give me a turn."

Chris dismounted and boosted Nan in the saddle. She shortened the stirrups and took off down the sideline. Halfway down the field, the crowd noise went into cheering again. Ali pumped up and stepped even higher than usual. Nan took him to the end of the field and turned him right to a spot behind the center of the goalpost. She stopped him and asked him to rear. He hopped on two legs twice before dropping down onto all fours and trotted back to the tunnel entrance.

"Oh, my! That was a thrill!" Nan said as she dismounted. "He was perfect. Let's walk him this time. There are some places I want him to see. There will be TV cables and stuff snaking across the sidelines behind the players' bench on game day. I want him to look at that so he knows it's there. There will also be giant cameras and cameramen in those elevated mounts all around the field." She pointed to the white structures above the sidelines. "I can't do much to prepare him ahead of time for them. As long as he knows they are there, he should be okay with them."

Chris and Nan began walking Prince Ali down the sideline. They came close to the players' bench, and several players were sitting down taking a break. One of the players noticed the trio. "Hey, Nan, who's that good-looking guy you're bringing onto our field?" he asked.

Nan laughed, "Henry, this is Chris O'Neal. He's the trainer for the lovely horse we're walking."

Henry laughed, "I was talking about that horse, but pleased to meet you, Chris," he stood and extended his hand. Chris was tall at 6 feet 1 inch, but Henry towered over him and weighed at least twice as much. Chris took the hand offered. His was swallowed in the grasp. "Nice to meet you too," Chris said. "My family are fans. We watch you every time you make it on the Sunday telecasts."

"Thank you very much, Chris. Tell me about this handsome horse," Henry asked.

Nan spoke up, "Henry, you probably know Lightning is out for a few weeks with an injury. I found Prince Ali to stand in for him. Prince Ali is the reigning National Champion stallion. I think he'll make a good substitute for Lightning, don't you think?" Several of the other players who'd been seated on the bench joined the group.

One of the men, another almost Henry's size, spoke up. "I saw him out of the corner of my eye when you came down the sidelines. I almost got my head knocked off because I wasn't watching my opponent for a second. He's sure a beautiful horse. Welcome to the team, Chris."

Henry walked closer and stroked Ali's neck. "Are you sure this horse is a stallion? He's so soft! And he's so nice."

Ali looked at the men in their practice uniforms. They looked huge in their shoulder pads and protective gear. This group happened to be linemen for the team, so they were all large men, to begin with. Henry's touch was gentle. Ali nickered at him. Henry stroked him again. The players all came closer when they realized Ali was friendly. Someone finally said, "I thought all stallions were hard to handle and aren't safe around people. This guy is nice. Who'd a thought?"

Chris laughed. "This one's best friend is a 12-year-old girl."

Henry looked dumbfounded. "You mean a little girl handles this stallion?"

Chris nodded. "She loves him, and he looks after her."

Henry shook his head. "Well, I'll be darned. My little girl loves horses. Maybe I should look into getting her one."

"Bring her by my ranch sometime," Chris said. "We'll introduce her to some lovely horses like Prince Ali. These Arabians do love people."

The lineman coach began blowing his whistle. Henry looked over. The coach was signally them to get back on the field. "We gotta go for now. Nice to meet you, Chris, and Prince Ali. See you on game day." The men dashed back out onto the field and got in formation.

At the end of their walk around the field, Chris asked, "How do you think Ali's going to do on game day?"

"Well, very well!" Nan said.

CHAPTER TWELVE

T he first game weekend arrived. The Howards flew into Denver on Friday evening, courtesy of the Mavericks Football Team. They rejected the offer of a weekend at the team hotel in Denver. They drove to Clearwater Creek Ranch and stayed there instead. Chris, Walter, Becky, and Todd went to Maverick Field on Saturday. Becky insisted on seeing Ali before the game on Sunday. The security guard recognized Chris immediately and allowed the group into the private area where Ali stabled. Nan was with him.

"He's going to do great tomorrow," she told them after meeting Walter, Becky, and Todd. "The TV cameras are in their mounts, so I took him through the routine a couple of times. He knows where those darned cables are, so we can avoid them tomorrow. Now, all we have to do is hope the Mavericks score. The team they are playing this weekend is the toughest match for the year. Their opponents are undefeated."

Becky looked concerned. "Do you mean that Ali won't get to charge out of the tunnel at all tomorrow unless the Mavericks score a goal?"

Nan smiled, "No, Becky. I will ride him out before the game even starts. I always ride Lightning out onto the field at the beginning to fire up the audience. This time, I'll be riding Prince Ali. I wrote an introduction for him and gave it to the announcer this morning. You will get to see your boy on the football field tomorrow. We also play a part in the half-time events. No matter if we win or lose, I always ride Lightning across the middle of the field when the game ends too."

Becky asked, "Can we see where he's going to be?"

"Sure," Nan said. "Let me give you the tour."

Nan took the group through the tunnel to the playing field. As they passed the staircase to the players' dressing room, she pointed it out. "They've been practicing today, so I won't take you in there right now. Someone could be in the showers or dressing," she told them. When they came out of the tunnel, the stadium looked immense to Becky. The stands were empty except for the people cleaning and getting it ready for the game. Food vendors scurried around, stocking their booths. Officials walked around looking the site over for areas that needed attention. The video people worked on the screenshots that would play on the video display screens during the game. Some of the players were still practicing throwing and kicking the balls around. Camera operators checked over their cameras mounted around the stadium. Even with a couple of hundred people preparing for the game the next day, the stadium looked huge.

"I've seen this on TV hundreds of times, but I never thought it was this big," Todd said as he looked around. "I've seen the football field at the high school. It's tiny compared to this."

Nan laughed. "Your football field is measured out the same way this one is, most likely. The difference is all the rest of it. I'd bet your grandstands are nothing like this!"

Todd nodded in agreement. "Neither is our snack shack."

One of the assistant coaches came out from behind them. "Hey, Nan. I've been looking for you. The head coach sent me. We're having a team dinner tonight at 6 pm. Coach wanted to know if you'd invite the owner of that horse and his trainer to join us."

Nan introduced the man to the group. "Since they are both here, why don't you invite them yourself?"

The man explained the dinner was early so players could get to bed and get sleep before the game. "Coach wanted you to know your horse made quite an impression on some of our players. They've asked to meet you. Dinner tonight will be a lot of "Rah Rah, Score

Points!" stuff. It helps get the players up and focused on the game. We'd love to have you join us."

Dinner that night included the wives of the players. There was a lot of juvenile joking around and kidding between the players and coaches. The Head Coach stood up and made a short speech about how important the game was for the Maverick's season, concluding with poking fun at the quarterback. The team manager introduced the players and their wives to the Howards and O'Neals. Many of the players stopped by to meet Becky in person and tell her they could hardly believe such a sweet little girl owned such a big, beautiful stallion.

Nan and her husband sat with the O'Neals and Howards for dinner. Nan told Chris she needed his help in the morning. "We need to get Prince Ali show groomed, tacked, and ready to ride by noon. The game starts at 1 pm, but they will announce Prince Ali before that. I usually ride Lightning around the entire stadium with the American flag at that point. We charge back into the tunnel and wait out of sight until the Mavericks score."

"Will you be in the tunnel when the players run out onto the field?" Todd asked.

"Yes, and there are a couple more things I should tell you. When the players come down the staircase into the tunnel, they slap the horseshoe mounted on the wall at the end of the stairs for good luck. Then, when they pass Lightning and me, they pat him on the butt as they run by. That's the tradition. I hope Ali doesn't jump around. I'll keep him as calm as I can. He's not a flighty horse, so he'll probably be a lot like Lightning. He'll stand there for me."

"Can I be there with him?" Becky asked.

"If your Dad thinks you can help keep Ali calm, yes," Nan answered and looked at Walter. Walter nodded his head. "Okay, then. I'll see you in the morning at the stall. And, so that you know, Prince Ali is guarded overnight here. Our security guards don't mess around, and they carry guns. No one will mess with your horse while he's here."

The following morning was a rush. Prince Ali had a bath, clip job, hooves sanded and polished, and a light coat of glitter spray added to his mane, tail, and body. Nan brought out Lightning's tack and adjusted it for Prince Ali. She slipped into the tack room and put her clothes on. They were ready by noon, one hour before game time.

Nan mounted Prince Ali and walked him around with the flag. There was a slight breeze that morning, so the flag fluttered. Ali ignored it completely. Nan kept checking her watch. Finally, she said, "Let's go. It's time to get in position." She walked Ali toward the tunnel entrance with Becky and Chris on either side. The rest of the group headed to the grandstand. They had seats behind the players' bench where the players' wives sat.

Nan knew the order of pre-game announcements even though the announcer's voice sounded muffled in the tunnel. She walked Ali a little in front of the entrance to the players' locker room and stopped. Suddenly the door to the locker room opened, and the team streamed out. The first player in line slapped the horseshoe plaque on the wall and rushed down the tunnel. He patted Ali on the butt as he passed. Ali flinched but didn't move. The second player slapped the plaque and patted Ali on the butt. It all happened so quickly, Becky couldn't believe it. All she heard was the wall slap from each player. Suddenly the last player passed them by with a gentle pat on Ali's rear end. When the first player reached the end of the tunnel and ran out on the field, the stadium burst into applause. The applause didn't end until the last man was through the tunnel.

At the opposite side of the field, the same scenario took place, minus the slap on the wall and the pat on Ali's rear end as the opposing team came onto the field. Becky could hear boo's from this side of the grandstand and cheers on the opposite side, nearly drowned out. Nan said, "It's time for us to get ready," and began walking Ali toward the tunnel entrance.

The announcer's tone changed. He made a different announcement. "Ladies and gentlemen, Mavericks fans, you probably know our beloved mascot, Lightning, is on injured reserve for a couple of games. In his place, we have a surprise for you. This young stallion is the current Canadian National Champion, the United States National Champion, and the World National Champion Arabian stallion. He's never lost to another. We are privileged to have him step in for Lightning for a few games to keep your spirits up. I'd like to present to you, Prince Ali! Let's give him a big hand!"

Nan cued Ali to the trot, and they streaked out of the tunnel into daylight. The crowd roared! Ali hesitated for a split second, then struck off in his high floating trot with the American Flag streaming beside him. Ali made the circuit around the entire field. The higher he trotted, the louder the crowd became. Ali had never heard 70,000 screaming fans before. It pumped him up with adrenalin and excitement, and he stepped higher and higher than he'd ever moved before. Ali began meeting the eyes of fans as they passed by. Fans started calling him by name. They chanted "Ahh-Lee! Ahh-Lee! Ahh-Lee!" He loved it. Ali was a little sorry when Nan asked him to return to the quiet of the tunnel.

The teams ran out on the football field and set up their formations across the line of scrimmage, and the game began. After the opening show, the Mavericks were on fire and made their first touchdown with half of the first quarter to go. Nan and Prince Ali trotted out to the field and made their pass down the Mavericks sideline with the flag snapping in the breeze. The fans in the grandstands stomped their feet, clapped, and screamed. Nan turned Ali right at the end of the field and stopped him in front of the goalpost. She cued him to rear up. Ali reared and pawed at the sky. Then he screamed the stallion challenge in his own language, loud enough to be heard over the fans. They, in turn, screamed louder than ever. "Ahh-Lee! Ahh-Lee! Ahh-Lee!" It took a few extra minutes to get the players on the field back into position for the extra point. The placekicker set up and scored again. Ali and Nan made another run down the sidelines, firing up their fans.

By the time the fourth quarter ended, Nan and Ali traveled down the sideline to the goalpost four more times. Ali screamed the wild stallion challenge from the goalpost each time. The previously undefeated opponent scored once. The Mavericks players scrambled onto the field in joyful celebration. One of them called down into the tunnel, "Hey, Nan, bring that horse out here! He's part of our team too." She trotted Ali out onto the grass. There 300 pound linemen were fist-pumping and chest-bumping each other and the quarterback. Ali joined right in, nose bumping and shoulder bumping players in fun. The head coach took a shower in Gateraide from a five-gallon bucket and laughed as he chased the players who soaked him. Everyone, including Prince Ali, was in high spirits before the team finally settled down and headed for the locker room. They walked down the tunnel as a group. Each player stroked Ali's butt again before turning up the stairs.

Chris, Becky, and Todd stood against the wall, out of the way. Becky finally said, "That was really something, wasn't it?"

Chris and Nan laughed. "Yeah, that was fun." The group headed out of the tunnel to Prince Ali's temporary stable. They just finished taking off his tack when the head coach charged out of the tunnel in their direction. "Oh, great! You're still here. The team wants you to come to dinner tonight. We have a lot to celebrate. Can you make it?"

"Where and when? We'd love it," Chris said.

The dinner was a raucous affair with lots of teasing and joking between players and the coaching staff. This time, nearly everyone in the group stopped by to meet and talk with Becky, the owner of "that fabulous horse." The quarterback and his wife stopped by to tell her how much they appreciated how Ali encouraged them to their best efforts. The head coach and team manager came by with two signed game balls. The manager explained to Becky and Walter, "One of these is for you. The other is for the horse. When he trounces it and smashes it flat, let me know, and we'll get you another one for him."

The TV cameras loved Prince Ali. Cameramen on the opposite side of the field from the Mavericks' bench zeroed in for closeups of him during his gameday performances. People across the nation saw him in brief clips before the commercial breaks in broadcasts of the games. Fans flooded the Mavericks Office with questions about Prince Ali.

At the team dinner following Prince Ali's final performance for the Mavericks, the Mavericks gave team outfits to every O'Neal and Howard family member. They awarded Prince Ali a Mavericks stall plaque listing his title as "Fan Morale Manager," along with a Mavericks saddle blanket, day sheet, heavy winter blanket, and polo wraps all in Mavericks team colors. As everyone got up to leave, the Mavericks manager pulled Chris and Walter aside. "If you ever want to come to a home game, give me a call. I'll get you in the family section, front row behind the bench. We'd be delighted to see you and your families again."

The sports section of newspapers across the country, including the New York Times, USA Today, LATimes, Chicago Tribune, Denver Post, San Diego Union-Tribune, and Wall Street Journal, all had stories and photos of Prince Ali during his game performances. Stories like "Horse Fires Up The Mavericks," "So-So Team Delivers No Fouls, No Errors – Could It Be The Horse?" "Is Prince Ali The Mavericks' Secret Weapon?" "Team Climbs Out Of The Hole – Because Of A Horse, Of Course?" The articles included photos of Prince Ali and Nan in action at a game. Some were photos of Ali rearing, some trotting, and all showed fans on their feet waving banners. One point the journalists made was the Denver Mavericks were a solid team but had a lack-luster record until Prince Ali showed up on their field. Since his first appearance, they won every game and showed no intention of falling back into their previous "win-some, lose-some" habits. They were on track toward the Super Bowl at the end of the season. In weeks following Prince Ali's final performance, so many people showed an interest in him the journalists began digging into his background. They wrote about his very human family and his 10-year-old owner Becky. They covered his unbroken streak of wins in the Arabian show ring, including his International success in Paris. The winning picture at the Salon de Cheval made the papers before other current news took him off the Sports Section's front page. Prince Ali was the most famous Arabian horse in the United States, a standing previously held by Cass Ole, the star of the highly successful "Black Stallion" film.

Back in his stall at Clearwater Creek Ranch, Ali was oblivious to the attention. He settled right back into his training routine with Chris. They had shows to enter and classes to win. Ali would never forget his time with the Mavericks. A stadium full of screaming fans is hard to beat for a ham with a capital H.

CHAPTER THIRTEEN

C hris hit the show circuit with Ali. Prince Ali was named Champion Stallion at the Canadian National Championships again. Ali also won their national titles in English Pleasure and Native Costume classes. Chris showed Ali to championships in Texas, Washington State, and California again before the US National Championship show. Prince Ali, as a 3-year-old, won the Halter, English Pleasure, and Native Costume classes for the US National titles again. Ali added his final Futurity win, too, paying Walter Howard back for some show and training fees that year. Chris brought Prince Ali back home to Clearwater Creek Ranch for two months of R&R before show season started back up in late January. Becky insisted on being in Colorado the last weekend in January for Ali's fourth Birthday Party. Becky's twelvth birthday was just a few days later, so they had a combined party for the two.

A year before, Becky started hinting loudly about riding Prince Ali. Her Mom, Dad, and Chris felt Ali needed to focus on his riding skills with Chris first. Chris wanted the horse to win his classes without distractions. He spoke with Walter and Caroline about putting Becky off for a year before riding Prince Ali. Becky accepted it grudgingly. Prince Ali was her horse. The entire year passed by. Prince Ali was four. In Becky's mind, she'd been patient long enough, so it was time for her to ride.

Becky flew to Colorado for Spring Break at Clearwater Creek Ranch. She was determined to ride Prince Ali for the first time that week. Chris agreed, so long as Becky rode Ali while he was there to instruct her. Chris had problems in the past with a couple of his show horses when the owners let their kids ride them. The kids allowed the horses to get by with sloppy habits. Chris spent hours fixing them so he could show the horses again. He had Prince Ali tuned up so well, he didn't want to go backward with all that training.

Chris was pleasantly surprised when Becky rode Ali for the first time. She was a good rider. She and Prince Ali fit well together. "You know, Becky, you can show Prince Ali in the youth classes without much more work. We should talk to your parents about that. Maybe we can get you two ready for Youth Nationals next year.

Becky was ecstatic about that. She thought about it and had the idea she could ride one of her parents' other horses with a coach to keep in practice. That way, Ali could continue showing with Chris while she polished up her skills for next year. When she stayed in Colorado, Chris could coach her. She had someone in mind to work with her at home. Caroline Howard had a great friend that used to show horses with her when they were girls. Ginny Hartley now owned a ranch where she trained horses and kids. Maybe Aunt Ginny could be her coach. The only problem with Aunt Ginny was she lived a hundred miles from them. Becky thought about that. Could she work that out with her parents? She hoped so. She mentioned it to Todd. He thought it was a great idea. He had his eye on a horse too. He wanted to show at Youth Nationals, but not in the same classes as Becky. Maybe they could work that out.

Just before the US Nationals show, Chris got a phone call. It was Sameer from Paris. "How are you doing, Chris? More importantly, how is Prince Ali doing? I've been following him since I saw him in Paris. He's been a busy horse. He keeps on winning for you. Do you think the owners have any interest in selling him?"

"Sameer, it's great to hear from you. Has it been a year already? Yes, Ali has been busy and is still doing well. I think he gets better and better all the time. But, I'm sorry to say the owners are not interested in selling him. Becky wants to ride him in the US Youth Championships next summer."

"Well, if that's the case, have you mentioned the syndication idea to them?" Sameer asked.

"Yes, I did. Walter Howard is looking into that but hasn't made a decision yet," Chris told him.

"Well, that's not what I called you for," Sameer explained. "I'm on the nomination committee for the World Championship for next year. Prince Ali will be a four-year-old then if I'm not mistaken. I have already placed his name on the list. I wanted you to know so you can make plans early this time. I would love to meet the owners in Paris. I can talk to Mr. Howard in person about syndicating their horse. I can direct him to an excellent lawyer friend I know who can help them. I have several friends who also want to buy shares."

"Oh, my goodness. That is good news. Do you have the dates yet? I need to clear our schedules and get in touch with the Howards. They will want to be there this time. Becky will never forgive them if they don't take her along. I will mention Syndication to Walter again and let him know you want to meet him and talk about it too," Chris grabbed a pencil and sheet of notepaper. He scribbled the dates down before thanking Sameer again for calling him.

Chris told Sharon about the phone call from the Arabian prince. He gave her the dates for the World Championship Show in Paris. Sharon pulled out her notes on the previous trip. She had the vet information for vaccinations, airline number for Ali's flights to and from Paris, and the phone number of the hotel Chris stayed in last time. She told Chris she would call Caroline Howard about the show in Paris and see if there was time to plan a more extended trip to include some vacation time.

Caroline was pleased to hear Ali had been nominated again for the World Championships, and they did have time to plan an extra week in Paris. "I wouldn't be able to send Ali to Paris without Becky again. She's a little older and a lot more persistent," she laughed. "Why don't you come along and bring Todd? I think the kids would have a better time with someone their age on the trip. I'll talk to Walter when he gets home so we can block out that time on our schedule."

Ali's fourth year flew by. Chris began showing him in Western Pleasure with as much success as he achieved with the English Pleasure, Native Costume, and Halter classes. Ali proved to be a horse who could perform slow and steady or show fast and hot. By the end of Ali's fourth year, Caroline Howard and Sharon O'Neal received calls from people interested in breeding their mares to Prince Ali. It seemed many people wanted a son or daughter of Prince Ali in their barn.

Walter and Caroline discussed it and decided to put that off until Becky had her chance at winning a National Championship on "her" horse. Becky had been very patient in waiting to ride him. Walter and Caroline didn't want the added distraction of breeding mares to interfere with Becky showing her horse. Walter did, however, contact the lawyer the Arabian prince recommended to discuss Syndication.

The Howards and O'Neals took advantage of the horse show-related travel to take Todd and Becky to places they'd never seen. In Paris, they walked along the Seinne, drove through the Arc de Triomphe, looked out over Paris from the Eiffel Tower, and studied paintings and sculptures in the Louvre Museum. In upstate New York, they visited Niagra Falls. In New York City, they rode the subway, in Chicago, they took a ride on the L-train. They saw the Grand Canyon on the way home from Albuquerque and made a side trip to Carlsbad Caverns. They took a 3-day Riverboat cruise on the Mississippi River from Nashville. They visited the Outer Banks in the Carolinas and the warm water beaches in Florida. They never got to stay long, and the arrangements were complicated with home, work, and school schedules, but well worth the effort.

By the end of that year, Prince Ali won the Senior Stallion Championship in Paris, won the Canadian National Championships in all four of his classes, and finished the year winning the US National Championships in those classes again. Becky was looking forward to Prince Ali's fifth year. That would be her year with him. After the US National Championship show, Becky begged her parents to bring Prince Ali home to give him a rest and let her work with him and her new coach, Ginny Hartley.

CHAPTER FOURTEEN

Ginny Hartley, "Aunt Ginny" to Becky, was a dear friend of Caroline Howard. They grew up together in the barn showing Arabian horses. Ginny had 14 National Championship Trophies of her own. She and her husband Mike lived in the High Desert community of Pinon Hills. They ran a training and breeding ranch on 70 acres of land on the northern slope of the San Gabriel Mountains. The high desert plateau separated the suburban communities of the Los Angeles basin from the southern end of the Sierra Nevada Mountains.

After high school, Mike Hartley, the second son of his Montana-born parents, went to college at Cal Poly in Pomona, California. He studied for an Agricultural Degree to take back home to Montana and help his parents run their Dude Ranch. As it turned out, Pete, his older brother, took over the Dude Ranch. His younger brother, Scott, took over all the computerized reservations and advertising. They didn't need Mike, and there would have been conflicts between him and Pete, so Mike stayed in California. He met Ginny at school. They married, found the 70-acre parcel, bought a well-used travel trailer, and moved onto the land. They built the ranch themselves. Ginny was a well-respected Arabian horse trainer twenty-five years later, while Mike was a nationally known Reining and Cutting horse trainer. They divided the ranch. Ginny had about 25% for the

Arabians. Mike had the other 75% for his Paints and Quarters and all those cows he needed for their training.

Caroline and Ginny remained close friends after college. Ginny was on that shortlist of trainers for Prince Ali in the beginning. She'd come to the Howard's place and seen Ali as a baby. Ginny advised Caroline to go with Chris O'Neal because he had a stronger reputation. For Ginny, it gave her time to take care of some business by cell phone on the 100-mile drive to San Juan Capistrano and a chance to get off the ranch for a day every week. "I miss the color green," she laughed. "I need to see grass and flowers."

Ginny loved Becky. They worked well together. The coaching sessions never ended in tears, always laughter. Becky was a talented rider. Ginny found her weak spots, and they worked on them. Becky got better and better every week. She practiced the exercises Ginny left her with and showed improvement at every session. Ginny encouraged her.

Occasionally, Ginny brought Clyde with her. He was a truck-riding dog. He loved going with Mike or Ginny. Clyde was a hundred pound, shiny black Laborador Retriever who loved horses and Ginny's son, Brody. He also loved birds, cats, and cows. What he didn't like were rodents that got into the feed room stealing feed from "his" horses. Becky always found a treat for him, so he liked her too. Clyde liked Ali very much. When Becky got off Ali and turned him out in the arena for a few minutes of relaxation, Clyde and Ali played soccer with Ali's giant soccer ball or played games of "chase the dog" or "chase the horse" for a while.

A few weeks after Prince Ali's fifth birthday, Ginny and Clyde drove down for a coaching session with Becky. After greetings, Caroline had some work to do on the Swallows Day Parade for the volunteer organization that set it up. She was in her office going over some of the schedules when her phone rang. It was the chairman of the volunteer group for the parade.

"I got some bad news today," she told Caroline.

"What happened, Toni?" Caroline asked, perplexed

"Our Grand Marshall just bowed out. Rex Taylor's new movie moved production up, so he needs to fly to Europe this weekend.

Rex's wife said he wouldn't be back for three months. He can't be our Grand Marshall this year. We haven't got anyone lined up who can step in, especially on such short notice," the chairman told her. "Do you have any ideas? The Grand Marshall is always a celebrity or one of the town's prominent citizens. We've already used up all of our prominent citizens, and no one wants to do a repeat."

"Have you talked to the rest of the committee about it?" Caroline asked

"Yes, I have. I've only had one suggestion. It's really out there, if you know what I mean. We can't find another celebrity who will be around on that date. We can't find anyone in town to fill in. So I'm going to throw this at you. The suggestion was that Prince Ali could fill that position. He's a resident of San Juan Capistrano. He's a celebrity in his own right. How would you feel about that? I know the idea grew on me when I thought about it. Some of the volunteers were excited about it. They saw him on TV when he filled in for Lightning at the Mavericks games."

Caroline sat back in her chair. Her head whirled with thoughts and ideas. She didn't know what to think. Toni finally spoke up on the phone, "Hey, Caroline, are you still there?"

Caroline cleared her throat, "Yes, I'm here. I was thinking that through. The Grand Marshall does other things than just riding in the parade. They are usually one of the judges for the beard-growing contest. They also attend the President's Ball on Wednesday before the parade. The Grand Marshall always attends the Opening Ceremony with the Mayor on the first day of Swallows Week. They are always with the Mayor and City Council members during the award ceremony after the parade. How would we manage all that with a horse?" she wondered out loud.

"We thought about some of that too. We could have you bring Ali to the Mayor's office for the Opening Ceremony. He could stand just outside, so he's in the pictures with the rest of the group," the chairman suggested. "We can cue the news photographers in for that, so they set up ahead of time."

"You forget about the guns," Caroline said. "You know they take their guns into the Mayor's office to threaten him to open the event, and they shoot off those guns with blank rounds the minute they get outside the building. It's all part of the fun for us humans, but I'm not sure about including a horse in that. Someone might get trampled."

Toni paused. "You might be right. Maybe we should leave him out of the Opening Ceremonies. Even the human GrandMarshals doesn't have much to do but stand there. But we talked about the President's Ball. It's always at the El Adobe Restaurant in the banquet hall on the lower level. That's right next to the garden area outside in the back of the restaurant. We always use that area too because we have so many people there that night. There is a nice-sized gate into the patio area. The trash collectors use it when they pick up the trash from the restaurant. It's big enough for a horse to walk through."

"What would we do with him all night while we're having dinner?" Carolina asked.

"You're right. I didn't think of that. But, my brother is the head chef at the El Adobe. He told me he has some fantastic recipes for horse treats, some apple treats, and some kind of carrot treat he bakes like cookies. He'd love to do them up for Prince Ali. He's a football fan, you know. He watched your horse at the Mavericks games. He'd love to meet him in person."

…Caroline laughed. "Toni, you must have known about this for a couple of days now. Why didn't you tell me before? I'm getting the idea you and your team are working hard to figure out how to get my horse in your parade." She chuckled to herself.

Toni admitted it. "Well, yes, we've known for four days. But you can't imagine how many volunteers would love to have Prince Ali step in as Grand Marshall. He's the most famous horse we know. He's so beautiful. As you suggested, I'm guessing we'd have to leave him out of the beard-growing contest and the Opening Ceremony. But we all think he'd be a great draw for our parade. We're ready to start advertising and letting the press know. All you have to do is say the word."

Caroline smiled. "Toni, I can't give you the answer until I talk to my family. I will do that the minute Walter gets home from work. I will call you and let you know one way or the other tonight. I will call his trainer right now to discuss it as well."

Caroline smiled as she glanced over at the trophy cases filled with awards Prince Ali won over the past four years. It never occurred to her their horse would be considered a celebrity in their hometown. She assumed no one outside of the Arabian horse industry heard much about him. She picked up the phone and called Sharon O'Neal. They chatted a few minutes, and Caroline told her why she called. Sharon promised to have Chris call her back. How would Chris feel about flying to California to ride a horse in a parade? She felt a little foolish for asking.

CHAPTER FIFTEEN

Caroline decided to talk to Ginny Hartley about the parade invitation and see what her opinion was. The minute she explained it to Ginny, her comment was, "Fantastic! That is great. You guys can share that beautiful animal with all your friends and neighbors. You did a great job breeding him, and Chris has done a wonderful job training him. But he is a special horse. I think you should let your daughter ride him in the parade."

"Don't you think Becky is a little young for that?" Caroline asked.

"Have you watched her ride Ali?" Ginny asked. "Those two are so good together. I know Ali loves her. If anything were to happen, that horse would take care of your daughter. She's one of the best young riders I've ever seen. Give her some credit, will ya?"

"I hadn't considered Becky riding him in the parade. I assumed I have to get Chris out here for the weekend to do that. Are you sure about Becky? If she was your daughter, would you let her ride that stallion in a parade by herself?"

"Caroline, that stallion is your daughter's best friend, and she is his too. If Becky were my daughter, I would definitely let her ride him."

"I haven't told Becky about this yet. Please don't say anything to her until I have a chance to talk to Walter and Chris, okay?" Caroline asked.

"Not a problem. But I think you will have a problem if you don't let Becky ride," Ginny chuckled. "I wouldn't want to be in the same house with you two if you told her no on this."

Twenty minutes after Ginny left to drive home, Chris called. "Hey, Sharon told me the good news. I think that's fantastic. Public appearances are the best thing for Ali. He loves all the attention."

"How would you feel if I let Becky ride him?" Caroline asked.

"I'm all for it. Don't get me wrong, I'd be honored to get on a plane to California and spend the weekend with you guys to ride Prince Ali, but you have his rider under your own roof. Remember, I was the first one to put her on him. I've seen them together. She is an excellent rider already. She is going to kill the competition in the show ring with him. She has enough confidence in herself, but that doubles when you put Becky together with Prince Ali."

"Okay. I haven't talked to Walter yet. I'll call you later and let you know what we decide to do. You might have Sharon pencil that weekend on your calendar, just in case."

"Caroline, it would be a silly waste of time and money for me to fly out for this when Becky will do a great job. All you need to do is get your farrier out a couple of days before the parade and have him put special non-slip shoes on Prince Ali. There are a couple of different kinds. Your farrier will know which ones to use. Those shoes will help ease your mind. Ali won't slip on the pavement in them."

When Walter got home that evening, Caroline invited him into the office and shut the door. She told him what happened that afternoon. "I haven't told Becky about this yet. I wanted to talk to you about it first. I have talked to Ginny and Chris. They both suggested we let Becky ride Ali in the parade. Both of them feel Becky is good enough to keep control of Ali and not get into trouble. Chris suggested we get special non-slip shoes put on him a couple of days ahead of time so he can get used to how they feel. What do you think?"

"You know he's only supposed to walk the parade route, don't you?" Walter said. "If both trainers feel Becky is qualified to walk her horse down the street, who are we to say no. I'm excited they think so highly of him to invite him. You do know this is the first time the Grand Marshall of the Swallows Day Parade is not some over-rated actor or self-important businessman."

"I can't believe you said that," Caroline chuckled. There had been some of those people before, but not as many as Walter's comment implied. "I like Rex Taylor. He's a plain ol' cowboy. I think he's a nice man too. Maybe next year will work out for him to step in. I was looking forward to having dinner with him and his wife, Robin, at the President's Ball. They are both a lot of fun to be around. I guess we let Becky ride her horse in the parade. We can tell her at dinner."

The minute Caroline told Becky over dinner that the parade committee asked Prince Ali to be the Grand Marshall this year, Becky interrupted her.

"Mom, Dad, can I please, please, PLEASE ride him?"

Caroline looked down at her plate. "Becky, you are pretty young to ride a stallion down the street in a crowd like we usually get. Maybe I should call Chris to fly out for that. You can sit with us and watch."

Walter had to turn his head away from the table as if something in the other room caught his attention. He was struggling not to laugh out loud and spoil Caroline's fun.

Becky began to plead. "Mom, Dad, I promise to get all my homework assignments in on time for this whole year if you let me ride Ali. Okay, I'll keep my room spotless too. Uh, and I'll clean the bathroom after I use it, so I don't leave a mess for Espi. I'll...I'll... I'll do anything you want, just please, PLEASE let me ride Ali."

Caroline couldn't hold back any longer and burst out laughing. "Of course, you're going to ride him. We've talked to Chris and Aunt Ginny. They say you are ready. So now we have to figure out what you two are going to wear. You're probably going to have to go with the Western stuff. That fits in with the entire parade. Everyone in it shows off the heritage of the Old West, including the Native Americans in our community. I don't think you have a costume for Western Pleasure, do you?"

"Mom, I have a great idea! Since everyone else is supposed to show off the Old Western heritage of our area, why don't we have Prince Ali show off his heritage? It's very different, but his Native Costume is so beautiful."

"I'd have to run that by the Parade Committee," Caroline told her. "But, that might be a great idea. We have the Grand Marshall placed right behind the Capistrano Valley High School Marching Band. I wonder if they have time or could find the score for the theme song from Lawrence of Arabia? That would certainly show you two off."

"Oh, Mom, that's a great idea. I watched that movie with you and Dad that one time. I loved that music. It fit with the camels walking. Why not a beautiful Arabian horse?"

"I'd better get right on that tomorrow, then," Caroline said. "If we use Ali's Native Costume, I'm going to have to have one made for you. I don't think you'd fit in the one Chris wears, and we need a different head covering for a girl rider."

Caroline called Toni the next day and accepted the invitation for Prince Ali and Becky. She sent Toni one of the photos of Ali and Chris in his native costume. Telephone wires and computer lines burned up all over town. Volunteers passed around the photos and shared the good news about the new Grand Marshall. They talked about the costume and agreed it would feel right to have Prince Ali share his heritage in the parade that celebrated theirs.

Walter called the principal of the high school. He was also a member of the Rotary Club. Walter talked to him about the music his students planned to use during the parade and suggested changing it as an introduction for Prince Ali. The principal thought it was a fantastic idea after he saw the photo of Ali in his costume. He talked to the music teacher who managed the marching band. The music teacher was able to locate the score for the movie. While burning the midnight oil for a couple of nights, he put together pieces of the score for the different instruments in the band. He shared the music idea with the students and showed them the photo of Prince Ali in costume. They accepted the challenge of learning the new music with enthusiasm. They scheduled band practice every weekday, plus Saturdays, until the day of the parade.

Caroline phoned the costume maker in Temecula about Becky's costume. The woman still had swatches of the material and suggested she order silver slippers for Becky to wear. Caroline had no idea where to get something like that. The best part was she could get the entire costume done on time for the parade.

Becky spent the next several weeks in a dither. She was going to ride Prince Ali in the Swallows Day Parade in her hometown. What could be better than that?

CHAPTER SIXTEEN

On Saturday before the Swallows Day celebration began, an old blue truck bounced down a rutted road on worn shocks and tires at one-thirty in the afternoon. The driver turned into the long, almost invisible driveway toward a falling-down cabin. A plume of dust followed, settling slowly into the countryside. Calvin and Danny Hix spent the morning working on a ranch 10 miles away. They'd mucked stalls and repaired several hundred feet of pasture fencing for the property owner who bred horses for the race track.

Calvin threw the truck in parking gear and set the brake before climbing out when they got to the cabin. He reached into the cooler in the truck bed for two cold drinks and tossed one across the bed to his brother. Danny caught it with one hand.

The two men sat down in creaking lawn chairs beside the cabin and stretched out their legs in the sunshine. They twisted the caps off their bottles and tossed them in nearby weeds. Each took a long pull of the cold liquid. The old truck engine ticked as heat dissipated. An occasional splat of oil dripped onto the gravel below. Neither of them said anything for a while. They just looked out across the hillsides surrounding the cabin.

Located in northern San Diego County, the hills were a vibrant green this time of year. February rains brought fresh grasses and wildflowers out among the scrub oaks and mesquite. The twenty-acre property was miles from the nearest town, Ramona, and the nearest neighbor as well. Calvin and Danny preferred to live "off the grid," so finding this abandoned place was a lucky accident.

The two brothers resembled each other with sandy hair and tall, lean frames. Calvin was the oldest, nearing thirty. Danny was the better looking of the two but had the mental capacity of a child in his twenty-five-year-old body. He could not survive without Calvin. They did anything to earn a living. Calvin had enough social skills to get them honest work on local horse ranches in the area. They cleaned horse stalls, painted barns, or mended fences. They could change the oil in a tractor. They knew how to fix a leaky faucet or toilet, build a new gate, clean up a yard or paint a room or a house. They were pretty good hands with horses too.

Danny closed his eyes under the mid-day sun and almost fell asleep until Calvin spoke.

"Ya know, Danny, we're goin' to have to scrounge up a few bucks pretty quick if we want to have your birthday party in two weeks. Our jobs'll only pay a coupla hundred, so we have to come up with an idea."

Danny kept his eyes closed but nodded his agreement and cackled out loud. He would be twenty-five in precisely two weeks, and Calvin wanted to throw him a big birthday party. He'd never had a birthday party in his life. He didn't understand why it was such a big deal, but he always went along with Calvin.

"Been thinkin' about it," Calvin said. "How 'bout we do like last time."

"Got any ideas where we can find a couple with nobody watchin'? We get work from lots of these ranches around here," Danny said thoughtfully.

"That Swallows Day Parade is next weekend in Capistrano. There'll be hundreds of them there," Calvin suggested. "You wanna go to a parade?" Calvin grinned and scratched, swatting a fly away with his other hand. "If we can put somethin' together in the next couple days, I can borrow gas money from someone at the bar. You know, the Drop Inn? We just have to promise them a real good time in exchange for the loan. Hey, we can invite them to your party!" Calvin chuckled.

"Well, we got nothin' better to do, and we're gettin' low on drinks and coffee," grinned Danny. "Let's take a drive up to Capistrano and check it out."

And that's precisely what they did. Calvin and Danny spent enough time in San Juan Capistrano to find the parade route, the staging area for livestock, and the on and off-ramps for the freeway. They confirmed the times for the parade, the awards ceremony in the park, and the Street Faire. They talked to a few locals at the Swallows Inn for good measure. Calvin thought about the timing carefully. They were going to try pulling this one off in broad daylight with many potential witnesses. He knew he had to get it just right.

CHAPTER SEVENTEEN

P arade week finally arrived. A troop of prominent citizens dressed as cowboys stormed the Mayor's office on Monday morning. Some of them had their six-shooters loaded with blanks strapped in their gunbelts. The last man to burst through the door was very tall and wore a black hood to obscure his identity, even though everyone knew it was Charlie "Slim" Baker. He had a long rope ending in a hangman's noose draped over one shoulder. The group demanded the mayor immediately announce the opening of the Swallows Day celebration, or else! Anticipating the confrontation, the poor mayor feigned surprise but allowed the "gang" to hustle him out onto the steps in front of the city office building. There he declared the celebration officially open.

The "gang" encouraged the celebration by shooting off their six-shooters and making a horrible racket on the steps of City Hall. The local newspaper photographer was there to immortalize the event in pictures. Everyone there overacted their parts for the fun of it. They promptly left with the mayor for the Swallows Inn for something "to wet their whistles."

City crews constructed iron cages in several areas on downtown sidewalks. Anyone walking on the streets without wearing an article of "Western" clothing was immediately arrested and put in one of the cages. They were allowed to use their cell phones to call for bail money from their friends or family. All bail money went to charity. No one stayed in the cages very long, but visitors and citizens of the community had a lot of fun with the "inmates" during their brief stay in City Jail, chiding and teasing them.

The "beard growing" contest began on New Year's Day. That was the last time men in the community wasted time shaving. By March, their beards had grown to some degree. One of the City Council members told the rest of the Council they all looked like hippies in shirts and ties at the February meeting. Some men stopped by the local barber and had their beards trimmed a bit, so they didn't look so scraggly. Once the contest was over and the best and worst beard declared, nearly every man who grew one dashed home to shave their's off.

The President's Ball on Wednesday was a formal event. Ladies dressed in long dresses in Western, old Spanish, or Native American styles. They added feathers, wide-brimmed hats, and fancy jewelry to their ensemble. The men dressed formally in string or bolo ties, Western-style jackets, polished cowboy boots, and hats. The dinner spread from the lower level banquet room into the patio area behind the restaurant.

Becky usually missed this event. She had a friend over for the night or went to a friend's house. This year, she wouldn't miss the event for any reason. The Grand Marshall of the parade was honored at the President's Ball. This year, the Grand Marshall was her best friend, Prince Ali.

Caroline took Becky shopping and found just the right outfit for her. They discussed what to do with Prince Ali and decided he would go Western as well. Caroline borrowed some expensive Western Show tack from another friend of hers. She and Becky spent hours polishing the silver on the bridle, reins, and saddle the day before the Ball.

The night of the Ball, Caroline drove her car to the restaurant early. With the help of the restaurant staff, they cordoned off part of the parking lot for the truck and horse trailer for Prince Ali. Becky, Walter, and Fernando brought Prince Ali in the trailer so Ali would be there on time. As soon as Fernando parked the trailer, Becky and her parents took him outside and tacked him up in the silver-trimmed saddle and bridle. Becky applied a little baby oil on his face while Caroline and Walter gave Ali a good brushing. Becky bathed Ali that afternoon. She put hoof polish on his hooves before they left home. When they finished, Ali looked stunning.

"Since you're going to ride him in the parade, you should be the one to walk him into the patio area," Walter said to Becky. "We probably need to do that now before it gets too crowded."

Becky took the reins and walked beside Ali to the gate. Walter opened the gate and stepped aside so Becky and Prince Ali could enter first. As soon as they walked into the patio area, the mayor noticed them and picked up the microphone. "Ladies and Gentlemen, I'd like to present the Grand Marshall of this year's Swallows Day Parade. Please join me in welcoming Prince Ali and his rider, Becky Howard." Everyone in the restaurant that night turned to look, then stood and clapped.

Becky curtseyed, then stood beside Prince Ali, smiling. Those at the party later recanted the horse smiled too. The head chef heard the announcement and grabbed a tray of his special treats for Prince Ali. He marched through the crowd holding the tray over his head with one hand. When he reached the patio, he used the other hand to pull a small folding table out to set the tray down. "Do you mind if I pet your horse?" he asked Becky.

"Oh, Ali likes it. Would you like me to show you where he likes to be scratched?"

"Perfect," the man said. He pointed to the tray. "These are a special recipe just for horses. I used a recipe with carrots for the round ones and apples for the flat ones. I hope he likes them."

Becky offered one of the carrot treats to Ali. He took it from her hand and began to crunch on it while Becky showed the chef where to scratch Ali's withers. Ali groaned with delight. He had someone scratching that itchy place he could never reach himself, and the cookie was absolutely delicious.

"I think he likes this," the chef said.

"I think he's enjoying your cookies," Becky answered.

"I watched that football game on TV," the man said. "We heard a horse from our hometown would be taking Lightning's place, so lots of us tuned in to see him. I wish they showed more of him. It was just a few seconds here and there, but he was spectacular to watch. He's even more handsome in person."

Becky laughed. "My dad always says Ali is a ham with a capital H. He likes to show off, especially when he thinks someone is watching him. He's never had so many people watching him at one time before."

"Well, I need to get back to my kitchen. Thanks for letting me meet him. If you run out of cookies, I have another couple of trays waiting for him. Just let me know," the chef said, smiling as he hurried back to his duties.

Other guests began to approach Prince Ali and Becky. Many wanted their pictures taken with the horse. Ali knew just when to prick his ears forward and open his eyes for the camera. Everyone who stopped by to see Prince Ali fed him treats, so the first tray emptied quickly. A waiter rushed another tray out.

An hour later, waiters hauled trays of food to the banquet table from the kitchen. Hungry diners filled their plates and looked for spots at the tables to sit. Walter and Caroline were on the patio with Becky and Ali. "It's time for Ali to leave for home," Walter said. "Let's take him back to the trailer. Fernando will drive him home for us."

Becky led Ali through the gate to the parking lot. "I'll go home with Ali, Mom. I'd rather stay with him if you don't mind. This is kind of a grown-up party. You brought your car over, so you and Dad can stay as late as you want to. I'll see you at home."

In step behind their daughter and her horse, Caroline and Walter looked at each other and smiled.

CHAPTER EIGHTEEN

P rince Ali stood quietly breathing in the fresh salty air and enjoying the early morning crispness. He stood tied to the side of his horse trailer while Becky and Caroline brushed him down on both sides. Ali yawned and stretched his neck when Becky reached his withers. *"I don't know what this 'parade thing' is,"* he thought to himself, pushing his withers into the brush. *"But it beats taking those cold baths at o'dark-thirty at the horse shows."* That morning Becky bathed him inside his barn with warm water. He enjoyed the luxury of a warm bath. Ali shivered involuntarily, remembering all the times his first class of the day was at eight in the morning. That meant he was in an outdoor wash-rack by 5:30 a.m., sometimes before the sun was up, getting his bath in freezing water from a hose.

Becky peeked her head around Ali's neck and under his head. "Mom, are the O'Neals or the Hartleys coming today?"

"Honey, Chris and Sharon have that whole training facility in Colorado to run. We talked about it and decided it didn't make sense for them to hop a plane to come out here for one parade when Chris has so many other horses in training. Ginny lives a hundred miles away, you know. She's been here twice this week to coach you and Ali already. She has her ranch work to do today. I told them I would get them a copy of the video. I'm on the parade committee. I can do that." Mom grinned at her.

The staging area was in the large Regional Occupation Program parking lot directly across from the famous San Juan Capistrano Mission. Caroline parked the rig in an area near the rear exit, next to the last building in the lot. It gave them room to take Ali out of the trailer and work on him between the building and the trailer for privacy. The building would also provide shade for Ali later in the day.

Becky was so excited about riding her Prince Ali down the parade route she hardly slept a wink the night before. Mom insisted she eat something for breakfast that morning. Becky was all business on the outside and nervous and jittery on the inside. Becky constantly chattered to Ali when she was excited. This morning it was non-stop. Caroline had seen it before many times. When Becky was on a roll, Ali would sometimes nod his head as if he were in agreement with her or shake his head as if he didn't. He would turn around and stare at her like he couldn't believe what she was saying, snorting at the same time. When Becky said something funny to him, he had a unique response. He blew through his closed lips and made a sound remarkably like a raspberry. Caroline swore that horse answered Becky back. Ali's appearance in the parade would be the first time most of Becky's school friends saw Ali under saddle. Walter and Caroline were happy they could show off their unusual "son" to their friends and neighbors at home for the first time.

Despite the tension and noise in the parking area, Ali stood still. He knew Becky was going to ride him. He loved riding with her and couldn't wait to get started. His motor was humming. The energy from the people getting ready for the parade was different from anything he'd experienced. He could hear it all as other animals were tacked, hitched, saddled, decorated, and groomed. High School bands tuned their instruments on the grassy area next to the parking lot. Horses whinnied, mules brayed, goats bleated. He could hear wagons rolling on wooden wheels, and carriages come out of trailers and truck beds, leather squeaked, shod hooves rang out on the pavement, people chattered as they climbed up on floats. Drivers began shuttling their animal-powered vehicles through traffic to their starting places. People gave orders, moved animals and gear around, and climbed into their costumes. There was action, noise, and color everywhere you looked on this beautiful early spring morning. Ali could hear it all but couldn't see it yet because the horse trailer blocked his view. His ears spun around like a helicopter taking in all the racket.

Becky applied lotion to Ali's face and ears to enhance the black of his skin where the hair was thinner on his muzzle and around his eyes. It defined his facial features and added shine to the silver hairs on his face. Caroline finished brushing him down and sprayed his coat with a shine and conditioner polish. She smoothed his mane and took tangles out of his tail. Becky applied hoof-black polish to his hooves, so they gleamed like patent leather.

Working on each side of Ali, Caroline and Becky put his costume on. The outfit was elaborate and took some time to complete. Ali stood still as they worked. When the last piece of the costume was in place, Caroline adjusted the crystal medallion on the brow-band to the center of Ali's forehead. She polished away any fingerprints on the jewel.

Caroline and Becky stood back and looked Prince Ali over, brushing loose hairs from the velvet and adjusting tassels. Ali looked gorgeous. This was the costume he wore at the United States and the Canadian National Championship shows last year. He brought home both trophies for the Arabian Native Costume Under-Saddle class.

The teal velvet of the costume contrasted with the silver of Ali's coat. The blanket covered Ali from withers to tail and hung just below his belly at the sides. The bottom edge of the blanket was scalloped. Long tassels hung from three places on each scallop. Hand-set Swarovski crystals in a floral pattern covered the blanket and the back of the abba, or cape, Becky wore. A geometric pattern followed the edges of the blanket and the abba in silver thread embroidery. They sparkled in the sunlight. The deep teal and silver tassels nearly dragged the ground along the bottom edge of the blanket. The tassels on the breast collar came to his knees. They swayed and glittered in the slight breeze. Shorter tassels on the reins and the headpiece hung down on either side of his neck.

"Well, it's time to get you in your outfit," Caroline told Becky. Ali was ready to get moving. He sifted his weight from leg to leg impatiently.

Caroline helped Becky step into the teal lamé jumpsuit, zipped it up, and tightened the sash at her waist. She fastened the abba around Becky's neck and adjusted it to show off the gorgeous rondel floral pattern in crystals on the back. She helped Becky put on the turban and tucked her blonde ponytail underneath it. She attached a sheer veil over the lower part of Becky's face. Becky slid her feet into silver slippers, pulled on her silver riding gloves, prepared to mount Ali.

"You pay attention to your horse and keep your eyes and ears open, hear me?" Caroline said seriously.

"Yes, Mom. You know Ali will take care of me."

Ali nodded his head in agreement. *"Yes, Mom, you know I always watch out for Becky."*

"I know that. But you also need to take care of Ali. He's never done a parade before. Don't be afraid to grab hold of the reins and stop him if he acts like he's going to spook. Then just talk to him until he calms down."

"Yes, Mom, I'll be careful," she answered, looking away and rolling her eyes.

"Just when did I ever spook while Becky was riding? I don't spook anyway!" Ali snorted, hurt by the suggestion.

"Okay, then. Now, up you go," Caroline boosted Becky into the saddle.

Caroline walked around the horse and rider one more time, adjusting little things. She had to admit these two were stunning. They were going to get a lot of attention on the parade route.

"Time to head off to the staging area. Do you remember your place in the parade?"

"Yeah, we should be about in the middle of the parade. I know we are right behind the Capistrano Valley High School band. Has Dad found you a place to sit yet?"

Caroline checked her watch. "He's there now. We'll be on the front porch of the El Adobe restaurant."

Caroline walked beside Becky and Ali through the trailer parking area toward the parade Staging Area. People stopped what they were doing to watch. Caroline and Becky heard bits of comments from people as they passed.

"Is that the Howard's famous Arabian horse? We heard he was going to be the Grand Marshall in the parade." one lady whispered to her friend. "He's beautiful! And they're letting a kid ride him?"

"Yeah, just look at that costume." her friend replied. "That's amazing! I heard that young lady has a lot of experience with that horse."

"He's sure better looking than ol' Rex Taylor," someone shouted. His friends laughed. "Say, Melba, maybe you can get that horse to kiss you like you wanted to lay one on Rex. He looks a lot younger anyway!" More laughter followed. Becky just sat up straight and kept Ali moving forward, smiling under the veil. She knew they were quite a sight and enjoyed the attention. This was going to be a fun day!

Heads turned as Ali passed. Ali also knew he was looking good. His necked arched, his ears pricked forward, his nostrils flared, and he strutted like a peacock. The tassels on the reins, headpiece, breast collar, and blanket swayed with his movements. Because of the crowds and all the activity, Becky kept Ali to a slow walk. For Ali, that was difficult. All he wanted to do was trot on. The soft morning sunlight sparkled on his silver coat and the jewels on the costume. He was picture-perfect.

"Hey, how about we have lunch at the El Adobe after the parade. I know how much you love their tacos. We can take Ali back to the trailer and haul him home after the parade. We can meet your Dad at the El Adobe when we get back. He'll hold a table for us."

"Good idea, Mom!" Becky's stomach growled at the thought of tacos. She was too excited to want breakfast that morning, but now she was glad Mom made her eat something.

She saw people and animals milling around the Staging Area. "We're here at our place now. We'll be okay if you want to join Dad.

Ali's feeling perfect this morning. He's solid as a rock," Becky stroked his neck, "aren't you, boy?" Ali nodded his head.

"Well, I was going to stick with you two until the parade starts, but if you are sure you'll be okay, I think I will go join your Dad. I'm ready to sit down for a while. It's been a long morning."

Caroline patted Ali's neck affectionately. "You be a good boy for me, you hear?" She hurried off to join Walter, not knowing how good Ali would have to be in a very short while.

CHAPTER NINETEEN

At eleven o'clock a.m., two Eagle Scouts marched down Ortega Highway toward Del Obispo Avenue. They carried the banner for the Swallows Day Parade.

The theme for this year's parade was "How the West Was Fun." The first entry was a large group of rodeo clowns. They had painted faces and crazy red, white and blue costumes. Some wore barrels held up by suspenders. They did all kinds of silly things. The crowds down the parade route cheered and jeered as they passed by. The louder the crowd got, the crazier the clowns acted. Three carts pulled by goats followed the clowns on foot. The drivers were face-painted clowns that dangled carrots in front of the goats' noses on sticks. The clowns in the carts threw hard-wrapped candies to the children along the parade route as they went by. Behind the clowns was the first of many school bands.

Equestrian groups in Western and Early California attire moved between bands and strolling mariachi groups. Walking "Soiled Doves" sashayed down the street with their "Cowboys." Several Color Guards from military and police units rode their horses down the streets. Draft horses or mules pulled floats. Miniature horses pulled carts. Individual and family groups of equestrians moved west on Ortega Highway to Del Obispo. The parade turned north on Del Obispo to Camino Capistrano. Then everyone turned east on Camino Capistrano to the finish of the parade route. El Mercado, the street faire, was near the end of the parade route.

El Mercado would start up right after the parade. Many vendors set up booths with items for sale, food, and plenty to drink. The City kept streets in town blocked off after the parade because of the people walking through the street faire.

Prince Ali and Becky followed the local high school marching band. When the band started to play, Becky was surprised at the music. She immediately recognized the Overture from the movie Lawrence of Arabia. The flutes, piccolos, and clarinets carried the soothing melody, highlighted by the xylophones and trombones and punctuated by the bass drums and tubas. It put Becky in the mood of an Arabian Princess. She looked the part, except for the blue eyes above her veil. She straightened her shoulders and moved with the music, waving at the crowd as they passed down the street.

Prince Ali and Becky were the only ones in the parade not wearing some kind of Western costume. Ali strode down the parade route proudly, looking to his left and right, making eye contact with spectators, especially the children. He kept pace with the marching band in front of him. He knew he was looking good. This was fun! The attention was what he loved, and he had his best friend along for the ride too. What could be better?

Fiona and her sisters followed Ali down the parade route. Ali knew Fiona was nervous. The sound of her hooves against the asphalt was more tentative than her companions at first. As the parade moved along, she was getting better and more relaxed, her stride more purposeful.

A two-year-old child beside the road lost her bright red Happy Birthday balloon. It drifted across the road in front of Fiona. It touched the pavement almost beneath her front feet. It exploded! The child screamed and began to wail. Fiona froze. She stopped in her tracks for a heartbeat, then screamed out in fear and began to shake. She scrabbled backward away from the noisy thing. Her shoes slipped on the pavement. She slammed into Sally, hitched behind her.

That caught Sally off guard. The impact drove her backward. She crashed into the buckboard. The buckboard jolted back several feet.

When Fiona threw herself in reverse, she dragged Peggy, hitched beside her. Peggy slammed backward. Her rear rammed Missy. That shoved Missy into the buckboard. The impact sent the buckboard several more feet backward. The first jolt tossed the Boy Scouts to the floor in the back of the buckboard. The second jolt sent them crashing into the front of the wagon.

Gloria hung on for dear life. Chuck hauled on the reins and hollered, "Whoa! Easy! Whoa! EASY! WHOA!" Gloria turned her head and saw the kids knocked about on the floorboards. She saw blood. Her heart raced.

The Marine Corps Color Guard marched behind the buckboard. The explosion stopped them in their tracks. The Marines held onto their Palomino mustangs. They grabbed flags and held them against the flag poles to stop flapping that could cause further distraction.

A Marine on the outside of the group spun his horse around and moved to the school band leader behind them. He asked them to stop the music until the horse situation was under control. The band passed the word backward person to person quickly. Everyone went silent, standing at attention. Word spread back from the band to every group behind them down the parade route. Every float, cart, carriage, walker, wagon, and band stopped in silence. The spectators watching this went quiet from shock. They watched with their hearts in their throats.

Fiona threw her head and brayed. Sweat poured down her neck and flanks. Her chest heaved. All four animals voiced their fear. They fed on each other's fright. The four danced and scrambled on the asphalt to keep their footing. The sound of metal shoes scraping asphalt screeched through the still morning air.

Fiona couldn't move backward because of Sally behind her. She started jumping forward. When her metal shoes hit the asphalt, they slipped. She started to go down. All she wanted to do was run away from this thing that was going to kill her. She shook all over, tossed her head around, and screamed in terror.

Ali saw what happened and was momentarily startled by the exploding balloon himself. He turned and walked calmly back toward Fiona. Becky could not change his direction. She finally understood and went with him. Ali stood sideways in front of

Fiona. His body became a granite wall she couldn't get through. He blocked her. He reached around with his muzzle and touched the side of her face and neck. He nickered at her. Fiona stood shaking, sweating, and ready to bolt.

"Hey, Beautiful, its okay! That thing is dead and can't hurt you." Ali was so calm and unruffled Fiona began to settle down. Her breathing slowed. Becky sat on Ali's back and spoke to the Hinnies in a soothing voice, "Easy ladies. Everything's all right. It was just a balloon. It can't hurt you. Easy, Whoa … Easy girls," Becky kept talking to the Hinnies in a soothing voice until the other three mares began to settle down. They stopped hopping around. *"Beautiful Fiona, I know you want to run away from that thing, but you can't do that. If you did, you could get hurt. Look around. There are many little people here that could get hurt too. It's okay. I promise you. Calm down, catch your breath. I'm right here. I'll look out for you."* Ali told her.

When Fiona was calm enough, Ali found a piece of the red balloon lying in the street in front of her and stomped on it with his front foot. *"See what I mean?"* Ali said to her. *"This thing is dead!"* He kicked it and stomped it again. Ali looked at the thing under his foot then looked at Fiona. He looked back down at the rubber thing and up again at Fiona.

She finally got it! She answered him at last. *"Oh, thank you. I was so scared. I don't want to get hurt, and I don't want to hurt anyone else either. I thought that thing was going to kill me! I can't thank you enough, sir. Thank you!"* She and her stable-mates felt consoled. Their breathing slowed to normal. They stopped sweating and stamping the pavement.

During the commotion, spectators on both sides of the road couldn't turn their eyes away. They remained quiet, holding their breath. The mother and father of the child who lost her balloon took the sobbing child away from the area. The crowd parted to give them room.

Chuck was blown away. He watched the interaction between Fiona and Ali. He knew positively Ali prevented a disaster. For a few seconds, he was sure he had a four-horse stampede on his hands. He thought his family, the scout troop, their buckboard, and the four Hinnies were goners and maybe some of the spectators too. His wife was next to him on the seat. A couple of their kids were in the back of the buckboard with the rest of their scout troop.

He and Gloria saw news coverage of a wreck caused by a four-horse hitch like his bolting at a parade a few years back. The news report said it destroyed the wagon. Some of the horses and several of the spectators were seriously hurt. One person in the wagon died.

Chuck had never seen an animal diffuse a situation like this. He had tears in his eyes. His hands were shaking as he held tightly to the four sets of reins. He leaned toward Gloria and she hugged him. She was shaking too.

Gloria checked on the boys in the back of the buckboard. She saw two bloody noses and a few scrapes. None were seriously hurt. There might be a couple of black eyes in the morning. All the boys were shaken, her sons included. Her eyes welled up thinking of that old TV newscast. She reassured the boys. They got back to their seats on the hay bales. She handed out Kleenex to those bleeding and helped mop up the bloody noses.

Fiona took two paces forward until she felt the tug of the harness on the breast piece then stopped. Sally moved forward the same two paces until she'd pulled the harness tight from the wagon. Fiona tightened up the rigging again and halted. Next to them, Peggy and Missy also moved forward and tightened up the harness. All four stood and waited calmly.

Ali resumed his place in the parade, but he looked over his shoulder at Fiona. When he was sure she was alright, he turned back and faced forward with his neck up and arched like nothing ever happened. He waited for Becky to signal him onward.

Fiona nickered to him, "*We're okay now. We're ready. Thank you again!*" All was right with the world. Everything froze in place for about ten seconds. Nothing moved; no sound was heard except the slight squeak of harness leather as the hinnies drew their breaths.

Chuck handed the reins to Gloria. He jumped down from the buckboard to check the rigging on the animals. He stroked and patted each one as he checked harnesses, breeching, saddles, breast collars, and reins. He straightened those he found out of place. He smiled up at Gloria when he discovered no damage.

"We're good to go," he said as he climbed back up and took the reins from Gloria. "We sure dodged a bullet that time."

Chuck leaned over and whispered in Gloria's ear, "We may want to consider switching to Arabian horses. I understand they drive beautifully."

Gloria whispered back, "I'll get in touch with the owner and see if any of Ali's foals are available. I want *his* breeding if we switch to Arabs. That kind of intelligence is inheritable!"

Walter and Caroline were right across the street from the incident and watched it happen. Both of them felt sheer panic in the first seconds. It all happened so fast. In the end, they were so proud of Ali and Becky they could have popped the buttons off their shirts. Caroline no longer worried about Becky with Ali. Ali demonstrated what he was made of – courage and intelligence. Becky showed her own courage. Caroline had tears in her eyes. Walter didn't know quite what to say. He sat with his arm around his wife's shoulders and let out a big sigh.

Becky squeezed her legs to signal Ali on. He struck up the pace. The parade resumed. Ali strutted on. The jewels on his costume glinted and sparkled in the light of the mid-day sun. He was having the time of his life. It was a gorgeous day – blue sky and sunshine with just a hint of crispness in the air. There were so many beautiful mares to see. That little Hinny wasn't a bad looker at all, and he thought she might like him a little too! He flipped his head, flared his nostrils, elevated his tail, and snorted like a bad boy.

For Ali, this whole parade thing was much easier than the horse show routine. There was no pressure to perform because all Becky wanted him to do was walk down the street. He was carrying his best friend with him. He knew there were special treats and extra oats in a bucket when he was done. He knew there was a dry barn, soft bedding, and a manger full of fresh hay. What could be better? *"Aaahhhh! Life is good sometimes."*

When they heard about the incident, the parade committee huddled together. Someone ran to get the Mayor and the City Council of San Juan Capistrano. Together they came up with an award for Prince Ali. At the end of the Awards Ceremony, the Mayor gave the Key to the City to a horse! And the day wasn't over yet.

CHAPTER TWENTY

The minute the Awards Ceremony finished, Becky led Prince Ali off the stage. She wanted to get him back to the horse trailer and give him his bucket of goodies. Walter and Caroline followed them.

Becky and Ali were mobbed. Chuck and Gloria wedged their way through the crowd and threw their arms around Ali's neck on both sides. With tears in her eyes, Gloria said, "Ali, you saved our lives today!" Chuck stroked his neck and scratched his withers. "That you did, young man," he told Ali. They wouldn't leave until Becky gave them a phone number so Gloria could call Mom.

The crowd around Becky and Ali grew larger as more and more people surrounded them. Caroline and Walter became separated from Becky and Ali. Those who knew the Howards owned Ali gathered around them to talk about Ali and Becky, especially those who saw the event mid-parade. That separated them from Becky and Ali even further.

Most horses would be nervous in such a large crowd. Everyone wanted to touch Ali, have their pictures taken with him, and talk to him. Ali was a gentleman. He reveled in the attention. With his lips, he tousled the hair of tiny children who could only reach his knees to pet him. He nodded his head in answer to people's questions about him. He watched where he stepped so he didn't smash toes. Becky answered a million questions about Prince Ali, his costume, how he came to be her mount for the day, etc. She and Ali managed to creep along a few feet at a time.

The street faire was in full swing across the street from the park. The street filled with people walking back from the Awards Ceremony and those attending the street faire besides those who wanted to see the celebrity horse up close and personal.

Becky became frustrated with their lack of progress toward the horse trailer. She finally announced that she and Prince Ali had somewhere to go. She asked people to give him some space so she could get him to his "goodie bucket." That seemed to do the trick, and they were finally able to make some headway.

That was not the case for Caroline. Walter whispered in her ear that he was going back to the El Adobe to save a table for them for lunch. He would meet her there when they got back from taking Prince Ali home. Dad wasn't thrilled with being stuck in that crowd. Crowds made him uncomfortable. Mom tried moving off toward the horse trailer and spotted Mrs. Grimes heading her way.

Caroline gulped and smiled at her, resigned to her fate. Every town has its own "Mrs. Grimes." This Mrs. Grimes was a lovely woman. In fact, she was the principal at Becky's school. She was always one of the most generous citizens in town, especially where the children were concerned. She gave of her time and opened her pocketbook for causes involving what she referred to as "her kids." At the same time, she was a notorious talker. What Caroline could say in ten words took Mrs. Grimes a hundred or more. Everyone in town loved Mrs. Grimes unless they were in a hurry.

Mrs. Grimes threw her arms around Caroline when she reached her. "Oh, your horse is so lovely and courageous!" she gushed. "I was across the street when that balloon thing happened, and I was so scared those horses were going to stampede. That gorgeous horse of yours, not to mention your lovely daughter Becky, was spot on! I never knew horses could think like that. Can you imagine?"

All Caroline wanted at that moment was to get to the horse trailer and help Becky get the costumes off. She just breathed a little sigh, smiled, and let Mrs. Grimes continue. It wasn't easy to get a word in the conversation. She couldn't shove one in sideways with this lady.

When Mrs. Grimes finally ran out of gas and slowed down, Caroline thanked her profusely for her kind words. She promised Mrs. Grimes she could visit Prince Ali at home. She explained she needed to get to the horse trailer so she and Becky could take Ali home. They wanted to come back and enjoy some of the street faire. Unfortunately, that opened another topic for Mrs. Grimes. She prattled on for another few minutes about some of the new vendors at the El Mercado this year.

Caroline didn't want to annoy Mrs. Grimes in any way, but time was flying by, and she didn't want to leave Becky and Ali alone for too long. She finally explained that to Mrs. Grimes, who completely understood. "Yes, sometimes I do chatter on a bit. You'd better head on over and take care of your family," the older woman insisted. She hugged Caroline again and hurried off to catch someone else she'd spied in the distance.

Becky got Ali back to the parade staging area and walked him around the trailer to the shady side nearest the building. She tied him to the side of the trailer and pulled his goodie bucket out of the dressing room. She also fixed him a fresh water bucket and sat it down on the pavement within his reach. Ali was no different from most males, guided by his stomach. He reached into the goodie bucket for a mouthful of grain before taking a drink of water. Chewing and with his muzzle still dripping, he turned his head toward Becky.

She jumped back, giggling, "No, you don't, Mister. You keep your sloppy mouth to yourself. We don't need your drool all over this nice costume." She began removing the costume from Ali and hanging up what she could in the trailer. She wondered what kept Mom but continued working while telling Ali what a good boy he had been and how proud she was. As soon as Becky finished pulling the costume off Ali, she stepped into the trailer to remove her outfit, closing the side door behind her.

The Hix brothers got off the freeway on the Ortega Highway exit and drove to the trailer parking area. They cruised the area slowly, looking for horses with no one around. There were still quite a few people putting wheeled vehicles in their rigs. A few were busy stowing tack. Some were getting their horses ready to load up for the trip home. They saw no unattended horses.

"I told you we shoulda been here an hour ago," whined Danny. "Looks like most everybody's gone or getting ready for the haul. There are too many people around here. What're we goin' to do now?"

"Just shut up and keep your eyes open!" Calvin snapped. "There were hundreds of horses here for the parade. They can't all be gone. We just need one or two that nobody's watchin'."

Danny simmered in silence. He was slipping into one of his dark moods. He began obsessing over a minor issue that could consume him for hours. He wasn't particularly crazy about this whole idea in the first place. He was angry with his brother for dawdling so long at the Drop Inn. They went over to borrow gas money for the trip. Calvin insisted on playing around too much and showing off his pool skills for some girl. It took forever to get his mind back on the job at hand.

They drove around the lot, looking at every rig left in the parking area. Just as it seemed they'd completely missed the boat, they spotted the Howard's truck and trailer at the end of the lot. They almost passed it by before they saw Ali tied to the far side of the trailer with no one around. It was perfect! They could sneak up on the horse, and nobody could see them.

"Here we go!" Calvin said as he set the parking brake on the old truck. "This one's it. There's no one around, and the folks on the other side of the trailer can't see. Get the tranquilizer ready, will ya? I'll just make sure there's nobody here."

Danny pulled the vial out of his pocket and got a syringe out of the glove box. He twisted a new needle on the syringe. He plunged the needle into the vial and turned the vial upside down. He pulled the plunger on the vial to fill the syringe. "I'm ready."

Calvin left the engine running, got out, and walked around the Howard's trailer. He saw no one. He waved Danny over. Danny hopped out of the truck leaving the door open and stepped around the trailer to the far side out of view. "How're ya doin' boy?" he asked Ali as he scratched him on the withers and patted his neck.

He had the needle in Ali's neck in a split second, pushed the plunger to deliver the drugs, and pulled the needle out.

"*Ouch!*" Ali felt the sting of the needle. He'd had shots before from the vet, but not by some stranger who just came up to greet him. That alarmed him. He snorted loudly to alert Becky.

Calvin stood on the other side of Ali, scratching his withers to divert Ali's attention.

"This will just take a few minutes," Danny whispered. "We should just stay here until he gets sleepy."

Becky heard Ali snort and quickly pulled on her tee-shirt. She opened the side door to the trailer and jumped out. She was startled by the two men standing on either side of Ali – then she noticed the syringe in Danny's hand.

"What do you think you are doing?" she yelled.

Ali heard the anxiety in her voice and became nervous and agitated. He pawed the ground and neighed loudly.

"You'd better get away from my horse right now, or I'll have the cops on you!" Becky shouted.

She saw a mean look cross Calvin's face, and she began to fear for herself and Ali. She was determined not to show it, so she stretched up all five feet, four inches, and one hundred ten pounds of herself and stuck out her chin.

"You two better get out of here before I start screaming my head off!"

Numbness began to settle over Ali. "*This isn't right. What are these people up to? I have to protect my Becky! But I don't feel so good… .NO! NO!*" Ali screamed a stallion challenge at them, but it didn't quite come out right. His vision was blurring. The noise in the parking area covered the sound of his scream. No one could see anything because the trailer hid them from view. No one took any notice.

Danny and Calvin had no great love for the police. And they needed the money for this horse. Danny looked over at Calvin, and Calvin waved him backward and pointed at the girl.

"Okay, okay little lady," Danny mumbled, "I'm leavin'." He backed up and walked around Becky. As he passed her, she stared daggers at Calvin, who hadn't moved away from Ali yet.

In a split second, Danny's pent-up frustration turned to panic and rage. He didn't like this situation one bit! He hated cops and jails! He was angry about his brother's dawdling around and getting them here so late. They were only getting half the horses they'd wanted. That cut the money they'd get in half. And now there was a witness!

Danny grabbed her from behind and gave her a violent shove.

The shove caught Becky off guard. She went flying toward the building. She wheeled her arms as she struggled to keep her footing. She tripped on loose gravel on the pavement. She stumbled. She crashed headfirst into the wall of the building. Her momentum bounced her off the building onto the asphalt. Her body rolled partially over and went still. A trickle of blood appeared on her forehead. Blood from the gash on top of her head began staining her long blonde hair a deep red. Her blue eyes closed, and her body twitched once.

Ali tried to whirl around and strike at Danny with his front feet, but his legs would hardly support his weight. He almost fell when he reached the end of his lead. He moaned, *"Oh my Becky! Becky, help me if you can. Becky, please get up. What's happening?"* The dark cloud became heavier on him, and he felt his whole body go numb. He began weaving on his feet to stay upright.

"Now you've done it!" spat Calvin. "All you needed to do is push 'er out of the way or hold onto 'er so we could tie 'er up or somethin'. But you maybe just killed 'er. We have to go NOW!"

"Hey, I only pushed 'er. She's the one who tripped," whined Danny.

Ali struggled to stay on his feet. His eyes were at half-mast, and he was beyond caring. His mind shut down with the drugs and the shock. Calvin untied him from the Howard's trailer and walked him to theirs. He opened the back door. Ali made several attempts to get his front feet up in the trailer. He finally succeeded. Calvin shoved Ali inside and closed the trailer door. Calvin had Danny grab the lead rope through the front window of the trailer and tie Ali inside. Then both men jumped in the truck, slamming the doors.

Calvin jammed the truck in gear and stepped on the gas. He sped to the on-ramp of the freeway a quarter of a mile away. He put his foot to the floorboard, hoping no one saw what just happened.

CHAPTER TWENTY-ONE

C aroline finally extricated herself from well-wishers and hurried to the trailer parking area. She noticed the rear trailer door was open. "Becky?" she called out and got no reply. She stepped around the truck to the other side and noticed the tack room door was also open, but Ali was not tied to the side of the trailer. He was gone! "Becky, where are you two?" There was no reply.

That's when she saw Becky lying on the pavement with her eyes closed, not moving. She saw the fresh pool of blood around Becky's head and began to scream, "No! No! NO! NOO!

Caroline ran and dropped to her knees beside her daughter and cradled her head in her arms, tears streaming down her cheeks. "Becky! Wake up, Becky! Honey, open your eyes! WAKE UP, PLEASE, DEAR GOD!" She got no response. It was then she noticed the blood on her own arms and clothes. Terror gripped her heart, and she began to scream in earnest, "HELP! HELP! HELP! My daughter's been hurt! SOMEONE CALL 911! PLEASE, SOMEBODY, PLEASE COME HELP US!"

People at the nearest trailers dropped what they were doing and came running. Two of the ladies were already on their cell phones dialing 911. "What's happened? asked one man.

Choking down sobs, Caroline cried, "I don't know. I just got here and found my Becky here and can't wake her up. There's blood everywhere, and our horse is gone. Did anyone see what happened?"

Prince Ali and Becky had been on the far side of their trailer, away from the view of the parking area. No one saw what happened.

"We didn't see a loose horse anywhere around here. He couldn't get far," answered the man.

"Hey, what color was your horse? I saw two guys loading a gray horse in a beat-up trailer right there in front of your rig," said a young man just walking up from the far end of the parking area. "They hauled out of here in a hurry. It looked like they were heading for the freeway. Maybe you shouldn't hold your daughter like that until the paramedics get here in case there's an injury to her neck or somethin'."

Fresh sobs came from Caroline. "Oh, my God! They stole Ali! They must have hurt Becky to get to him. NO! NO! NO! Can someone call the Sheriff and get an ambulance?"

She sat beside her daughter as tears streamed down her face. "Can someone get my husband? His name is Walter Howard, and he's waiting for us on the porch of the El Adobe."

Two women in the forming crowd were still talking with the 911 dispatch operators when the first siren wailed through the afternoon air. A couple of bystanders took off running for the restaurant to find Walter. Some of the people there were trying to give advice. The rest of them watched in stunned silence. The locals were shocked. Things like this just didn't happen in San Juan Capistrano!

When the first fire engine arrived, six firemen jumped out. By-standers directed them to Caroline. They asked Caroline to move back and give them room. They checked for pulse and respiration. They checked her pupils and probed for wounds finding a large gash near the top of her head and a small patch of "road rash" where her forehead came in contact with the asphalt. By that time, the paramedics' ambulance arrived. The paramedics applied bandaging to her head and a neck brace. They slid Becky onto a backboard. They started an IV in her arm and hoisted the backboard onto a portable stretcher.

Caroline stood back and watched in horror. Walter came, out of breath from running, and wrapped his arms around her holding her tight while she cried. "What happened?" he asked.

"Ooohh, I don't know," she sobbed. "I found her lying there on the pavement with blood everywhere and Ali gone. Someone said they saw two men load a gray horse in a trailer and take off, so they might have stolen Ali. Becky must have gotten in their way." She cried as if her heart were breaking.

"We're taking her to Mission Hospital," the paramedic told Caroline and Walter. "She's got a head injury, and we think she's in a coma, but she's breathing, and her pulse is strong and steady. That's a good sign. Are you her mother? You can come with us. We need to get some information anyway." Looking at Walter, he said, "If you're her father, can you follow us in your vehicle?"

Walter steadied Caroline as they walked to the ambulance. Becky was already loaded inside. One of the paramedics helped Caroline inside and showed her where to sit to be with her daughter and out of their way as they worked. The other paramedic riding in the back took out his clipboard and gathered Becky's chart information. The driver hit the siren switch again as they pulled away from the curb heading for the hospital.

The wail of the siren cracked the air like thunder. Grief struck Walter hard as he watched the ambulance get smaller and smaller in the distance. He almost fell to his knees. He was watching the two most precious things in his life, leaving him on the curb alone. It took his breath away.

Walter stood watching the ambulance until it disappeared, then decided it was time for him to find the courage and get moving. He locked up the truck and trailer and ran to his car, hoping there would be some good news waiting for him at the hospital.

CHAPTER TWENTY-TWO

T wo Orange County Sheriff's cars showed up at the staging area just as Dad drove away. The deputies talked to bystanders, trying to figure out what happened. When they heard who the victim was, they were very concerned. "That is an important family here. We'd better get the Watch Commander involved right away," one of them said.

They called their Watch Commander. They told him about Becky Howard. They told him a famous horse owned by the Howards was missing. They didn't have much information on the case yet but thought he'd want to get involved now.

The Watch Commander's ears perked up when he heard the name of the victim. "Would that be the daughter of Walter and Caroline Howard?" he asked. He knew and liked Walter Howard and knew the Howards' reputation. They were heavily involved in their community, state politics, and local charities. He also knew about their horse and instantly wondered if this could be a horse-napping for ransom.

He called the Detective Commander and his superiors immediately. The DC assigned four detectives. Two went to the crime scene to interview witnesses and gather any evidence they could find. The Lead Detective on the case went with his partner to the hospital to interview the Howards. The DC assigned other people to the case. Calls went out fast and furious to different agencies.

The U.S. Border Patrol received a call immediately. They could stop the horse at the border if the suspects tried to get him out of the country that way. To help identify the horse, the Border Patrol requested photographs. The Sheriff's Department promised to get them copies when they got them. The DC called the State Fish and Wildlife Department because they handle cases that involve animals. He also promised them a photograph of the horse when one was available. The DC also called Orange County Sheriff Nolan's office because of the high-profile nature of the family involved. The Sheriff's Department Public Information Officer was alerted in case the media contacted him. The deputies at the parking lot asked all bystanders who might have information to wait until the Detectives got there. Detectives Sharp and Newsome arrived with lights flashing. They looked over the crime scene and collected anything they thought was evidence. They did find some long blonde hairs and some blood on the side of the building. They picked up the syringe Danny dropped. They bagged a cigarette butt found lying on the pavement in front of the Howard's truck just in case.

They interviewed bystanders. After they talked to the young man who saw the two guys loading a gray horse into a trailer and take off, they made some calls. They set him up with a Sheriff's Department sketch artist. They got a verbal description of the truck, trailer, and the two men and called it into their Commander. He had an All-Points Bulletin (APB) issued to every law enforcement agency in the State.

Darryl Finn owned and ran the local newspaper for San Juan, Dana Point, and several small surrounding cities. He was at the parade with his photographer to cover the story for his newspaper. His photographer had many pictures of the parade, the crowds, and the awards ceremony.

Finn heard a rumor something was going on in the trailer parking lot. He hurried over to check it out. When he spoke with people in the lot and heard what they knew, he rushed back to the El Mercado to inform the Mayor. The area was closed to cars but filled curb to curb with crowds of people going this way and that.

Finn and Mayor Sterling elbowed their way back to the parking area. They found the Detectives working on the case. Detective Newsome brought them up to date with all they knew at the time. They swapped cards so they could stay in touch.

Finn scribbled in his notebook. He asked his photographer to take pictures of the Howard's empty truck and trailer for the story. Newsome asked him if he had any photos of the missing horse. They reviewed the digital images on the photographer's camera. Newsome asked, "Why don't you guys jump in my squad car. I can get through the barricades quicker. If we go back to your office and transfer the images to my department, it will save us a lot of time." The photos were of Ali in his costume, but they were all they had right now. As soon as the pictures were transferred to the Sheriff's Department, Newsome dropped Finn and the photographer back at the parking area.

On the way, Newsome called his DC and asked if Detectives Nelson and Bentley could get better photos from the Howards at the hospital. Darryl Finn overheard and made a note to himself to ask the Howards for pictures for his story too.

When Detectives Sharp and Newsome finished their investigation, Darryl Finn rushed off to the newspaper office on foot to make some phone calls. He'd parked his car there because of the street closures. He'd need it to get over to the hospital too.

Finn was well-connected in the media world. Before retiring to San Juan Capistrano, he'd spent 40 years as a headline reporter for a major East Coast newspaper. Finn made a phone call to a reporter friend, Marcia Phillips, who worked for local network TV. He told her what he knew at that point and gave her the background on the Howards and their horse. He suggested she bring a truck and cameraperson to the hospital. He told her Mayor Sterling was on his way with several members of the City Council so she could look them up for updates.

Finn contacted newspaper reporter friends from the Orange County Register, LA Times, Chicago Tribune, USA Today, Dallas News, San Francisco Chronicle, Denver Post, Boston Globe, and the New York Times. He set up a large conference call so he didn't have to repeat himself so many times. He promised to funnel them information as he got it. Finn knew Prince Ali had a national, and possibly international, fan base. He promised to transfer the digital images he had. One was a nice picture of Ali with the Howards and Mayor Sterling. His photographer took that image an hour before the incident. It would definitely be an excellent human interest photo. It included a happy, smiling Becky Howard hugging her horse.

Finn was satisfied when he hung up the phone at last. He suspected this was going to be a media circus. He was excited to be the one who got the story out. He grabbed his car keys, locked up the office, and left for Mission Hospital to see what was happening there.

Walter caught up with Caroline in the Emergency Room at the hospital. She was in the waiting room. "How is she, honey? Do you know anything yet?" he asked, out of breath again.

"The doctors are working on her now. They asked me to wait here." Caroline replied, now dry-eyed and pale. "She wasn't responding in the ambulance, but she is breathing on her own, and her heart is stable."

They sat side by side, Walter holding her to him with one arm as they waited for news. The minutes dragged on and on and on. They sat wrapped in their own thoughts and just waited.

CHAPTER TWENTY-THREE

C alvin drove north on Interstate 5 in the slow lane at the speed limit. He didn't want to call attention to themselves. They were both sweating from the adrenaline rush.

"Phew, we did it, little brother! I'm thinkin' he probably weighs nine hundred to a thousand pounds, so that's ...., let's see ...., at fifty cents a pound ...., maybe four hundred fifty to five hundred bucks. Looks like we goin' to party after all!"

Danny had a hard time controlling his emotions. He wasn't sure if he was mad, scared, relieved, or what. He was very anxious. He thought about that little girl lying on the asphalt with blood in her hair. She looked so small. He wanted her to be okay. He didn't want to be responsible for killing her.

Danny turned on the radio and fiddled with the dial until he found a station he liked. Danny turned the volume dial up on the radio, "Hey, I LOVE this song," and he began tapping to the beat on his knees. When the song was over, he turned the volume back down.

"Hey, Cal, why do you keep saying he's worth fifty cents a pound anyway? We both know he's worth more than that. Can't we get more for him?"

"I told you I met this guy, Ed Tweedy, at Red's a coupla weeks ago. He buys and sells horses all the time. He's got a 60-acre ranch in the High Desert where he keeps 'em. He buys 'em at horse auctions for a coupla hundred bucks, and puts some weight on the skinny ones.

Some of them, if they're good horses that he buys legit, he can sell for more than he paid for 'em. The others he just fattens up and hauls to Mexico for slaughter. People give him horses they don't want no more 'cause they're old or crippled. Some people sell him horses. He don't ask no questions. There are horse buyers that insist on Bill-a-Sale or papers of some kind to prove you own the horse. They only buy at auctions that are legit. Not this guy. He'll buy anything! That works for us 'cause we don't have no papers on this guy."

"Why take 'em to Mexico?"

"'Cause we don't do no horse slaughter in this country. Horse people got laws passed to stop that. But Ed told me the President signed a new law that might bring slaughter plants back. It'll make his job easier, won't have to leave the country to make his money, just head for Missouri or Wyoming."

"But, why Mexico?"

"Only two places you can haul horses for slaughter from the States is Canada or Mexico, and Mexico's only three hours away for him. Like I said, he takes horses and don't ask no questions. If he gets one he thinks could be hot, he dummies up some paperwork and hauls them across the border. Over there, they're just meat, hides, and hooves in a coupla minutes. No way to trace 'em, and he makes a quick dollar a pound and is back in the States before anybody knows the horse is missing."

"Do people really eat horses there?"

"Well, it's cheaper than cow, and if you're hungry, you'll eat anything. Most of it prob'ly goes to dog food, and they might ship some overseas. People in some countries in Europe eat horse meat. Speaking of which, hand me my cell phone. I gotta call and let him know we're comin.'"

Danny handed Calvin the cell phone, and he made the call. "Right, know where that is….be there in about two hours. See ya then." Calvin snapped the phone shut. "He'll be waiting for us," he told Danny.

"Well," grumbled Danny, "I still don't get why we can't get more for this guy. He sure is a pretty one."

"Haven't you been listenin' to me? We don't got no papers on him! He's hot! We gotta dump him quick. And this guy don't ask too many questions, you big dummy. It's fast cash for us. All we had to do was snatch 'im and drop 'im off and collect our money." Calvin looked at Danny with irritation.

Danny never was the brightest bulb in the box. But eventually, he understood their position and sat back to listen to the radio as Calvin drove the old truck up the freeway.

"Ya know," Danny said quietly, "I feel kinda bad about this guy," poking his thumb backward over his shoulder. "He didn't do nothin' to deserve this. He's goin' to be dog food in a few days like ya said. And I like horses. In fact, I like horses more than most people."

"Well, don't get your panties in a twist! You don't know this horse from Adam, and we need the cash," answered Calvin. "You are going to enjoy that birthday party. Just think of it that way and don't go stewin' over it."

As they rumbled northward through Saturday afternoon traffic on Interstate 5, neither of the brothers had much to say. The drive across the Los Angeles area was uneventful except for slow traffic at the interchanges where they changed freeways.

Ali was half-conscious most of the way. He was used to being hauled, so this was nothing new to him. One knee at a time would buckle on occasion, and the trailer swayed a bit as he regained his footing. He began to come back to himself slowly the further they went. When they merged from Interstate 405 onto the Antelope Valley Freeway, his head was mostly clear.

He was in an unfamiliar trailer and had no idea how he'd gotten there. He whinnied loudly a couple of times but settled down to pick at the stale hay in the hay bag. He wondered where he was going. This didn't look like any place he'd been before. He could see the countryside from the trailer window. The hills looked bare and rocky, not at all like the area near his home, or around Boulder,Colorado.

In the truck cab, the news came on the radio. Danny was just about to change the station to something he liked when the newsman announced "Breaking News." Danny's hand was on the dial when he heard, "The most famous Arabian horse in the country was stolen this afternoon from the parking area in San Juan Capistrano following the Swallows Day Parade."

"Oh, crud!" Calvin exclaimed, "Turn that up!"

Danny turned up the volume.

"Prince Ali, a gray International Champion Arabian horse, was taken from his owner's trailer this afternoon by two men driving an older blue truck towing an older blue and white horse trailer. It was reported this horse had just been awarded the Keys to the City of San Juan Capistrano for bravery in stopping a potential stampede during the parade. The horse was also the Grand Marshall of the parade."

"The men are suspected of causing serious injury to the owner's 13-year-old daughter who is currently in Mission Hospital in San Juan Capistrano fighting for her life."

"The suspects are two men described as white, mid-twenties to early thirties, both with blonde hair wearing ball caps and blue work shirts and jeans. In a highly unusual attempt to recover the horse, police have issued an Amber Alert. Anyone seeing these two men or their truck and trailer is encouraged to call the California Highway Patrol or their local law enforcement and report their location…. and the weather today in the LA Basin will be generally sunny and mild with slight breezes, 72 degrees in downtown LA….."

"Holy cow!" Calvin shouted. "We're in big trouble! We'd better get off the freeway quick. I know there are several back roads into the High Desert from here, but some are just dirt roads. The longer we stay on the freeway with that horse, the better our chances of getting stopped! We prob'ly stick out like a sore thumb." He began to sweat again. He'd been in jail before, but this would get them a long stretch in prison.

"Danny, get out the map. I'll take the next off-ramp and park under it where we can't be seen 'till we figure out which way to go."

Danny fumbled through the glove box for a map. Calvin turned off the freeway at the next exit and parked the rig under the freeway overpass. "Better call Ed and tell 'im we're goin' to be a bit late.

Wish I had a cold one. Need somethin' to calm me down. I gotta think about this."

"Oh, man!" Danny shouted, "You really got us into it this time! Just take any horse, you said. It won't matter. It's just meat on the hoof. Well, we took the wrong darned horse! And that little girl is in the hospital. What're we goin' to do now??" He was shaking and sweating and scared to death.

"Just shut up and give me the phone," Calvin growled. "I gotta call Ed."

"Okay …. Okay! Here!" Danny tossed him the phone. "Here's the map too! See if you can figure a way outa this mess you got us into." He sat back and crossed his arms over his chest. He crossed his legs. He nervously twitched his raised foot.

Calvin dialed the phone, and Ed Tweedy picked it up after two rings. "Hey, Ed. We're on our way, but we might have a little problem. Just heard a breaking news story on the radio, and we might have a famous horse in our trailer ….. yeah, he's gray. …. yeah, I understand …. You've seen it on TV?? Holy crud! …. Too hot for you to handle?? …. yeah, I get it. …. We're under the over-pass at Vasquez Rocks right now. ….dump the horse? …. You got any ideas where we can take 'im and get rid of 'im?" Calvin listened for a minute, then asked Danny for a pen and piece of paper. "Yeah, I'm writin' it down. Can you give me those directions again?" He scribbled furiously on a scrap of paper Danny found in the glove box. "Okay. See you another time," he said as he closed the phone.

Calvin looked over at Danny. "Ed Tweedy won't take this horse. Says he's too hot to handle and doesn't want to get caught with him, takin' stolen property and all. Says we'd better dump him quick. He gave me the name of an old guy he knows not far from here that'll prob'ly give us a coupla hundred bucks for him as a packhorse. Says the guy's a crazy old prospector out in these parts who keeps lookin' for the gold Vasquez, the bandit, was supposed to have hidden in these rocks. I got directions. Let's head on over and see what kind of deal we can do."

Calvin turned the truck around and headed east until he came to the dirt road Ed Tweedy told him to look for. He turned left and headed north into the hills. The dirt road looked like it never saw much traffic. The hills were almost entirely bare except for the rocks and squat-growing desert plants. A few California poppies struggled to poke their heads above ground in the arid desert soil this time of year. There wasn't much to look at. The truck bumped along the desert track, mile after mile, climbing as they went.

"Better to be a packhorse for some old fool than what you had in mind for 'im," Danny said thoughtfully. "Better to work in this heat and rocks than be turned into dog food in couple days."

"Oh, shut up, ya big dummy!" Calvin spit out. "I told you not to get your panties in a twist over it. You're in this just as deep as I am. And, you're the one that tossed that little girl into the building in the first place! Sure wish I had a cold one 'bout now."

They bounced along in silence after that. Ali, in the trailer, struggled to keep his footing as the trailer bounced over ruts and rocks, so the trailer swayed back and forth. He whinnied his discomfort loudly, but there was no one to hear him except the Hix brothers, and they could have cared less at this point. All they wanted to do is be rid of him; the sooner, the better.

CHAPTER TWENTY-FOUR

When Caroline arrived with Becky, the emergency waiting room was empty. As the news spread, more and more people came. The emergency waiting room was now filled. People were standing around in little clusters. More people were outside the doorway, talking quietly in small groups as they waited for news.

Finally, a door opened, and a tall, slender older gentleman in a white lab coat over scrubs stepped out, looking around the room. "Mr. and Mrs. Howard?" In blue lettering, *D Spencer* was embroidered above the left breast pocket of his lab coat, and he had a stethoscope draped around his neck. His graying hair was neatly trimmed, his blue eyes behind dark-framed glasses were soft and compassionate.

"We're here," said Walter as he stood and helped Caroline to her feet. They walked toward the doctor. He escorted them to an empty conference room near the emergency room waiting area.

"I've just been with your daughter, and you can go in and see her in a minute after we've had a chance to chat about her condition," Dr. Spencer said quietly. "I thought a little privacy would help."

Caroline's eyes filled with tears again, and she began to shake as she and the doctor took a seat at the small conference table. Walter stood behind her with his hands on her shoulders. "How is she, doctor?"

"Becky took a tough blow to the top of her head, right about here," he answered. He pointed to a spot about the midline of his skull and just a bit forward of center on the top. "It looks to us like she hit her head on some kind of building because we found stucco debris in the wound. We've done skull x-rays and a CAT scan. She has a fracture under the wound site but no displaced bone. In other words, the bone is cracked; all of the pieces are still intact."

"She has bruised her brain in that area. There is some bleeding inside her skull, and her brain may be swelling some. We've given her medication to help with that for now, but we need to watch it for the next 48 hours closely. If her brain swells too much, there's nowhere for it to go inside her skull. We may have to remove a piece of her skull to give it more room until the swelling goes back down."

"If she bleeds inside her skull too much, it will put extra pressure on the brain. We'll have to relieve that pressure by drilling a hole into her skull to allow the blood out. We are doing what we can right now to stop the bleeding."

"She is breathing on her own, and her heart is strong. We couldn't find any other injuries. But she is in a coma right now. There's no way for us to know how long she'll be in a coma. These brain injuries are difficult to predict. She could wake up five minutes from now, or it could be five weeks from now. All we can do at this point is give her body the best medical support we can and hope for the best. She's young and strong, so she has that going for her."

The doctor looked directly into Mom's eyes, "And, many of my patients have told me prayer works when medicine doesn't. I've been around long enough to believe that myself."

Dr. Spencer took off his glasses and pinched the bridge of his nose, looking tired. "Is there anything else you'd like to know before I show you to her room?"

"Is she going to be okay?" asked Caroline with great concern and anxiety.

"I wish I had a guarantee for you," answered Dr. Spencer, "but there are no guarantees here, just a gut feel from an old man who thinks she'll recover just fine. As I said, the next 48 hours are the most critical. She's in a fight for life. We'll do everything we can medically to support her. The rest is up to her and the Man Upstairs."

"Thank you, doctor," Walter said quietly. "Can we see her now?" He steadied Caroline as she got to her feet.

"Right this way" Dr. Spencer led them down a hallway into the ICU. "She'll be here in ICU until we control the bleeding and swelling in her brain. The nurses here will tell you that you can see her for five minutes every hour, but give me a call if you have any trouble with them. I can arrange for a folding bed in the room so one of you can stay if you'd like. Please keep the other visitors to family only. I'd rather not get on the bad side of the nurses."

Walter and Caroline followed Dr. Spencer into Becky's room in the Intensive Care Unit. They were shocked at what they saw. Her head was swathed in bandages, and she had tubes running into her body from everywhere. Her eyes were closed. Bruises were forming underneath them. She was going to have a pair of "shiners" by tomorrow. She wasn't on a respirator, but she did have a tube inserted in her nose and taped in place.

Machines beeped and chirped as they monitored her vital signs. One large screen above her bed kept pace with her heartbeat, blood pressure, blood oxygenation, and respiration. IVs dripped medication into each arm. Becky looked small, helpless, and so pale. Caroline broke down in quiet sobs again.

A nurse walked in and introduced herself. "Hi, I'm Joanne. I will be Becky's nurse for the rest of the day. I get off at midnight, and another nurse, Susan, I think, will take over for me. If you have any questions or concerns, please let me know." Joanne checked the monitors, typed something in Becky's chart, and left the room.

"I know this looks a little scary to you, so I'll try to help you navigate some of the stuff we are doing for your daughter," said Dr. Spencer. "We cleaned her wound and stitched it, but we did have to shave off quite a chunk of her hair. Sorry about that, but it will grow back."

"We are feeding her a high protein supplement to keep her body healthy. That's what the tube in her nose is doing. It goes directly into her stomach. We have an IV line in one arm with saline solution to keep the vein open for medication we have to inject. The other IV is for the medication I talked to you about for the swelling and bleeding in her brain. She is getting some steroids, antibiotics to prevent infection, and something to keep her sedated for a while."

"If she stays in a coma for more than a week, we'll have to put in something else. IV lines go into veins. We must reposition them every couple of days, or the veins collapse. The monitors here tell us that her heart is beating strongly, her blood oxygen level is excellent, her blood pressure is good, and her heart rate is fine."

"Now I do have something else to talk to you two about. We have a firm belief that patients in a coma are aware of their surroundings. I have a feeling that Becky hears every word spoken in this room. She knows you are here. She may not respond to you, but I believe she knows what goes on in this room. My advice is that you talk to her, read to her, and sing to her. Let her know you are here and that you love her. I think knowing you are here to help her fight will make a difference." Dr. Spencer said softly. "Do you have any questions before I get back to the ER?"

"Oh, and before I forget it," he reached into his pocket and took out two business cards handing one to each of them, "here's my card. You can reach me on that number 24/7. If I don't personally answer, my service will, and they can track me down. If you need me, I'll be here. I also want to assure you we have excellent doctors here that will assist me."

Dr. Spencer left the room and closed the door. Walter and Caroline were left alone with their daughter. Caroline began to cry again, and Walter put his arms around her and held her tightly. Once she stopped crying, she took a chair next to the bed and held Becky's hand. Walter stood across from her and held Becky's other hand. They both talked to Becky and told her how much they loved her. Mostly they just held her hand and prayed.

Joanne poked her head into the room. "The Sheriff's Detectives are here to speak with you," she told them. "I got you a conference room near the ICU, so you have some privacy. It would probably be better if they conduct their interview with you in another room, not in here with Becky."

CHAPTER TWENTY-FIVE

Joanne led Walter and Caroline down the hall to a small conference room. When she opened the door, two men in suits sitting at the conference table stood up. Joanne held the door open for them.

A tall, nice-looking man of about 40 reached out his hand to Walter. "I'm Detective Brian Nelson, and I'm the lead on this case. This is my partner, Ron Bentley." Ron, about the same age as Brian Nelson, but a little heavier, nodded in their direction.

Walter took his hand and shook, "I'm Walter Howard, and this is my wife, Caroline."

"Please take a seat. We need to go over a few things with you," Detective Nelson said. "First of all, I need to get your address, and any contact phone numbers you have, and any other names you go by."

Walter gave the information while both detectives scribbled it down in their notebooks. Caroline sat dry-eyed and numb during this exchange.

"We understand Caroline was the one who first found Becky," said Detective Nelson. "Can you tell me about that?" He looked at Caroline with raised eyebrows.

"Well, after the parade, Becky walked Ali, that's our horse, back to the trailer to give him some water and grain and take off his costume. People in the crowd delayed Walter and me, so I didn't get there until maybe fifteen or twenty minutes after Becky and Ali got there. I got tied up talking to people who wanted to know more about our horse. Walter doesn't like crowds, so he went back to the El Adobe to hold us a table. Becky and I were going to take Ali home and come back for the street fair and lunch." Mom sniffled. "I should have been there with them."

"Take your time," Detective Nelson reassured her and handed her a tissue from the box on the table. "I understand. I have a 14-year old daughter."

"Becky left the feed and water out and took off Ali's costume and her own before whatever happened happened." Caroline broke down. All the guilt and all the fear suddenly washed over her in waves. "I was chatting to people about our horse when someone attacked our daughter and stole him!" she wailed.

Walter put his arm around her and held her close while she sobbed. "Give us a minute, okay?" he asked the detectives. He held his wife, whispering to her while she cried as if her heart were broken.

Caroline pulled herself together in a few minutes, dried her face, and blew her nose. She looked at the two detectives with red, swollen eyes. "Let's get on with this. I know you have a job to do." She sniffed and mopped her eyes with the tissue.

"Okay, you went to the trailer parking lot from the street fair area to check on your horse and your daughter, that right? You were going to take the horse home and bring Becky back for the street fair and lunch. And you found her unconscious and the horse was missing? Do we have that right?" asked Detective Nelson. "Do you know about how long it was from the time you last saw Becky and the horse until you got back to your trailer and found her?"

"When I last saw Becky and Ali, I checked my watch. It was 2:10. I probably got to the trailer and found Becky about 2:35 or so. I didn't check the time." Mom blew her nose again, then wiped at her eyes.

"That's when I found my baby girl lying there bleeding, and I couldn't wake her up." Fresh sobs tore through her. Walter held her close and comforted her.

After a few minutes, Caroline regained her composure. Detective Nelson said, "Well, this is what we know right now. Your daughter was walking the horse to the trailer at 2:10. We have a witness that saw two men putting a gray horse in a blue and white horse trailer right in front of your truck about 2:25 to 2:30. You found your daughter unconscious about 2:35, and your horse was missing." The Detective referred to his notes. "We found a cigarette butt that looked fresh next to your trailer. Either of you smoke?"

Both Walter and Caroline shook their heads, "No."

"Okay, it could have been left by the suspects. We'll have it checked for possible DNA. We also found a syringe next to your trailer. It's too large for human use, so we're assuming it was for livestock. Could it belong to you?"

"No, we have the vet out when our horses need shots for anything," Caroline explained. "We wouldn't have one in the truck or our trailer."

"Okay, then we assume the suspects could have left it. We'll have the lab check it to see what was in it and look for possible fingerprints."

"Now," Detective Nelson said, "with what we know, it looks to us that the horse was the target, not your daughter. She might just have been in the wrong place at the wrong time, got in the way, or interfered. We won't know for sure until she wakes up and we can talk to her. Do you know of anyone that might have a grudge against you or anyone in your family? A business associate? Another family member? A neighbor you don't get along with?"

"Not that we know of," answered Walter. "So you think Ali is what they were after?"

"Let's talk through some scenarios. How would your horse react to strangers? Would he go willingly with someone he didn't know?"

"We have no idea. Ali's never been in that position that we know of. Many people he didn't know have seen him, and he's always friendly. But Ali loves our Becky, so he wouldn't be happy with anyone that tried to hurt her. He's a big boy. If he got angry or upset, he could be threatening." Walter said.

"Well, assuming your horse was the target, there are some facts we know. If they left that syringe behind, maybe they drugged him to make him easier to handle. First, tell me about the horse. What is his value anyway?" asked Detective Nelson.

"Ali is something of an anomaly. He's only five years old. We started showing him in large breed shows when he was a yearling. He's done extremely well, nationally and internationally, because he has excellent conformation for his breed. He is extremely well-bred on both sides of his pedigree. Ali's very talented, a very handsome individual, and has a lot of natural charisma. We were offered 1.3 million for him as a two-year-old. That was when he won his first World Championship at the Salon du Cheval in Paris, France. He won his second world title a few months ago. We were approached three months ago about syndicating him for somewhere close to 2.5 million dollars. We would never consider selling him for any amount of money. If you are looking purely for his dollar value, you'd have to use the syndication offer," Walter explained.

"How does syndication work?" asked Detective Nelson.

"When you have a top-performing stallion of any breed, many mare owners want to breed to him hoping to create a top-performing horse for themselves," Walter explained. "If every superior horse produced nothing but superior horses, the breeding business would be easy. But it doesn't work that way. Syndication legally limits the number of mares bred to the stallion. 'Breeding Shares' generally run into five or six figures, depending on the horse. The share-holders pay annual 'maintenance fees' for the stallion and 'mare care fees,' which run pretty high. That helps ensure the stallion is bred only to the best quality mares for the highest quality babies. It also limits the number of babies. Supply and demand keep the value of the babies high as well," Walter explained.

"We're not ready to 'retire' Ali to stud just yet. Becky wants to ride and show him herself."

"Wow," whistled Detective Nelson. "That's 2.5 million reasons to snatch your horse for ransom. "We need to focus on that angle here."

Detective Bentley cut in, "I'd say we'd better get a wiretap on your phone now. Don't want to miss the ransom call."

"The more I think about it, Ron, we'd better put out an alert on the airports as well, in case they try to fly him out of here. Can you call the Commander and have that wiretap done a.s.a.p. and see who at the Federal Aviation Authority we need to get a hold of to put a watch out at the airports?" Detective Nelson spoke to his partner, "I'll get the Howards to sign off on the authorization for the wiretap before we finish here. We might also put extra patrols on their home, just in case. And it would be a good idea to have someone at the house 24/7 until we know more."

"Is that okay with you two?" he asked Walter and Caroline. They nodded their agreement.

"Is there anyone at your home right now?" Detective Nelson asked.

"Yes, Esperanza, our housekeeper/nanny is there, and Fernando, our groundsman, is there. I called Esperanza a while ago to tell her what happened to Becky and what we know right now. Fernando is taking care of the horses and keeping an eye on the place." Walter answered.

"Oh, and we need some better pictures of the horse. The news photographer at the parade took the only ones we have now. He's wearing some kind of costume, and you can't see the horse very well. Do you have pictures of him without the costume that we can use?" Detective Nelson asked.

"Yes, in my office at home," answered Caroline, dabbing at her eyes. "Esperanza can show your officer. They can take whatever they need to help find Ali. Finding him is important to us. You have to understand, I think of him as a son, and he is Becky's best friend."

"Ron, when you talk to the Commander, can you see that someone gets over there and picks up a picture of the horse for us?" Detective Nelson asked.

"Sure thing. I'm going outside so I can use my cell phone. Is there anything else I should report or get handled now?" Detective Bentley asked.

"Not that I can think of, but I'll be outside with you in a couple of minutes. I just have one or two more questions for these folks, and I know they want to get back to their daughter," answered Detective Nelson.

He looked at Walter. "Can you call your people at home and let them know we're sending officers over to work on the phone lines and pick up the picture? You might also let them know we'll be keeping an eye on the house and doing extra patrols of the neighborhood."

Walter nodded, "Sure."

The final questions asked and answered, authorization forms signed, the Detective looked directly at Caroline and said, "I want to assure you we are going to do everything in our power to find out who did this to your daughter and find your horse. As I said, I have my own 14- year-old daughter at home. I don't know how I'd feel in your place, but I have some idea. I'm leaving our business cards for you. If you, either of you, think of *anything*, any little detail, no matter how insignificant, please call us. A lot of crimes get solved by putting together little details. And my family and I will pray for Becky's recovery."

Walter and Caroline headed back to the ICU, and Detective Nelson hurried to the hospital entrance.

When Brian Nelson got to the hospital lobby, it was packed with people. Through the glass doors to the outside, he could see three network TV news vans parked with their antennas reaching skyward. Reporters with their cameramen milled around with news photographers and newspaper reporters. He recognized the Mayor and City Council members. He didn't recognize others he assumed were friends or family of the Howards.

Finally, he saw Ron Bentley outside the entrance talking on his cell phone. He headed toward Ron but was stopped by Mayor Sterling. The Mayor noticed the badge Brian had clipped to the left breast pocket of his suit coat. After exchanging names, the Mayor asked, "Do you have an update for me? I'd like to schedule a news conference in about forty-five minutes."

"Let's go outside. It's too noisy in here," Detective Nelson said. "My partner, Ron Bentley, is on the phone with our Commander right now. Let's see what he has."

The two men strolled outside the hospital lobby into the waning sunlight. Ron noticed them as he spoke on his cell phone and nodded in their direction, holding up his finger to signal he'd be with them in a minute. Brian checked his watch. It was only 4:45 p.m. So much had been done in a short time.

"The Commander is notifying the FAA people now to get a watch set up at the airports. They made sure Border Patrol was watching the Canadian border as well as the Mexican border. The wiretap is on its way to the Howard residence, and they're sending someone to pick up the picture of the horse and get it back to the station. They've assigned a team to stay at the residence and monitor the wiretap. There are two units at the house already, keeping an eye on the place. The Sheriff is setting up for a news conference at the station in San Juan as soon as he can get there. He's on his way with lights and siren. We might want to get the Mayor and some of these media people over there so they can get set up."

Mayor Sterling spoke up, "I'll get my people right on that. I didn't know the Sheriff's Department was holding a news conference, so I was going to set one up. I'll cancel mine and meet with Sheriff Nolan's people and join theirs." He hurried off.

"Do you believe what a circus this place is?" Ron asked Brian. "There were already thousands of people in town for the Parade and Street Faire, and now we've got this going on too. I guess we'd better call home. Don't think we're going to get there for dinner tonight."

"Yeah, you're right about that," said Brian Nelson. "It's got the makings of a long night," shaking his head.

About that time, people began streaming out of the hospital lobby heading for their cars. The news vans dropped their antennas; reporters jumped in with their cameramen and sped off toward the Sheriff's sub-station in San Juan Capistrano.

Brian and Ron stood on the curb watching the madness as everyone jockeyed their vehicles for position to leave the single exit to the parking lot, wishing they'd had a traffic control officer there for the moment. They waited for the crowd to thin out before heading to their car to drive back to the station.

When Walter called, Esperanza answered the phone on the first ring. He used a phone at the nurses' station in the Intensive Care Unit. "Espie, it's me. I wanted to bring you up to date. Becky is in a coma, but she's holding her own. There's nothing we can do except wait. They said the next 48 hours are critical, but she's young and strong otherwise. We just have to wait and pray."

"Will my little one be okay, Señor Howard?" Esperanza asked, sniffing back her tears. She'd helped Caroline take care of Becky since she came home from the hospital two days after she was born. Esperanza loved Becky.

"We don't know," Dad replied softly. "All we can do is pray and hope she recovers. You know Becky is tough. She'll fight to get back to us."

"Señor Howard, you know I'm already praying and my whole familia too." Esperanza blew her nose. "What can I do?"

"The Sheriff's Detectives that just talked to us are thinking the guys who did this were really after Ali. They may have taken him for ransom. If that's the case, they may call us for money in exchange for Ali. They are sending over some of their people to put a tap on our phone. They will record all our calls. When they get to the house, please let them in and show them whatever they need. Okay?" Walter explained

"Oh, Si, Señor Howard," Esperanza replied, nodding her head.

"Another Sheriff's officer will be coming to the house looking for a good picture of Ali. Can you show him into Caroline's office? Let him take any of the pictures he wants."

"No problemo," Esperanza sniffed through her tears. "Is there anything else I can do?"

"Please ask Fernando to watch over the horses. Caroline and I will be here at the hospital. We need him to feed and bed them down for tonight and in the morning. I'll talk to him sometime tomorrow. If you need us, call our cell phones. We'd appreciate it if you two would keep an eye on the house and grounds while we're here. The Detective told me they would send over some Deputies to help watch over the place, and they will be sending extra patrols in the neighborhood. If either of you sees anything that looks suspicious, be sure to let them know, or call 911." Walter instructed

"Will do, Señor Walter," she replied. "Please kiss my little one for me. Tell her I love her too. And tell Caroline not to worry. Fernando and me will take good care here." She blew her nose again.

Esperanza went directly to her room. She had a small altar along one wall with a statue of the Virgin of Guadalupe. She knelt in front of the figure, closed her eyes, and bowed her head. She said her Rosary, fingering her beads as she prayed.

CHAPTER TWENTY-SIX

H ow much farther are we goin' anyway?" whined Danny. "We've been on this blasted dirt road forever already."

"Oh, quit yer gripping"! Tweedy gave me directions. He told me this guy lives up in the mountains where that Station Fire burned everything up a coupla years ago. He must be sorta like a hermit. I'm looking for a signpost that points to Little Rock. We turn there and follow the road for another 10 miles or so."

Calvin was feeling the effects of the day. He was jumpy and jittery, and his mind was going a thousand miles an hour. It was difficult for him to focus. He almost slammed them into a ditch and a hillside in separate near misses had Danny not yelled at him to watch where he was going.

"We'll be lucky if we get there before dark."

"Might be better if we don't. If the cops are looking for us, they might miss us in the dark. I just don't like the idea of driving this rig around these mountain roads at night. If we do get down to civilization 'for the sun goes down, we should prob'ly look for someplace to hide out 'til it does."

"You got us in a fix this time! Picked the wrong darned horse for sure!" Danny muttered under his breath. It was starting to get cold as they climbed in elevation. He rolled up his window and hugged himself to keep warm. "Should'a brought jackets or somethin.'" Danny was feeling the effects of the day. His mind was jumping around.

"Like I said before, quit yer gripping. We just gotta get rid of this animal and skedaddle home." Calvin snapped. He rolled up his window. They were starting to see a few patches of snow on the ground.

Another 45 minutes passed as they bumped along the dirt track, twisting first one way then another. Thousands of twisted black skeletons of trees and shrubs covered the sides of the hills from the forest fire a few years before. Some regrowth had started, but it would take decades to grow back.

Ali kept his footing as best he could in the trailer, with the trailer rolling and swaying from side to side over the rough rocky ground. He was fully awake now and didn't know where he was or how he'd gotten there. The last thing he remembered was his Becky getting pushed and hitting her head into the building and falling. She didn't move. *"Becky, I miss you. I have to get home! I have to find you. I don't know where I am, but I will get home somehow. I promise you, Becky!"* He wasn't sure what happened to her, but he would recognize the man who hurt her. He hated that man! He saw that man push her, and he saw his expression when he did that. He would never forget!

After a time, Ali locked his knees and dozed off, jerked awake only when a particularly hard bump jostled him. That started the replay in his mind again, and he watched Becky sailing headfirst into the side of the building. It made him sick at heart.

It was almost 4:30 p.m. before they found the turnoff Ed Tweedy told Calvin about. Just as he made the turn, he slammed on the brakes and shouted, "Looky there! It's a big black bear right up on that hillside," pointing his finger towards it.

"Oh, wow! Yer right! It is a bear. We'd better get outa here," Danny said. "I hear bears can come right on in through the window if they want to. I don't feel like tanglin' with anything that big or that mean."

The she-bear had just wandered out of her winter den looking for water and something to eat. She only weighed 300 pounds, about 75 pounds less than she weighed when she went to sleep. She had two cubs waiting for her, and her food search hadn't been successful. She climbed up the hill and slowly lumbered her way back to the den.

The Hix brothers bounced, jounced, twisted, and turned their way down the dirt road to the final turnoff. Once they made the turn, they could see the camp before them. It wasn't much to look at. It consisted of a makeshift cabin built of whatever lumber the old guy could scrounge up. The roof was a patchwork of tin sheets in all sizes and didn't look very water-tight. An ancient pick-up truck stood beside the cabin. It could be from the 1950s by the style of the fenders. It was covered in more rust than paint. There was trash on the ground everywhere, old cans, bottles, cardboard food packaging, clothing, and stuff that defied identification. A corral built of whatever the man could cobble together, including tree limbs and rusty wire, stood beside the cabin. It had a three-sided shelter from the weather. The side walls had holes in them you could put your fist through. A lone chestnut horse stood in the corral and called out a welcome.

Calvin leaned on the horn to raise the owner of this mess. As he looked around, he looked dejected. "We're sure not going to get much for the horse from a place like this," he said.

Just then, the cabin door opened, and an older man stepped out, clutching a shotgun in both hands. The man, of indeterminate age, had long matted gray hair with a matching beard down to his chest. He wore a stained thermal undershirt partially tucked into grimy jeans. His feet peeked out from under his pant legs in dirty socks.

"What's your business?" he said as he lifted the barrel of his shotgun slightly and aimed it at their truck.

"You Nixon?" Calvin asked. "Ed Tweedy sent us. Said you was lookin' for another horse for packin.'"

"Oh, if Ed Tweedy sent you, come on in," said the old man with a grin that showed missing front teeth. "I called him from down below when I lost that last danged horse."

Calvin turned off the engine. He and Danny climbed out of their truck and walked over to the cabin door. The old man waved them in. The inside of the cabin wasn't in much better shape than the outside. It sure smelled worse.

"Can I get you somethin' to drink?" Nixon asked. "I got some coffee just made this morning' …. Or was that yesterday morning? … or something stronger? Got some whiskey, but I don't have ice and don't have any clean glasses."

The offer of whiskey tempted Calvin, but after looking around the cabin, he decided to pass on it.

"No, thank ya, sir. But thanks for the offer. We're needin' to get our business done pretty quick so we can get back down out of these mountains before it gets too dark. I'm not familiar with these roads." Calvin replied. "Why don't you come on out to our truck and take a look at the horse we brought ya."

Carl Nixon followed Calvin and Danny back to the door and stashed his shotgun just inside it. They walked out behind the horse trailer, and Calvin opened the door. Danny went to the front of the trailer and opened the feeder door to untie Ali. Calvin stepped inside the trailer, on the other side of the divider wall from Ali, snagged the lead-rope, and pulled Ali out of the trailer backward.

Ali was compliant. He came out of the trailer quickly. He stood quietly and looked around, seeing not one familiar thing. Then Danny stepped around the side of the trailer to stand beside his brother. Ali screamed and lunged at him, kicking out with his front feet as he tried to take a bite out of the man who hurt his Becky. Danny scrambled backward, hit the trailer, slipped, and fell flat on his butt. Calvin choked up on the lead rope and pulled Ali away from Danny.

Nixon laughed. "Looks like he doesn't like your partner there," he said. "But he's sure a pretty one. Where'd you get a horse like this anyway?"

"Danny, go sit in the truck. I'll finish up here," instructed Calvin.

Danny happily scurried off and jumped in the truck, slamming the door.

Calvin looked at Carl Nixon, "I don't own horses. I just drive the truck. Couldn't say where this horse came from."

Nixon walked over to Ali and stroked his neck, then scratched his withers. Ali turned his head and nickered at the old man like he usually did when someone found his itchy place. The old man walked around the horse and looked him over carefully, checking his legs and feet. Then he stroked his face and pulled down his lower lip for a quick look at his teeth.

"Young one, isn't he? 'Bout five or six maybe?" he asked Calvin.

"Looks like it to me, but I don't know for sure. I just haul 'em, don't own 'em," Calvin answered. "You interested?" he asked.

"I asked for a packhorse, and you bring me a pretty boy. I don't know." The old man stroked his beard while he admired Ali. "What are you asking for him?"

"Like to get four hundred fifty or five hundred for 'im, but we can talk," Calvin said.

"The deal I had with Tweedy was for a packhorse for two hundred, not a pretty boy. I only have two hundred in cash on me right now." Nixon answered.

"Well, what else ya got?" asked Calvin, standing slump-shouldered. This was not going well. They needed more cash.

"All I have right now is maybe a few hundred in gold flakes. It hasn't been assayed yet, but it's pure. I've been panning it. I could add that to the two hundred in cash. Will that make you a deal?"

"Oh, what the heck. Sure. Deal! Go get your cash and your gold, and you got yourself a horse." Calvin had no idea in the world what they were going to do with gold flakes. But it had to have some value, didn't it?

Carl Nixon went to the cabin and came back out with a stack of dog-eared bills and a tiny pouch tied up with a leather thong. He untied the thong and opened the bag, pouring a bit of the content into the palm of his hand. It glinted like gold in the waning sunlight. Calvin nodded his acceptance, and Nixon poured it back inside the pouch, re-tied the leather thong, and handed it to him with the stack of bills. Calvin tucked the pouch into his jeans pocket and counted the bills. It was all there.

"Guess you got yourself a horse." He said and handed the lead rope to the old man. "Now, can you tell me which way to get down this mountain? From the maps, I think we're looking for Highway 138, so we can go east and pick up Interstate 15."

Nixon gave him directions, and Calvin headed back to the truck. "Been nice doin' business with ya," he said to Nixon as he started up the truck and turned back toward the road hauling the now empty trailer behind.

The old man watched the truck and trailer leave, heading downhill, and turned back to the horse. "Don't know what your name was before, but you're my Buddy now. Let's get you into the corral, and you can meet your new friend Max," he said as he led Ali to the corral. He opened the improvised gate and led Ali in. He removed his halter and coiled the lead rope in his hand. "Now, you two get acquainted. I'll get you both some hay and freshwater," as he walked out and latched the gate. He returned with hay and filled up the water barrel with fresh spring water.

Carl Nixon had been very fond of the last packhorse. She was a sweet-tempered bay mare and was always easy to deal with and sure-footed as a mountain goat until that last trip. They were on their way back from panning in his secret stream when she slipped on the trail and fell into a ravine. He'd climbed down to see if there was any way to get her out and found she'd broken her front right leg. And he'd forgotten to bring his gun on this trip. So he'd taken what he could carry from the pack and had to leave her there. She'd screamed when she fell, and she'd screamed when he walked away. But there was nothing he could do but let nature take its course. He still felt terrible about it. He'd never take a trip again without taking his gun.

Ali was cold. He'd always lived inside a tight, warm barn and worn a winter blanket when the outside temperature got below 50 degrees. As the sun dropped below the horizon, the temperature at this elevation plummeted down near freezing. There was no bedding to lie in, no blanket to keep him warm, and he missed his people terribly.

He and Max became acquainted somewhat. Max was a bit stand-offish, not much for words, but he didn't try to bully him; he just wasn't much company for a heartsick, homesick horse. Ali didn't get a bit of sleep that first night. He spent the night staring at the stars.

Calvin and Danny bounced down the dirt road, twisting and turning for a while. Calvin finally pulled to a stop. "Ya know we gotta dump this trailer for a while. Makes us stand out like a sore thumb. Let's get out here and see if we can find a place to leave it. We can come back in a month or so and pick it up again. I'll borrow a truck from someone at the Drop Inn. Can you hand me the flashlight in the glove box?" he asked Danny.

"It's cold out here. I didn't bring a jacket or nothin'" Danny whined.

"Let's find a spot and get this done so we can get outa here, then," snapped Calvin. "Stop yer snivelin' and help me find a good hiding place."

Danny and Calvin found a place in some trees off the road they could back the trailer into. Danny stood outside with the flashlight to help Calvin get the trailer spotted, then both of them worked to unhook it from the truck. The two men dragged some brush in to cover the front of the trailer so it wouldn't be easily visible.

The truck made much better time down the mountain relieved of the extra weight of the horse trailer and the horse. Calvin eventually found himself on paved roads. He followed the directions given to him and turned onto the highway he was looking for.

The sun dropped below the horizon, and dusk came over the hills. Full darkness was right behind. Calvin turned east and stopped at a convenience store with a gas pump out front. "Good thing we got some cash, anyway. We're not gonna get home on what we got in the tank. You want anything besides a cold one?" Calvin asked.

"A sandwich would be good. I'm starved! And a coat, but that don't look too likely in there," mumbled Danny.

Calvin walked inside the store to look for drinks and sandwiches. As he walked to the counter, the TV behind the clerk started the 5:30 p.m. news broadcast with a Breaking News story. The next thing that flashed on the screen was a photo of the horse they'd just sold.

The reporter announced, "Prince Ali, probably the most famous Arabian horse in the country, was stolen this afternoon from the trailer parking area after the Swallows Day Parade in San Juan Capistrano. The Orange County Sheriff is looking for two men, mid-twenties or early thirties, blond hair, wearing blue work shirts and jeans, driving an older blue pick-up truck with an older blue and white horse trailer for questioning in the case. The horse owner's 13- year-old daughter was with the horse when it was stolen but is now in a coma at Mission Hospital in critical condition at this hour. The Sheriff's office is asking anyone who sees the two men or their vehicle and trailer to please call ….."

Calvin didn't wait further. He grabbed a ball cap from the display next to the counter and pulled it on, tucking his hair in on the sides. He walked back to where he'd seen a stack of hoodie sweatshirts for sale and picked up two of them in bright colors. He pulled one on himself and walked back to the counter carrying the other one.

The evening clerk was not paying much attention. He was a young kid busy texting on his cell phone. He rang up the sale for the drinks, sandwiches, ball cap, and sweatshirts with hardly a glance at Calvin. Calvin paid for the purchases in cash, including an extra forty dollars for gas. He went outside to pump gas into the truck. He tossed the drinks, sandwiches, and sweatshirt in to Danny. He pumped gas into the tank, jumped in the driver's seat, slammed the door, and started the truck.

"We gotta get outa here," he told Danny. "They got us on TV now. That kid in there was too busy texting to notice. We gotta get home. It's a good thing we dumped the trailer up there. The cops are looking for the truck and trailer together."

He headed down Highway 138 and turned south on Interstate 15. The stars were lined up just right. They saw no highway patrol cars, no sheriff's cars, no police squad cars of any kind all the way home.

CHAPTER TWENTY-SEVEN

Ali's first night at the mountain camp was cold and lonely. He spent the entire night at the north end of the corral staring up at the stars, occasionally glancing at the lights twinkling in the plateau off to the East and West of his location. He was freezing cold. He'd never spent a night outside of a warm barn in his life. A few lights were on the plateau in front of him, but they were few and far between. He was heartsick. He had no idea where he was, and he worried about Becky constantly. His attempt at conversation with Max failed. Max would answer his questions with a single word and sometimes not even that.

Ali went over and over the previous day in his mind. He and Becky had a wonderful time in the parade. People all along the parade route seemed to enjoy seeing the two of them. But those two men at the trailer were different. He remembered the look on that one man's face as he shoved Becky. He wanted to hurt that man. He was scared for Becky. The last thing he remembered seeing was her lying on the ground with blood in her hair. She didn't move. Was he to blame? Should he have stomped that man who stuck a needle in his neck? Why couldn't he protect Becky? How did he get here? He had no recollection of leaving San Juan Capistrano. He didn't recall much until the terrain along the highway was rocky with little vegetation. The stink in that trailer would haunt him forever. It was the stink of fear. This place was terrible. It was surrounded by creepy and scary sounds he'd never heard before. He had no idea where he was or how he could get back to his Becky.

Ali heard his first owl that night as the giant bird flew between the trees hunting for mice or rabbits. Far off in the distance, he heard the snarl of a large cat. That snarl gave him the shivers. He didn't know what made that sound, but he instinctively knew it was something to be avoided.

Far down in the desert below, he heard the songs of the coyotes. He listened as the breeze sloughed through the needles of the pine trees near the corral. There were few other sounds at night. It was still, dark, and very cold.

As dawn broke, turning the sky pink and coral in the East, he finally went for a drink. The water was chilly but fresh. He nosed around looking for a tidbit to chew on but found little to his liking. Hunger set his stomach growling and did nothing to improve his mood. He was scared and depressed and very unhappy.

He missed his barn stall, his blanket, his siblings, and his mother, but he missed his Becky most of all. His world had been turned upside down, and he didn't know why.

A few hours after dawn, with the sun climbing toward its zenith, the old man came out of the cabin and brought fresh hay to the horses. Ali could smell him before he saw him. The old man's odor didn't particularly put him off; he just thought it was interesting. The old man filled up the water barrel with more fresh spring water.

He unlatched the gate and walked to where Ali stood. He patted and stroked his neck and found the itchy place at his withers again. "You're sure a pretty boy," he said to Ali. "I got the best end of that bargain!"

Carl Nixon spent a few more minutes admiring his new purchase, petting him and speaking to him in low soothing tones. Then he spent a few minutes with Max before heading back to the cabin.

Carl Nixon was a reader. There was not much in this world he liked better than getting lost in the pages of an old classic. His favorite was Dickens. The life he made for himself on the mountain gave him plenty of time to read.

He once had a life down below, as he referred to the towns and cities at either end of the high desert plateau. The old man spent his best reading time working for a living, getting to or from work, or taking care of his property and his family. Sometimes he felt like a hamster on a wheel, running as hard as possible but never getting anywhere.

The one really bright spot in that old life was his little girl. He was completely hooked the minute he laid eyes on her. He'd do anything for her. He loved his wife, but his daughter was the center of his universe. The day after his bright, beautiful and delightful little girl turned twelve, she and her mother were both killed instantly in a head-on automobile collision.

During the black days that followed the accident, he lost touch with reality. He drove the old pick-up truck he'd spent years restoring up into the mountains for the solitude.

One day he packed his truck with a few things he thought he might need, cleaned out the last few thousand from his bank account, and disappeared off the face of the planet. He walked away from his home, job, and everything he'd worked for. He no longer felt tethered to the world as most people see it.

It was quite by accident he discovered this little valley in the pines. And another accident that he found his secret stream held real gold that was easy to get. The first afternoon he'd panned for gold in that stream, he put the gold he collected in a small leather pouch like the one he handed Calvin. He took it down the mountain to a friend who owned a pawn shop in Palmdale. His buddy measured it and gave him three hundred eighty-five dollars for that one afternoon's work.

He was astonished, and he was very pleased with himself. He'd found a way to live the life he wanted. He could work two afternoons a month and have all the money he needed. He had no rent to pay. He used very little gasoline. He was surrounded by all the wood he needed to keep warm in the winter. And he was only feeding himself.

He rarely spent all of the money he dredged up out of that stream every month. In fact, he had sacks of the stuff sitting under his bed in the cabin. Some of the sacks were so heavy he had a hard time moving them. And he had bags of unspent bills sitting under the bed next to the gold. It does tend to accumulate over twenty years.

Carl Nixon didn't know that the owner of the pawnshop had been cheating him for years. He paid him cash for his gold at prices established twenty or more years ago. The actual cost of gold escalated a lot over that time. What Carl Nixon received for his gold was less than a quarter of the gold's real value. Carl didn't know he had almost enough to buy Ali at his actual value sitting under his bed in that ratty old cabin.

The only thing Carl Nixon bought in the last twenty years just because it was pretty was Ali. He was struck by the horse's beauty when he first came out of the trailer. There was nothing in or around his cabin except nature that was especially pretty. He thought it was odd he could be attracted to an animal in that way. He just knew he wanted him when he saw him, and he would have worked any deal necessary to keep him.

After feeding the horses their morning hay, Nixon brought a cheap plastic patio chair out behind his cabin. He turned over an old broken bucket for a footstool and settled down with his current book. He wanted to be outside in the fresh air, but he also wanted to look at Ali.

As he read, he glanced up every few paragraphs just to admire the horse. Ali stood quietly in the north end of the corral, staring out at the vista below. He ate little and seldom drank.

Carl fed the horses that evening as the sun was sinking below the horizon. He gave them fresh water and went into the corral to pet and scratch them both, talking to each in his soft, comforting voice. Then he went inside for the night, stoked up the wood stove, had his evening meal, and took his book to bed, reading until he fell asleep with the book opened on his chest.

Ali faced a second night like the first one on this mountain. The only difference was he was sinking deeper into depression.

CHAPTER TWENTY-EIGHT

Walter hung up the phone and joined Caroline in Becky's room. As he entered, he was shocked all over again at how small and pale Becky looked. He also knew Caroline was an emotional mess. She was desperately worried about her only child. But he also knew how much she loved Ali. She thought of him more like a son than a horse. He didn't know how Caroline was holding up as well as she was, with one child in a coma and the other missing entirely.

Both Walter and Caroline were anxious about Becky waking up and finding Ali gone. Becky would be wild to find him. Walter was a little ashamed of himself when he thought it might be for the best that Becky was "asleep" right now. He hoped that would give them time to find Ali and get him back home where he belonged before she woke up.

"Do you really think someone would take Ali for money like that?" Caroline asked after a while.

"Well, that's one theory," Walter said pensively. "If that's what happened, I have more hope of getting him back safely, in one piece. We can afford to pay. That seems to be the theory the Sheriff's Department is working on. They are operating strictly on his dollar value. I know *we* don't think of him that way, but to most people, he's just an animal worth a lot of money."

"I know, I know," Caroline said plaintively. "But it's like one of my kids has been kidnapped. I don't know where he is, I don't know how he is, and I don't know if they're taking care of him. It just makes me sick. And they hurt our daughter to get to him. What I wouldn't give to be left in a room all alone with them right now, whoever they are. I'd take them apart with my bare hands."

"I feel the same way you do, Mama Bear," Walter told her. "Let's hope they call soon. I want them caught – the sooner, the better. I really don't want to have to tell Becky he's missing."

Joanne stopped in to check on Becky and typed notes in the chart. "We did get an order from Dr. Spencer to move in a folding cot, so at least one of you can stay through the night with her. It should be here in a minute."

"Thank you so much, Joanne."

Walter, who preferred action to inaction, was antsy and restless. Finally, he could stand it no longer. "I'm going outside to take a walk. I just need to get moving right now," he told his wife.

Caroline understood. Walter was never one to sit around waiting for something to happen. That was why he was so successful in business. He *MADE* things happen.

"You go ahead, Papa Bear. I'll take the second shift going home. I don't want her to wake up alone." Caroline said.

"Think I'm going to bring my running clothes back with me when I go home to shower and change. I need to check on the home front anyway. I can always change here in the bathroom. Running helps me relax. I can't stand just sitting around worrying." Walter told her.

"You do whatever you need to. I'll be right here because that's what I need to do." Caroline responded. "If she wakes up while you're out, I'll send up a flare. Be on the watch for it." she smiled at him.

"I love you both, you know," he said quietly. "I don't know what I'll do if anything happens to either of you."

Caroline replied quietly, "I know. I know."

Walter left the hospital and took a long walk in the dark. The action felt good. He'd been sitting too long. He breathed deeply of the damp, salty air. He looked up at the stars and sent his own prayer to the heavens. As he moved, he felt the tension leaving his body, and he became more aware of the chill in the air. He'd have to remember to bring a windbreaker with his running clothes tomorrow. He should include one for Caroline too. He knew she'd forget it. He was very worried about Becky, but somehow, he knew she was going to be all right in the deep recesses of his mind. She'd wake up, and they would find no damage to her brain. She'd be the same bright, happy child she'd always been. The only question was how long it would take? And could they find Ali before then?

What he didn't know was that Ali stood in a make-shift corral on a mountain top, not so far away, looking at the same stars and wishing he was home too.

Walter passed the hospital gift shop on his way back to the ICU. He spotted a small white teddy bear in the window that had Becky's name written all over it. The shop was about to close, but he got inside just in time and bought the bear. When he walked into Becky's room, the cot was alongside the wall under the window, made up and ready with a pillow and blankets. He stopped by Becky's bed and tucked the little bear in the crook of her arm so it would be the first thing she saw when she woke up.

"Any change?" he asked Caroline, who looked up from a paperback book and shook her head.

"No, it looks like she's sleeping peacefully," Caroline said. "Why don't you try to get some sleep first? I'll wake you up if anything happens, but for sure, I'll wake you up about 2:00 a.m. so you can take a turn. That okay with you?"

"Yeah, that sounds fine," Walter said as he stretched out on the cot. He tried as best he could to sleep, but his mind kept spinning with the events of the day. He did close his eyes and got some rest but never fell completely asleep before Caroline shook him at midnight. "She's trembling," Caroline said. "Take a look. I don't know if I should call the nurse," she said.

Walter jumped off the cot and stood beside Becky's hospital bed, staring down at his daughter. All of a sudden, Becky began to shake. She scrunched up her face and tried to move her arms but didn't have the strength. Caroline felt her feet under the blanket.

"She's cold. Her feet are cold." Caroline reached under the blanket and touched Becky's upper thigh. "Walter, she's freezing. Please hit the nurse call button. Something's not right here."

Joanne flew into the room, "Is there a problem?" she asked.

"Please look at Becky," Caroline said. "She's trembling. I put my hand under the covers and her feet are freezing. She's cold. Is that normal?"

Joanne lifted the blanket and felt Becky's feet. "No, this is unusual. I'll get blankets," she said as she dashed out the door. She returned quickly with a stack of warmed blankets. Caroline helped her put them over Becky's trembling body. Becky stopped trembling a a few minutes.

Joanne and Caroline changed the blankets to freshly warmed ones until the hospital shift changed at midnight. Susan took over for Joanne then, and teamed up with Caroline throughout the night to keep warm blankets on Becky.

Becky stopped shivering at dawn. Caroline was exhausted. Susan monitored Becky's vital signs since her shift began. There was nothing in them that suggested a problem. Becky never opened her eyes or moved throughout the night. Caroline finally layed down on the cot a few minutes before 6:00 a.m. Walter grabbed his book and sat down in the chair beside Becky to read. It was hard for him to focus. When he realized he'd just read the same paragraph three times, he closed the book. He reached through the bed rail and held Becky's hand, leaning his other arm on the top of the bed rail. Within a few minutes, his head rested on his forearm as he sat there; he too drifted off.

Becky lay in the hospital bed, silent and motionless. She was in a deep fog but heard her parents' voices far, far away. She heard another male voice and another woman's voice off in the distance but try as she might, she could not understand a word they were saying. She wanted to get up and find her Mommy and her Daddy, but she could not make her body move no matter how hard she tried. After a while, she gave up and slipped back into the fog, and heard nothing for a long time.

Walter woke with a start when Susan, Becky's night nurse, came into the room at 8:00 am. She was holding two trays. "I took a chance that you and your wife would still be here at breakfast time," she told him, "So I ordered you both a breakfast."

Walter looked over at Caroline. She was just opening her eyes. "Any change?" she asked.

"No, nothing," Walter said as he took the tray from Susan. She walked the other tray to the cot and handed it to Caroline, who'd just sat up and stretched.

"Thank you so much," Walter said to Susan. "It was kind of you to think of us."

Susan checked on Becky and typed notes in her chart. She said, "There's coffee at the nurses' station. She invited them to "Help yourself. Cups are next to the machine with the creamer and sugar." as she left the room.

"You want some coffee?" he asked Caroline.

"Yes. I'm dying for a cup of coffee," she answered. He brought two cups back to the room.

Walter said, "I think I'll take off in a few minutes and go home to shower and change. I'd like to check on things at home. I'll make the phone calls to our families and bring them up to date. I can be back here in two hours so you can take the car and do the same," he said, "unless, of course, there are any changes here. I can be back here in ten minutes if you need me."

"We need to make arrangements to get the truck and trailer home too." She suggested.

"Thanks for reminding me. I'll talk to Fernando about that. Maybe he and his brother can handle that for us. If we are taking shifts, we don't need more than one car here. Give me the keys to the truck, and I'll take them to him."

Caroline dug around in her purse for the keys and handed them to Walter. He kissed her on the cheek and left the hospital.

CHAPTER TWENTY-NINE

Walter left the hospital Sunday morning and drove home. Esperanza met him at the door, wiping tears from her eyes. She threw her arms around Walter and sobbed. Walter held her until she calmed down.

"Espie, she's going to be alright," he said softly. "She's in a coma right now, but everything else seems to be fine. The doctors are doing all they can for her."

"Señor Walter, can I see her?" Esperanza asked.

"At the moment, the nurses will only allow family in to see her, so Caroline is staying with her until I get back. In a couple of days, I'll ask the doctor to let you in. You know you are family to us, but the nurses have their rules. I'm sorry."

"I understand," Esperanza said sadly. "But I will pray to the Virgin of Guadalupe for her recovery. I will pray as hard as I can."

"I know you will, Espie," Walter said. "I don't know what Caroline and I would do without you."

"Señor Walter, there are two men of the policia in the living room waiting for you. They came, as you said, to put something on the phones. There are also four others outside watching the grounds. The policia in the living room are recording all the phone calls that come here. So far, it has only been familia and your office calling. I have a list in the kitchen for you. The policia outside talked to Fernando. I let them put their cars in the garage."

"Perfect. Thank you. I'll go talk to the deputies and see what they want us to do."

Walter walked to the living room and introduced himself to the two deputies sitting on the couch with the recording equipment. They went over the procedures and explained what they did and how they needed to handle phone calls. They instructed Walter what to say when the kidnappers called, suggesting ways to keep them on the phone long enough for the wiretaps to locate the phone they were calling from. They also talked to Walter about possible suspects. Did he know anyone with a grudge against them, maybe an employee or ex-employee, a neighbor, another family member, a client?

Walter assured them he couldn't think of anyone in their circle of family, friends, neighbors, or at his work that would do this. He was as perplexed as they were. He told them he was confident he could raise any ransom in a short amount of time. He told them one of his calls today would be to his banker and stockbroker, just in case.

He excused himself and went to the master bedroom for a shower and change of clothes. He packed a gym bag with his running clothes and took it down the hall into Caroline's office with him. He sat at her desk and made his phone calls. He looked sadly at the blank spots on the walls where the photographs of Ali were missing.

Once he wrapped up his business at home, he stopped in the kitchen to let Esperanza know he was leaving for the hospital. She was cooking like a mad woman. "I can't just sit here with nothing to do," she explained to him. "So I'm making lunch for the policia and Fernando." She paused for a minute while chopping an onion.

"You do what you need to do," Walter told her. "I understand. Sitting waiting for something to happen is hard. I know you'll take care of things for us here. Caroline will be back for a shower and change of clothes when I get to the hospital. We will let you know how Becky is doing. If anything happens here, call us on our cell phones. We're only a few minutes away."

"Si, Señor Walter," Esperanza said, "Fernando and I will take very good care here. You no have to worry. Please tell the niña I love her and give her a kiss for me." She sniffled and wiped her eyes with the back of her hand. She resumed her chopping.

Walter patted her ample shoulder and left through the kitchen to the barn area, where he spoke briefly with Fernando before he left for the hospital.

Walter entered Mission Hospital's main lobby with his overnight bag in one hand, and Caroline's windbreaker tucked under his other elbow. He was a man on a mission, so he headed directly to the elevator.

"Walter," he heard and stopped in his tracks. He turned and faced Ginny Hartley rushing toward him with tears in her eyes.

"Oh, Walter, I'm so, so sorry," Ginny said to him as she hugged him. She sniffled back tears. "How is Becky? And is there any word at all on Ali? Has anyone seen him or heard anything at all?"

Walter hugged the woman and comforted her. "There's been no change with Becky so far. She has a concussion and is still in a coma," he said gently. "The doctor said the first forty-eight hours is the most critical, and we are just about halfway there now. She doesn't respond to Caroline or me, just lays there sleeping. As far as we know, there's been no sign of Ali, and everyone in the state is looking for him, maybe in the country by now. Last evening, I heard the Sheriff held a news conference, and the national TV news and newspapers picked it up. With all the publicity, we're hoping someone has seen him and will come forward soon."

"Yes, we all saw the coverage on TV last night. It broke our hearts. My nephew, Brody, was a lot more concerned than I expected. He called Chris and Sharon's son Todd last night about it. How is Caroline holding up?" Ginny asked.

"Caroline is stronger than she thinks. She doesn't want to leave Becky's side and insists at least one of us is with her at all times in case she wakes up. We want to find Ali before she comes around. We don't want to tell her that he is missing, and we don't have a clue where he is. You know yourself how she feels about Ali."

"Boy do I! Telling her that would devastate her. She and Ali have been training so hard for the Youth National Championships. That's all she talks about when we are working. Those two are so in sync; if she thinks it, he does it. It is the most amazing thing for me, as a coach, to watch."

"Well, I'm heading on up to the ICU. I'll let Caroline know you are here in the lobby. She'll be down in a few minutes," Walter told her.

"Wait a sec. Sharon O'Neal and I cooked up a scheme, and I need to tell you about it. My clothes are packed and in my truck. Sharon is flying in from Denver this afternoon," Ginny checked her watch. "In fact, she is in the air right now. She and I plan to stay at your house and take care of your horses so you and Caroline can stay with Becky. Now, this is not up for negotiation!"

"That's really not necessary, Ginny," Walter said. "Fernando and Esperanza are at the house. I know they will take care of things there while we stay with Becky."

"Well, you know Sharon feels like Becky's other mom. She can't sit fourteen hundred miles away and wait to see if she comes out of this okay. Chris and Todd talked it over with her. They need to stay in Colorado to run their ranch, but they want Sharon here close to Becky and you and Caroline since you are all family as far as they are concerned. As for me, not only is Becky my star student, but I feel like family too. She calls me Aunt Ginny. I love that kid half to death. I don't want to be a hundred miles away. And then there's Ali. I don't have to tell you how we all feel about him. We want to be here for him too."

Walter thought about what Ginny said, then hugged her again. "It means a lot to me to have you here, and Sharon too. Thank you. I'm going back to the ICU. I'll tell Caroline you are here, and she will be out to meet you. Thanks for being here for us. I will talk to Sharon when she gets here."

Caroline walked out of the elevator into the hospital lobby ten minutes later. Ginny jumped to her feet and rushed over to hug her. Caroline just held onto Ginny and cried. Ginny held her and comforted her, sniffling her own tears back.

When Caroline got herself under control, she stepped back and looked at Ginny. "I can't thank you enough for being here," she told her. "It means a lot to us."

"Hey, the way I was raised, that's what you do for friends and family."

"I know, but you and Sharon are making quite a sacrifice for us. You really don't have to stay. I know both of you have other things you should be doing."

"Woman, you couldn't blow us outa here with dynamite," Ginny chided. "Our families are all in agreement, so we'll stay for as long as it takes."

Ginny put her arm around Caroline's shoulder. "Hey, let's go. My truck's out in the lot, and I'll drive you home. We can talk more on the way. I'll be picking Sharon up in two hours, but that should give you time to shower and change. I can drop you off here before going to the airport to get her. In the meantime, you can bring me up to speed on your other horses so Sharon and I can keep their routines on schedule. Sound okay?"

"Thanks, yes, that sounds great. Please be sure to let Sharon know how much Walter and I appreciate what you're doing for us. I will call the house later this evening and give you an update. If you hear anything from the Sheriff's office, please call us on our cell phones," Caroline said.

At home, Caroline showed Ginny to one of the guest rooms to put away her things. "This will be your room any time you stay over here," Caroline told her. "Please make yourself at home. Sharon can have the room across the hall. I will let Espie and Fernando know you'll be staying. We're all family here."

Caroline spoke briefly with Esperanza and Fernando and the two officers in her living room. She introduced Ginny to the officers and let them know she would be staying at the house while they were at the hospital. The officers gave Ginny and Caroline the same talk about incoming phone calls they gave Walter. Caroline went to take her shower. She quickly put on clean clothes. Ginny drove her back to the hospital then drove on to the airport.

***

Becky lay in a deep fog. She heard Mom and Dad talking in the distance, but she couldn't make her body move. She struggled to speak but couldn't form words. She tried and tried and finally gave up, exhausted. She slipped back into the fog.

Sometime later, Becky didn't know if she was dreaming or just remembering, but she felt small. She was eight years old and standing on a bucket in the feed room in the barn. It was late at night and cold, but she didn't care. She was looking through a window into the foaling stall at Spirit, Mom and Dad's prized mare. Spirit dropped down in the straw as contractions became severe. Becky saw the two little feet and squealed, "Mommy, Daddy, there's the feet. He will be here soon. I can't wait!"

Mom smiled at her. "I agree with you. I think it'll be soon."

Becky felt herself sitting in the straw against the wall of the foaling stall, watching the new baby struggle to stand up. She was grinning from ear to ear. "Mommy, can we see whether the baby is a boy or girl yet?" Becky knew for a long time this baby was a boy. She'd already picked out his name, Prince Ali. She knew it wasn't a girl, so she didn't bother picking out a girl name.

Becky watched as the baby horse got to his feet. Fernando and Daddy helped him find his mother's udder so he could eat for the first time. Daddy looked the baby over and confirmed the baby was a little colt. "Looks like Prince Ali is here," he told Becky with a grin.

"He's going to be my very best friend in the whole wide world!" Becky announced. "He's the handsomest colt in the whole world too."

Becky spent days playing with Ali. They played soccer with a giant ball Mommy bought for them. They "jumped" over old fence posts Fernando replaced around the back of the property. Becky dressed him up like a toy doll. She was out in the barn before Fernando fed the horses their breakfast. Mom had to threaten her to get her in the house for meals and bedtime. She hated going back to school in the fall because it meant she couldn't spend the day with Ali.

Happiness circulated around Becky for a while and faded as the fog enveloped her again. The voices in her hospital room receded.

CHAPTER THIRTY

S haron O'Neal stepped away from the baggage carousel and almost walked into Ginny Hartley. "Hey, don't run me over, buddy!" Ginny laughed. "I'm your ride." The two women laughed and hugged and strolled out of the terminal together.

"How's Becky?" Sharon asked.

"I talked to Caroline just before coming to the airport. She said there is no change. Becky is still in a coma, but her vital signs are all good. The doctor is a little worried because there was some bleeding in her brain at first, but the latest scan showed nothing more, so it's the concussion they're worried about. He has no idea when she will wake up. Of course, the police want to talk to her too." Ginny explained.

"Has there been any word at all on Ali? Any ransom demand, any sighting? Chris and Todd are worried sick about him too," Sharon said.

"The only phone calls to the house have been reporters or friends," Ginny told her. "It's like he vanished off the face of the earth."

"This sounds awful, but maybe it's just as well Becky is in a coma right now. I wouldn't want to be the one to explain this to her. You know how she feels about that horse."

"Yes. Absolutely. But I also know how Ali feels about her. I'm really worried about him too. If possible, I know that horse would break down walls to get back to Becky if he could. I hate to think about what he's going through right now. If he's still alive at all," Ginny almost whispered.

"Oh, let's not go there," Sharon said quietly.

Ginny and Sharon settled into guest rooms at the Howard estate. Sharon got instructions about answering the phone from the officers assigned to the house. Esperanza, who quickly became "Espie" to all, prepared elaborate meals three times a day because she couldn't sit still from worry. Walter and Caroline took turns coming home to change and shower each morning. There was nothing to report. Walter and Caroline became more haggard as the days dragged on with no change in Becky's condition.

No ransom demand came by phone, mail, or any other way. Brian Nelson and Ron Bentley, the detectives on the case, were frustrated. The lab did finally identify the drug used in the syringe found near the Howard horse trailer. It was Acepromazine Maleate and Butorphanol Tartrate, a combination used by veterinarians to tranquilize or sedate horses, dogs, and cats. The size of the syringe pointed at use for a horse. To the detectives, it confirmed Ali was drugged, so he was the target, substantiating their kidnapping theory. The Sheriff's Department transferred the fingerprints they got off the syringe to the FBI to run through their database, hoping for a match. Local law enforcement didn't find a match in theirs.

People were on the lookout for him everywhere. Evening national news broadcasts on TV showed photos and videos of the 2.5 million dollar missing horse during his performances. All reported sightings anywhere in the country were immediately checked. None were Ali. The Sheriff's office called at least twice a day for updates on the case. Brian and Ron had nothing to tell. Media pressure was on the Sheriff, so he transferred the pressure to his detectives.

Ginny and Sharon fell into a routine. They had breakfast and headed to the barn to turn out, exercise, ride, bathe and groom the Howard's herd of Arabian horses. They worked until late morning and took a dip in the pool before lunch. After lunch, they helped Espie clean up when she would let them, then returned to the barn until dinnertime. After dinner, they cleaned up the barn and shared some time in the spa to soak aching muscles.

In the spa one night, Sharon asked, "I've been meaning to ask how your lessons with Becky and Ali are going?"

"You know Becky is determined to ride Ali at the Youth National Championship show this July. Those two work really hard. Ali is ready. He's had all that experience with Chris, so he knows what to expect. Becky rides very well. All we are working on now is some ring strategy. Those two ride like one. She can change leads, change gait, or change direction by just thinking about it. It is awesome to watch." Ginny explained.

"This situation is so sad. I hate to think about what will happen if we can't find Ali. Or what if we do and Becky can't ride?" Sharon replied.

"I can't even go there. All I can do is pray." Ginny said.

Spa time was about the only time Ginny and Sharon had to talk with each other. They shared tales about their husbands, spoke about their ranches, talked about their kids. One night Sharon asked Ginny, "Did I ever tell you how we got involved with Ali?"

"No, but I always wondered why Walter and Caroline sent him to Colorado when there are local trainers here."

"I've never asked them about that either. They hired a professional horse photographer to come and do a video of Ali when he was about seven months old. We got it in the mail. It sat on my desk for a couple of days before we got around to it. We watched it after dinner one night. Chris watched that video six or seven times. He just had a feeling he was looking at his once-in-a-lifetime horse. He called Caroline that night and had me book him a flight to California to see Ali in person. He told me he was absolutely sure the minute he laid eyes on him."

"I've never heard of a trainer flying out to interview a horse before!" Ginny exclaimed. "I don't think it would even occur to my husband, Mike."

"I keep the books for our place, and I'd never heard of it either. I got a little cranky about the expense at the time. But I have to admit Chris was right."

"I'll bet. Didn't I hear you guys had to add on an extra barn and an indoor riding arena to keep up with new clients after Chris and Ali's first year on the show circuit?"

"That was crazy!" Sharon exclaimed. "It started slow but got to the point all I could do was answer the phone. It just rang off the wall. I actually had to hire myself a secretary if you can believe that! We went from doing a decent business with Chris as the only trainer to being so busy we now have three trainers that work for Chris and two he is bringing along to show horses under our name because he can't be in more than one place at a time."

"How does he do that?" Ginny asked. "Mike trains cutting and reining horses. I don't remember him ever letting someone else show his training horses except for the owners in the amateur classes."

"Chris is demanding. He shows them what he expects and demands their best for our clients. It is working out."

The first Friday evening after the parade, Sharon was upset when she stepped into the hot bubbling water of the spa for their soak.

"Hey, what's up with you?" Ginny asked.

"It's Todd, our son," Sharon explained. "He is really upset about Becky and Ali. He and Becky are very close friends. That all started when the Howards brought Ali to our place two months before the big Scottsdale Show, his first year of showing.

"How old is Todd now?" Ginny asked.

"He's fourteen, almost a year older than Becky. They met when she was eight, and he was nine. At first, he thought she was just a pretty, stuck-up little snot. Then she beat the pants off him with his favorite video game," Sharon chuckled. "You know how it is. If you want a man's respect, you just have to beat them at their own game."

"Yeah, I remember me and my little Arabian gelding could outride Mike on his favorite cutting horse back in the day," Ginny laughed.

"Becky insisted on being at every show Ali entered. She and Todd spent a lot of time together. Becky stayed with us over part of Christmas break, spring break and summer vacations from school. They were inseparable. He is also very fond of Prince Ali. This situation is hard on him. I'm doing my best to keep his spirits up. The longer this goes on, the more difficult it becomes. He wants to be here, not 1,400 miles away."

"What are you telling him?" Ginny asked.

"The truth. Becky needs this time for her brain to heal from being bruised. With Ali, everyone in the country is looking for him. We will find him!"

CHAPTER THIRTY-ONE

C alvin crawled out of bed Sunday morning at seven. He fiddled around in the kitchen, brewing up a pot of coffee. When the coffee was done, he poured himself a cup and walked out on the porch. He liked having his first cup of coffee outside.

He leaned on the porch rail for a while, looking out over the hills that surrounded the cabin. The morning light was soft on the green of the grasses and the bright colors of the wildflowers in bloom. It was quiet. He could hear the birds as they started their day. A slight breeze stirred the leaves in the trees around the cabin. After a while, he backed up and sat down in his chair.

As he sat down, he felt the pouch he'd stuffed into his jeans pocket the day before. He almost forgot about that. He pulled it out. The leather pouch made a small lump in his hand but was surprisingly heavy for its size. He wondered what the value of the gold flakes inside really was.

He and Danny went through eighty dollars of the two hundred Nixon paid them for the horse, so they didn't have much left for anything. After all the hard work and the risk, he was depressed. He'd seen sketches of them on TV. He was anxious. He knew the police were looking for them. He'd have to figure this out.

Danny joined him with his coffee a few minutes later. "What're we goin' to do now?" he asked.

"I thought I'd take the gold to that coin shop in Escondido in the morning," Calvin answered. "I know they buy gold. Maybe they can tell us what this stuff is worth."

"Well, we can't eat it like it is."

Bill's Coin Shop opened Monday morning precisely at nine a.m. Through the windshield of their truck, Calvin and Danny saw a hand turning the sign from "Closed" to "Open." They'd been waiting nearly an hour. They sipped convenience store coffee with stale donuts to kill time.

They climbed out of the truck and walked into the shop, looking at the displays of coins in the showcases.

"May I help you?" asked the young lady behind the counter.

"Yeah, we got some gold we'd like to sell," Calvin answered, pulling the leather pouch out of the pocket of his jeans and placing it on the counter.

"Let's see what you have," she said as she reached for the pouch. She untied the leather thong, opened the bag, and poured a small amount of the contents into a small round tray she'd brought to the counter. The tiny flakes shined golden in the light.

"I'd better go get Bill. He's the expert on this stuff," she said after examining the contents of the tray. She turned and walked through a doorway into the back of the shop while Calvin and Danny waited anxiously.

The young lady returned a few minutes later, followed by a spectacled older gentleman with thinning white hair.

"Fellas, what can I do for you?" he asked pleasantly when he reached the counter.

"We did a job for a guy, and he was short o' cash, so he finished payin' us off with this gold. We have bills to pay, so we need the cash. Can you tell us what this stuff is worth, and will you buy it from us?" Calvin answered.

Danny was busy looking at the coins in the display cases across the store from the counter.

"Well, let's take this one step at a time," answered the old man. "First, we need to weigh it and see how much is there. Gold, you know, is sold by weight and then by purity. Do you know if this was assayed?" he asked. "That tells us how pure it is."

"The guy said he'd found it prospectin' and hadn't got it … what you called it? … Assayed? … yet."

"Okay, let's see how much you have here," the old gentleman said as he poured the remainder from the pouch into the little tray. He took the tray over to a digital scale and weighed it. He was surprised at how much it weighed. He looked carefully at the tiny flakes in the tray, spreading them around with a small metal probe. He didn't find rock dust or gravel in the tray. It was surprisingly clean.

He turned and brought the tray back to the counter. "How much did this guy owe you anyway?" he asked.

"Coupla hundred bucks," Calvin said. "Why? Is there that much gold there?"

"What you have here is over two ounces. At today's gold price, if it's real gold, and depending on how pure it is, that could be several thousand dollars worth."

Calvin's heart jumped in his chest "Several thousand dollars!!?"

Danny heard that from across the room and hurried back to the counter to join Calvin.

"Well, before you get too excited, let me test it to be sure it is real gold," the old man said. "By the way, I'm Bill, the owner of this shop. I've been in the precious metal business for over fifty years now. This is just a simple test I'll do, but it involves some pretty nasty chemicals and a tiny bit of your gold. It won't hurt it if it's real gold."

He pulled on a pair of disposable gloves from under the counter and grabbed a bottle of liquid. He bent over for a better view of the shelf below the counter and located a small glass Petri dish. Then he found a pair of tweezers. He plucked a small sample of the gold from the tray and placed it carefully in the Petri dish. He unscrewed the cap from the bottle of liquid and squeezed out a single drop onto the sample. Nothing happened. He turned the sample over and looked at the bottom side. He noted a very slight discoloration there.

"Well, it's real gold." He announced. "And this little sample looks to be fairly pure."

"Exactly what does that mean for us?" asked Calvin.

"Gold is generally mixed with other minerals or metals when you find it. The only way to get pure gold is to refine it. That requires specialized equipment and someone that knows how to use it. But that's how raw gold is sold, as I said, by weight and by purity."

"When I get raw gold, I usually send it to a refinery that has an assayer. The assayer tests it to establish how pure the gold is. The assayer finds out what other metals are mixed with it and how much is included. He can establish the weight of the gold and give a true value based on the price of gold that day. Then the gold goes off for refining and gets turned into jewelry or bullion."

"How long does that take?" asked Danny.

"I can get that done for you in a couple of weeks," Bill said.

"Oh, man, we can't wait that long! We got bills to pay." Calvin pleaded. "What could ya do for us today?"

Bill took his glasses off and pinched the bridge of his nose. He wiped his glasses on the tail of his shirt and put them back on, running his fingers through his thinning hair.

"Without an assayer's report, I can't tell you what the gold value in this tray is. The one little sample we just tested looks good, but there's no guarantee all the rest of it is the same." Bill leaned on the counter and shifted his weight from one leg to the other. "So, if I make you an offer, it will be a gamble on my part."

Calvin was restless. Danny was thinking about the "several thousand dollars" Bill mentioned earlier, and he was busy spending it in his head.

"Since this is a gamble, I'm going to offer you eighteen hundred in cash right now. And I'll take the risk someone didn't salt this sample, and I just tested the only real piece of gold in it." Bill looked through piercing blue eyes at Calvin as he spoke.

"Up to you now. Take it or leave it!"

Calvin and Danny expected to make two hundred dollars on the gold in that little pouch. When Bill said it might be worth as much as several thousand, their heart rates sped up, and they got excited. This offer slowed their heart rates considerably, but it was still more than they expected.

"We'll take it," said Calvin emphatically as he slammed his palm down onto the counter. Danny stood there, nodding his head in agreement.

"Okay, then," Bill said. "I'll go get your money. Be right back," as he disappeared through the doorway into the back of the shop.

Ten minutes later, the Hix brothers turned out of the driveway in front of Bill's Coin Shop and headed toward home with eighteen crisp hundred dollar bills on the seat between them. They began whooping and hollering. It was going to be one fantastic birthday party! Now both of them were spending the money in their heads. For the moment, they forgot they were Wanted Men.

CHAPTER THIRTY-TWO

T he longer he stayed in the makeshift corral on the mountain, the more depressed Ali became. He missed his world, his people, and especially Becky. He wasn't eating or sleeping well. He froze at night and shivered during the day. After the parade, the last thing he remembered was Becky flying headfirst into the building wall and rolling into a heap, not moving. He had no memory of being shoved into a trailer, but he did remember parts of the trip into the mountains. His first attempts at questioning Max were met with monosyllable answers that told him next to nothing. His future looked so bleak he wondered how he would ever survive it. Sadness enveloped him like a dark cloak.

Max watched him from the far side of their corral for the first day and a half. Finally, he spoke. *"Hey, Sonny Boy, you don't look so good. You have no hair, so you must be freezing. You got no hair in your ears either, and the gnats up here will drive you crazy. Where in the heck did you come from anyway?"*

"Wish I knew the answer to that myself. I have to get home. I have to know how Becky is!" Ali told him.

"Who's this Becky?" Max questioned.

"She's my very best friend. She just rode me in our first parade. We went back to our trailer to go home. She was in the trailer changing her clothes when two guys came up to me. One stuck me with a needle. That really hurt! I didn't know what they were up to. Becky came out of

the trailer and told them to leave me alone. One of the guys pushed her. She hit her head and fell. She didn't move. That's about the last thing I remember before waking up in a strange trailer on the way to this place."

Max snorted. *"Well, Sonny Boy, this ain't no palace, but it's home, and the old man is kind to me."*

"I got that impression, but I miss Becky!" Ali almost whispered. Then raw anger struck him. *"Sure wish I could get my teeth and my feet on the guy who pushed her. I'd make him wish he hadn't!"*

"Well, that ain't likely to happen!" Max snorted. *"You might try standing under the shelter with me when the winds come up. You'll freeze your fanny off out there in the open. I'll share the space with you."*

Ali and Max continued their conversation while Carl Nixon sat in his chair reading and staring at Ali every few paragraphs.

Carl thought long and hard about his new horse. He knew "Buddy" was not a two hundred dollar packhorse. He wasn't a four hundred dollar horse at all. He wondered what the story was. Did someone steal the horse? How did he end up with those two rascals who brought him here? Why did the horse try to attack one of them? He wondered if he shouldn't check in with the Sheriff's Office in Little Rock and see if someone was looking for his newest horse. Then he would stare at Ali and admire him again, pushing those thoughts out of his mind.

By the third day on the mountain, Carl Nixon noticed Ali's coat was dusty, and there were tangles in his mane and tail. He got his ancient truck out, poured gas into the tank from a red five-gallon can, and drove down the mountain to the feed store in Little Rock, where he bought hay for the horses. He searched around and found two body brushes and a mane and tail comb. He purchased them and a sack of grain and drove back up the mountain.

Carl took the brushes into the corral and brushed Ali down top to bottom. He stood back admiring his work. "You sure are a pretty one," he told Ali. He stroked the silken neck and found the itchy place on Ali's withers. He gave it a good long scratch. Ali dropped his head and closed his eyes. It felt good. Then Carl patted him on the shoulder and walked over to do the same for Max. When he finished grooming both horses, he gave each of them a measure of grain. He left the corral, re-latching the gate behind him.

Carl picked up his book, settled back into his chair, planted his feet on the bucket, and tried to read for the rest of the afternoon. He glanced up every few pages just to look at Ali. Thoughts nagged at him. He remembered how anxious those two guys were to get rid of him. His suspicion the horse was stolen didn't explain the horse's reaction to Danny, so maybe that was the reason they were so eager to sell him. He kept pushing those thoughts out of his mind every time he stopped to admire Ali.

One day rolled into the next. Carl fed the horses each morning and gave them fresh spring water. He brought out the new brushes and worked each of them over in turn. Max seemed to benefit most because he hadn't seen much brushing in years. Ali nibbled on the hay and grain, drank some of the water, and spent the balance of the day at the north end of the corral looking away from this place.

Ali could see an occasional vehicle drive on one of the dirt roads down on the plateau. Vehicles always threw up a rooster-tail of dust in their wake. There wasn't much to see down there but barren, arid desert. He could hear some kind of highway below, mostly because of large trucks using their jake-brakes to slow down for a traffic signal a few miles to the west. With the lack of buildings or foliage in the area, sound traveled for miles.

Rabbits and squirrels were the only living creatures he saw regularly besides Carl, Max, and a myriad of birds of all shapes and sizes. Two bolder rabbits crept into the corral to steal bits of hay and grain dropped by the horses. They high-tailed it out of the corral if either of the horses moved at all. The squirrels were braver. They only hurried out of the corral if one of the horses moved in their direction.

Nights were awful for Ali, although he finally accepted Max's invitation to share the shelter when the winds came up. Several more times that week, he heard the snarl of a large animal. It made him shiver. The she lion was hunting and snarled loudly when she missed the mark, and her dinner got away. She stepped on something sharp a week or more before and cut the pad on the bottom of her left front foot. It wasn't life-threatening, but it did slow her down a little. She was missing more meals than she was eating.

She had a belly full of kittens and needed the nourishment. During the day, she settled herself on a large granite boulder in the sun. She licked her sore paw to keep it clean. It was healing but would take another week or two, and her kittens were growing fast.

She already selected the den where she would give birth. It was beneath the boulder she used to sun herself. Instinctively she knew they would be born soon. She spent more time hunting while she tried to build herself up to the level she knew she would need to nurse a growing litter. Missing meals because of a sore paw made her nervous, hungry, and angry.

Ali heard the grunting cough of the she-bear Calvin and Danny saw on the way to this valley. She was coming out of her long winter sleep hungry. She had two cubs born in February to nurse. Bears are omnivores and will eat anything. This particular black bear had been out of her den for about two weeks, getting her metabolism working again after hibernation. She ate shoots of trees and shrubs, nuts, or carrion she could find. She was an opportunistic eater.

On occasion, Ali also heard the haunting chorus of coyote packs as they brought down their prey. They sounded vaguely dog-like, but there were so many voices in the choir he wasn't sure what to make of them.

Nights were cold. Ali wasn't used to that. He was always inside at night. His stall was secure, warm, and dry. This place was surrounded by scary sounds, and he was out in the open, subject to freezing temperatures. He never slept at night, always listening to the night sounds. Ali wasn't cowardly, but he was uneasy about what he didn't know or understand.

The monotony also bothered Ali. He was used to doing things every day. He'd go riding on trails or in the arena for practice. He got a bath several times a week. There were always people around and lots of other horses. Here his only companions were Max, Carl Nixon, and a few rabbits and squirrels. Carl just stared at him much of the time, and Max kept to himself and ignored him for the most part. Ali never got out of the corral.

Carl wondered more and more every day about his new "Buddy." The horse looked depressed to him. He wondered if animals could feel things like that. He wished the horse could talk to him and tell him the real story. His suspicion about the horse being stolen grew stronger and stronger every day. He woke up each morning trying to decide if he should drive down the mountain to the Sheriff's Office and check, and every morning he put it off.

On Ali's second Saturday evening in the mountains, Carl Nixon fed the two horses as usual and gave them fresh water. He forgot to latch the gate. Neither Max nor Ali noticed the oversight until much later that night. Max dozed off, locking his knees and hocks to support his weight.

It was a windless night, so Ali stood at the corral's north end, looking out over the high desert plateau and gazing up at the stars. About eleven, he walked over to the water trough for a drink and noticed the gate to the corral was standing open. A slight breeze must have blown it open.

"*Max, come on, let's go,*" Ali whispered. Max snorted. Ali had startled him awake.

"*What are you talking about?*" he asked.

"*Max, the gate is open. Come on, let's get out of here.*" Ali insisted.

"*Sonny Boy, let's think about that first,*" Max replied. "*I know you want to get back to where ever you came from, but I'm an old horse. My legs aren't as swift as yours, and my heart is not as strong. If you really want to take the chance, I would only slow you down.*"

"*No, Max. We can do this together,*" Ali encouraged. "*Two heads are better than one any time.*"

"*Really? Just think about it,*" Max got serious. "*We don't know where we are, and we don't have any idea where you want to end up. It is nighttime in the mountains, and there are plenty of dangers out there, some we don't even know. I'm a pokey old horse, and you are an inexperienced youngster. What kind of chance do you think we'd have leaving here like that? Who's going to feed us? Who's going to make sure we have fresh water? Who's going to protect us from predators? The old man is kind. He feeds us and gives us fresh water. He will protect us. Sonny Boy, you might want to think about staying right where you are.*"

"*Max, if I don't take this one chance, I'll never see my Becky again. I understand what you are telling me, and my head knows you are probably right. But my heart aches to be back with my family, and I'll never get there if I don't leave now."*

"Okay, Sonny Boy. I wish you the best of luck. I hope you find what you seek."

Ali walked through the gate into the unknown forest. He found the tracks of Carl Nixon's truck and followed them several miles away from the camp before losing them in the darkness. It was pitch black all around him. He had no idea which way to turn. He heard rather than saw a stand of tall trees to his left. He listened. He didn't hear anything rustling in the leaves or pine needles, so he thought it might be a safe place to stop for the night. Carefully he walked over and stood beneath the tall Ponderosa pines shivering in the cold. He knew he would see better in daylight. He resigned himself to stay where he was until first light.

CHAPTER THIRTY-THREE

C onnor McGrew and his assistant Darlene had a busy morning the Saturday after the parade. They did pregnancy checks on a small group of Angus beef cattle for a farmer, did horse vaccinations for another client, and ended up with three young horses to castrate for a third. All of the work was dirty, sweaty, and difficult. Cows are unpredictable and don't appreciate the invasion of privacy at all. Vaccinations were the most straightforward job they had to do, and none of the horses were especially cooperative. After doing their work at each ranch, Connor and Darlene had to change scrubs after hosing off as much as possible.

By the time they got to the last ranch for the day, the sun was almost at its highest point. Shade was nowhere to be found in the pasture where Connor sedated the young horses so he could do the surgery. Darlene stood over him, holding up the rear leg of each horse and handing him tools as he worked. They only got a bit of relief from the bright spring sunshine while they watched the young horses, to be sure they woke up and didn't hurt themselves getting back on their feet.

As with every call they made that week, the topic of conversation rolled around to the horse missing from the parade in San Juan Capistrano. Darlene and Connor spent their time at the parade with Walter and Caroline Howard and liked them, so their feelings about the theft were much more personal. The fact the horse had not been spotted, or no ransom demands had been made to the Howards worried them all. The area around Ramona, where Connor's veterinary practice was located, had suffered a few missing horses in recent memory. Those horses simply vanished as well. All the ranchers were nervous about it.

When the last of the three newly castrated young horses got to his feet, Connor checked his watch. "I just about have time to get to the soccer field and watch the last of my son's game. Do you mind if I just drop you off at the office and head on over there?" he asked Darlene.

"Oh, no. You go ahead."

"I'll drop off the truck there too. Maybe you and I can get together sometime tomorrow morning and clean things up and get it restocked. The other vet is taking all the emergency calls for the rest of the weekend. I want to spend it with my family."

"All I have is a stack of laundry waiting," Darlene said as she climbed back into the truck.

One of the reasons Connor picked the office he rented was it came equipped with a shower. After Connor dropped her off, she decided to use the shower before getting into her car and dragging all the stinking debris from the morning work into it. She still had another set of scrubs to change into.

Refreshed from a quick shower, Darlene decided to stop at the local watering hole for a cold drink before going home. The Drop Inn was a friendly local hangout, and she recognized most of the people who stopped in, at least by the first name. After placing her order, she noticed Linda sitting at the end of the bar and smiled at her. Linda picked up her drink and sat down next to her.

"Hey, what are you doing this afternoon?" Linda asked.

"Just laundry," quipped Darlene as she took a sip.

"How would you like to go with me to a birthday party for a handsome guy I met here a couple of months ago? He's single, and he's adorable?"

Darlene pondered that for a couple of minutes while Linda offered up more and more reasons why she should accompany her.

"Okay. Guess I don't have anything better to do." She acquiesced.

"Great. Let's take my car. You can leave yours here. We don't need two cars."

Darlene locked her car and climbed into the passenger seat of Linda's car. Linda drove down the main road in town into the countryside. About a half-mile outside of town, she turned down a road Darlene had never noticed before. The road was paved just a short distance and then became an unpaved and bumpy track through the woods. Linda drove fast. Several bumps would have sent Darlene airborne had she not buckled her seat belt. She began getting an awful feeling just a little way down the road.

Linda was excited. Parties were what she lived for. She had a boring job in a small town that offered almost no nightlife. She found herself a designated driver in Darlene. Everyone who knew Darlene even slightly knew she was a bit straight-laced, didn't drink much and didn't do anything else either. If this party got going the way Linda hoped, she would need that designated driver to get herself home later.

Six miles on a barely marked dirt road took forever! Linda continued driving much faster than Darlene liked. She became more and more alarmed as they bounced and jounced along. Darlene's "this is not going to end well" feeling got stronger.

"Just exactly where is this party anyway?" she asked Linda in concern.

"Oh, we're almost there," Linda grinned and gunned the engine a little harder. She almost missed the driveway, and the car went up on two wheels making a sharp turn suddenly. Darlene gasped and hung on. Linda slowed as she came to a clearing in the oak trees. There were lots of cars parked in front of an old falling-down cabin.

Getting out of the passenger side of Linda's car, Darlene looked around. Besides the cars parked willy-nilly everywhere, lots of people were milling around. One look was all it took for her to know this was not her kind of party at all. These were not her kind of people. She reached into her purse and found her cell phone missing. She remembered she left it in her car parked in front of the Drop Inn. Her heart sunk. She was stuck here! It was too far to walk back to town. She couldn't call anyone else for a ride. Oh, what had she gotten herself into?

"Come on, I'll introduce you to the hosts and the birthday boy," Linda encouraged, grabbing Darlene's arm and escorting her to the porch of the cabin. Several men were standing talking as they approached.

Darlene was a pretty woman with flawless skin and almost no makeup. Her glossy brown hair was pulled into a pony tail that hung nearly to her waist. Her figure showed through the scrubs with little animals printed on them. She stood out in this crowd. Darlene noticed a couple of men leering at her as the two women walked to the porch. "Keep your mouth shut and try to be invisible," she admonished herself.

Darlene endured the introductions and accepted a coke from the birthday boy, Danny Hix. Linda spotted some other friends and wandered over to talk to them. Darlene looked around and saw an old barn a bit away from the cabin with a couple of oak trees beside it. That offered some shade and distance from the other partygoers. She headed off and settled herself at the base of one tree to keep an eye out for Linda, hoping she would be ready to get out of there soon.

Every few minutes Calvin Hix would escort a couple of people into the barn. They would be inside with the doors shut for a few minutes and wander out again. Once or twice she saw Calvin stuffing what looked like a wad of cash into the pocket of his jeans as he followed his guests back to the cabin area. "Holy Cow," she thought. "There must be something bad going on in there."

She looked at the cars parked around. They were, for the most part, what she and her friends would call "junkers." She also had time to observe the partygoers. She saw lots of messy clothes and hair, bad teeth, tattoos, and body piercings. She heard lots of rough language. These people were not the kind she associated with. She couldn't wait to get out of this place.

After a while, Darlene noticed the one called Danny walking toward her. She sat very still, hoping he wouldn't notice her at all. Unfortunately, he did. He sat down beside her and leaned his back against the tree. "Darlene, isn't it?" he asked.

"Yea."

"Whatcha doing over here all by yourself"

"Just people watching. I had a headache when I got off work. I just needed a few minutes to decompress," she answered.

"Hey, I know what you mean," he said. "I had a bad headache when I woke up this morning." Danny laughed to himself. That's when Danny started talking. Darlene wouldn't have been able to squeeze a word in if she tried, so she sat there and listened incredulously.

Danny talked about his parents being in jail and he and his brother in foster care. He talked about his first contact with "the law," as he called it. He talked about what he and Calvin did to get the money for this party. He talked about the little girl in the hospital trying to chase them off. He talked about the horse they stole. He talked about hearing the news on the radio. He talked about taking the horse to an old prospector in the mountains. He talked about the value of the gold he paid them for the horse. He talked and talked and talked. He finally ran down like a wind-up toy and just sat there for a few minutes. He saw someone he wanted to talk to in the distance and just got up and left Darlene sitting there in shock.

A few minutes later, gunshots rang out. Darlene jerked to attention and spotted several men on the cabin porch using a handgun to shoot at branches of the trees down the driveway. Either the men were impaired by something or horrible shots because they missed everything they aimed at. Every time someone missed, the group laughed like fools. One wild shot blew out the windshield of a car. Either the owner was the shooter at the time, or just didn't notice. Calvin came out of the cabin with a long rifle and passed that gun around to his buddies. None of them did any better with the rifle than they did with the handgun.

As dry as everything was in that area with the drought, Darlene was scared to death one of them would miss and set off a spark that could burn the whole area down around them. They were so far back in the woods she wondered how long it would take for the fire department to get a call on fire out here. She was relieved when the shooting stopped.

Just before dark, Linda came staggering over to Darlene's tree and asked if Darlene would drive her back to the Drop Inn. Darlene didn't have to be asked twice. She hustled Linda over to her car and helped her buckle into the passenger seat. She grabbed Linda's key and fired up the engine, backing out of the driveway as quickly as possible. She turned the car down the dirt road, hoping she could remember the way back to town.

Darlene got to the paved road just as dusk fell. She turned the car toward town and drove straight to the Drop Inn. Linda was asleep. Darlene took the car keys to the bartender. "You can try bringing her a hot cup of coffee or call her a cab. I'm going home."

Darlene picked up her cell phone after buckling her seat belt. Low battery! She'd forgotten to plug it in. She had just enough battery to make one call. As she pulled out of the Drop Inn parking lot, she dialed the number.

CHAPTER THIRTY-FOUR

J ohnny, it's me," Darlene almost shouted when her brother answered his phone. "I just got back to the Drop Inn from a party in the woods, and you won't believe what's out there. I can't believe I was stupid enough to go in the first place. Linda from the Drop Inn invited me. I don't even know her last name. I didn't know she was into that stuff either." Darlene finally had to stop and catch her breath.

"Hold on, sis, I don't have a clue what you're talking about."

The words began tumbling out of Darlene in a rush she couldn't have stopped had she wanted to. "Oh Johnny, there's a place out in the woods just north of town with a run-down cabin that two men are living or probably squatting in … and they threw some crazy kind of birthday party for the youngest one … I think they are brothers … There were probably fifty or sixty people out there for that "party" doing all kinds of things ….I knew they weren't my kind of people the minute I got there, but I didn't have a way back to town, and I forgot my cell phone in my car, and I left my car at the Drop Inn, and I rode with that Linda woman … I mean to tell you those people were low-lifes … Some were trying target practice on the oak trees and were so high they couldn't hit anything ….I hid out away from the crowd until my ride was ready to leave, but one of the brothers found me sitting under a tree. He sat down and told me everything," Darlene rambled until she had to stop to catch her breath again.

"Hey, slow down, sis. What is everything? What were they doing out there that has you so upset?"

The rush of words from Darlene continued. "Oh, Johnny, there was drinking, of course, and I'm sure there was other stuff too….

The older brother kept taking people into the barn and closing the door. I'm positive I saw him shoving a fistful of cash in his pocket several times when he left. They're up to no good, if you know what I mean. I couldn't wait to get out of there but, you'd have to see if it is what I think it is … And the really horrible thing is he told me how they raised the money to have that "party" in the first place….you remember that horse everyone's been looking for since the parade last week? Well, he told me they drugged it, and stole it, and planned to sell him to the kill buyer for fifty cents a pound….He was the one who hurt the little girl … That creep told me he felt a little bad about that … Can you imagine?... That beautiful creature was going to be turned into dog food! … And that poor little girl … I think she's still in a coma … I just can't believe anyone would do something like that … He told me they did that a few times before and just stole horses out of pastures to sell for slaughter … But their buyer told them that horse was too hot for him to take, so they sold him for four hundred bucks to some old coot up in the mountains to use as a packhorse…. Johnny, I sat at the parade with the owners of that horse and parents of that little girl….I just can't imagine how they would feel if he'd been shipped off to a Mexican slaughter plant and ended up as dog food….And I can't imagine that poor horse being a packhorse in the mountains….He's so beautiful and so talented … You have to do something so they can get him back, Johnny!"

Darlene had Deputy John McGrew's rapt attention at the mention of low-lifes and a secluded barn out in the woods. His heart rate began to race when his sister mentioned the horse. "Hey, Darlene, are you sure you heard that right? Did he specifically mention the 2.5 million dollar stallion that was stolen from the Swallows Day Parade?"

"Oh, yes! I did hear that very specifically."

"Can I get you to hold on a minute while I find a pad and pencil? I want to go over this with you again so I can take some notes. I have to call my Watch Commander right away."

Darlene slowed down and took several deep breaths, keeping her hands on the steering wheel of her car so tightly her knuckles turned white.

Deputy McGrew came back on the phone line and began asking questions as he scribbled down her answers.

He was shocked by what she told him. Law enforcement agencies across the whole state had been looking for the horse thieves and that horse. Darlene, his baby sister, just broke the case wide open. He couldn't help but think how it would also help his career when he became the first law enforcement officer to get any kind of lead in this case.

John thanked her for keeping her eyes and ears open. He told her to go on home and relax. He assured her he'd take care of everything.

Darlene drove home and jumped in the shower the minute she got home. She needed to wash off the dirty feeling she got from being at that "birthday party." She stood under the hot water for a long, long time. She didn't hear her home phone ring forty-five minutes later.

*****

Deputy John McGrew had just arrived home following his watch when Darlene's call came in. His wife, two kids, and their brother's family were at the pizza parlor waiting for him. He made a call to his Watch Commander, who asked him to come back to the station right away. John called his wife's cell phone and let her know he wouldn't make the pizza party for the soccer team that night.

In the meantime, the Watch Commander reached his superior by phone, which set off a flurry of calls ending up with San Diego County Sheriff Tishman. Sheriff Tishman organized a Major Case Task Force of his people and called Orange County Sheriff Nolan and filled him in. Tishman asked Nolan to join them at the North San Diego County Sheriff's Station. Orange County had an Assault, Attempted Murder, and Grand Theft case hinging on the information. It was a very high-profile case. Sheriff Nolan wanted it solved. He was getting pressure.

Nolan called Detective Brian Nelson and asked him and his partner Ron Bentley to join them at the Task Force meeting. Nolan told Nelson they might have information to break the case on the stolen horse and the little girl in a coma.

Nelson called his partner as he left his driveway and told him to meet him there. By the time John McGrew arrived back at his substation, the place was a madhouse, and he heard both Sheriffs and a Major Case Task Force were on their way. He was surprised this was coming together so fast. Once everyone arrived, they went into the conference room for a briefing. Sheriff Tishman put Deputy McGrew in front of the group. He told them what he knew. He'd tried to call his sister but got no answer. Darlene was in the shower and didn't hear the phone.

The two Sheriffs asked John to hang around and keep trying to reach his sister while they held their private meeting. They planned what action to take and when. A lot of that depended on John's sister being able to lead them to the site. They discussed strategy. They decided they'd bust an illegal party and take the two suspects in for questioning. San Diego County and Orange County Sheriff's Departments would both take part.

The Orange County Sheriff's Forensic Lab was working with FBI Records. They finally got a match to the print on the syringe found by the Howard's horse trailer. Danny had a record, and his fingerprints were on file. Bingo! They now had a name to go with the evidence.

Brian Nelson had been working the case as a kidnapping for ransom. Now they had a live suspect. He was thrilled. According to the Deputy's sister, these two suspects had stolen the horse for money to have a birthday party.

The stupidity of it all and the amount of time and resources wasted on a wild goose chase made him mad and sad at the same time. In the meantime, there was a little girl in Mission Hospital in a coma.

*****

John McGrew finally reached his sister by phone. He told her he was at his station. San Diego County Sheriff Tishman asked him to get her to the station so he and the Major Case Task Force could get information directly from her about the horse theft and the party she'd been to that day. She dressed in a hurry and flew out the door.

She was amazed and intimidated by all the officers in the conference room waiting for her. There were Deputies and Detectives from Orange County and San Diego County, Federal Drug Enforcement Agency (DEA), Hazardous Material Handling (HAZMAT) staff, and Federal Alcohol Tobacco and Firearms (ATF) members. Both Sheriff Tishman from San Diego and Sheriff Nolan from Orange County were in the room.

All eyes in the room were on her. Deputy McGrew stood up and introduced Darlene. He gave the group a general outline of what she'd told him that evening on the phone. Darlene felt stupid for getting herself into the mess in the first place and was horribly self-conscious about speaking to such a large group of people.

Questions began flying at her. She answered each one as honestly as she could. Yes, she'd personally seen people going in and out of the barn. Yes, she'd seen what looked like wads of cash Calvin Hix shoved in his pocket after trips inside the barn. It was in the old barn on the property. No, she didn't know what went on inside that barn because she hadn't gone inside herself, but she was pretty sure they weren't having a Tupperware party.

Yes, she'd had a conversation with one of the residents, a man named Danny. He admitted he and his brother Calvin stole a horse from the Swallows Day Parade the week before. Yes, Danny did describe the horse. He told her it was a pretty gray stallion. Yes, Danny told her they stole the horse to raise money for his birthday party. Yes, he told her they planned to sell the horse to a kill buyer who intended to trailer the horse to Mexico for slaughter.

Yes, there were guns on the property. She watched several men taking turns shooting branches off trees. They were so drunk or otherwise impaired it scared her to death. And so on, and so forth.

The questioning went on for more than an hour. Finally, one of the deputies asked her to describe how to get to the place. She told him they left the Drop Inn on the main road heading west until they were about a half-mile past the 7-11 at the end of town. Then they turned onto a dirt road she'd never noticed before, heading south. She said they drove five or six miles to the driveway.

"I know that place," Deputy Jones said. "That's the old Miller place. Bill bought that property way out in the woods so he wouldn't have to put up with neighbors. He was always a hermit type. Real nice guy, though. I ran into him in town every week or so. He built that barn for his two horses. It was just him and those two horses and one old dog. He's passed on. I heard he had a heart attack about six or seven years ago."

"Thanks, Darlene, for your help on this. We all appreciate you being here so we could get the story straight from you. Do you mind if we call you with any more questions that come up?" Sheriff Tishman asked.

"No, not at all," Darlene answered. "I'm just glad I'm able to help. Maybe you can find the missing horse. Those people are scary. I think Danny is not right in the head. I think that he could get dangerous with little provocation. His brother is the brains of the operation."

"I think that's all the questions we have for you right now. Again, thank you for coming down and talking with us. You are free to go home now. Would you like an escort?" Sheriff Tishman asked her.

"No, but thank you. I'll be fine. I'm just tired and feeling pretty stupid for getting into that mess in the first place." Darlene answered.

Sheriff Nolan spoke up. "Darlene, it was ill-advised of you to go to that party, and we are certainly glad you got home safely. You showed a lot of courage in coming forward with what you know. Without your help, we would still be wondering what happened in that parking lot a week ago. We now have a chance to recover the horse and tell the young girl's parents what happened. I believe, with your information, we will solve this case. Thank you for being so courageous."

"Sheriff Nolan, it was the right thing to do. Now I'm going home. Call if you need anything else from me," Darlene said.

Sheriff Tishman announced a fifteen-minute break. He told the men in the room to be back by 9:30 p.m. so they could plan the raid. The men left the room searching for fresh coffee.

Sheriffs Tishman and Nolan led the meeting assembled in the conference room at nine-thirty. They had a map of the area blown up. They set up teams of Deputies with their assignments. They pointed out where they wanted the Haz-Mat Teams. They gave Drug

Enforcement Agency teams their assignments. Alcohol Tobacco and Firearms received their instructions. The time set for their arrival at the cabin was 5:30 a.m. the following day. Anyone on the property was to be arrested, not just the Hix brothers. Sheriff Nolan and his Detectives of Orange County planned to participate because the Hix brothers were suspects in the Orange County cases for Grand Theft, Attempted Murder, and other charges.

They had a current aerial map of the Miller property enlarged and printed. The various teams were assigned a specific sector, so no one on the property escaped. Deputy McGrew marked assignments on the property map. Sheriff Tishman brought in their command and control vehicle, which included phones and computers. The Public Information Officer got the go-ahead to notify the media of a Press Conference set for 2:00 p.m. the following afternoon.

One of the supervisors called the San Diego County District Attorney. He could start setting up his staff to handle the cases. The Sheriffs made another call to the Orange County District Attorney. The meeting adjourned close to eleven-thirty. The two Sheriffs told everyone to get some sleep. Everyone was to be back at the substation by 4:00 a.m. They needed to get their gear together and get to the property before 5:30.

Men poured out of the conference room, got in their cars, and left. The Orange County Detectives and Sheriff got a local hotel room for the night, so they wouldn't spend the rest of the night driving.

Brian Nelson and Ron Bentley were anxious to get their hands on the Hix brothers. They wanted to find out where the horse was. They wanted to know why those two saw fit to put a 13-year-old girl in the hospital so they could steal him to raise money for a stupid birthday party. Brian personally wished he could choke the life out of Danny Hix for what he'd done to Becky Howard.

CHAPTER THIRTY-FIVE

etectives Nelson and Bentley arrived at the substation in their bulletproof vests. They pulled their Orange County Sheriff's Department jackets over them to help identify themselves to other officers. They'd checked their weapons and made sure they had the right gear. No one had any idea what they would be walking into out in the woods.

The parking lot was full of Deputies gearing up. The Haz-Mat teams checked their gear and had everything loaded in their three vans. They left plenty of space in the vans for hauling out evidence. The Command and Control vehicle was idling and ready. The DEA teams brought several dogs along if someone headed for the woods to escape. ATF Teams had their weapons checked. Everyone was tense and ready.

The parking lot began to empty, all vehicles following the Sheriff's cars. Deputy Jones led. He was the only one who'd been to the property. Everyone parked quietly off the road a half-mile from the cabin. The Haz-Mat teams and their large vans parked across the road from the others. Deputies, ATF, and DEA Agents got out of their cars. Everyone crept to their assigned positions around the property. Everyone was quiet; radios turned down, dogs muzzled, all lights off.

As the teams approached the property, they noted people in sleeping bags in the dirt in front of the cabin. Others had fallen asleep in lawn chairs around and on the porch. Some slept in their cars.

At 5:30 a.m., Sheriff Tishman gave the signal. He shouted, "GO! GO! GO!" Officers assigned to the cabin drew their guns and jumped on the porch. They announced themselves as they busted the door off its hinges. They ran inside with guns drawn. Both Danny and Calvin were asleep, half-dressed in bed.

Calvin and Danny stared at the Deputies. Both had that "deer in the headlights" look of shock and fear. There was no one else in the cabin. Deputies handcuffed them and marched them outside.

K-9 Agents with dogs stood over the people in the open. They pulled the dogs' muzzles off when Sheriff Tishman gave the signal. The dogs came alive with snarling and growling. The Agents and their dogs maintained control. Deputies stood suspects against the walls, legs spread. Officers searched and handcuffed each suspect, then force-marched them to waiting vehicles. Officers rolled suspects already on the ground onto their bellies. They searched and handcuffed them, hauled them to their feet, and force-marched them to patrol vehicles. Most were too startled or terrified of the dogs to put up resistance. Dogs barked furiously, straining to get away from their handlers. Startled and scared partygoers screamed and shouted. Officer shouted commands. Dogs barked and growled. All in all, there was a terrible noise in the empty forest that night.

One man broke ranks and ran for the woods. An agent turned his dog loose and told the dog to find the man. The dog's handler ran to keep up. When the dog caught the man, terrified screaming echoed through the woods. The dog brought the man down. The dog, snarling savagely through clamped jaws, held the man down on his belly. The man's upper arm was in the dog's mouth. The dog stood on his back. His handler arrived and sat on the man as he cuffed him. The officer hauled him to his feet and escorted him back out of the woods. The dog continued snarling and snapping at the man's heels the whole way. The man sniveled and cried in fear.

Deputies assigned to vehicles searched for suspects inside with flashlights. When they found someone inside a car, a Deputy smashed out the side window with his nightstick. Startled suspects were helped outside by Deputies with their guns drawn. One Deputy leaned them across the hood of their car at gunpoint while his partner searched and cuffed them.

The officers rounded up a total of twenty-nine people. Thanks to the dogs, no one escaped. Every suspect sat in a car or van waiting for the drive to jail. One by one, officers checked each person for their identity. The officers took that information to the Command and Control vehicle. Those operating the computers ran each suspect through the system, looking for Wants and Warrants.

Everyone at that party had Wants and Warrants for Failure to Appear in Traffic Court, suspected Child Abuse, Burglary, Drug Sales and Possession, Parole Violation, Sex Crimes, Auto Theft, etc.

One of the DEA Agents checked out the barn. He kicked the door in. He went inside with his gun drawn. He found no one there. "Clear!" he shouted to the others.

The Agent confirmed what Darlene suspected. This was a meth lab. It was full of product ready for sale and all the equipment needed to make it. He backed out and called the Hazardous Material teams up to start loading their vans.

The Sheriff sent Deputies back inside the cabin to gather evidence. All vehicles on the property were checked for ownership and ran through the computers. Low and behold, two stolen cars were sitting there. Deputies went through the cars looking for evidence. Other Deputies went through the sleeping bags. They tagged and bagged many items as evidence. The Deputies in the cabin found one handgun and one rifle, both recently fired. They were bagged and tagged. The officers found a lot of contraband in pants pockets, sleeping bags, purses, cars, and inside the cabin.

All in all, it took several hours to collect the evidence at the scene. Officer started processing suspects through the Command and Control Vehicle in the meantime. Those processed transferred to jail for lock-up.

The Sheriff called the operation completed when all the evidence was collected. The officers headed back to the substation. They needed to process the rest of the prisoners and set up the evidence against each of them.

The substation was a flurry of activity within a few minutes. Deputies connected suspects to evidence. Officers and staff gathered incident reports and evidence they had on each prisoner. They sent them to the District Attorney's office for filing charges. Other officers made the bookings and moved prisoners into jail cells. There weren't enough cells in the small substation, so Deputy Escorts took some prisoners to other facilities nearby.

The Sheriffs had the Hix brothers separated at the property. Calvin and Danny were locked in interview rooms, chained to the tables inside.

Brian Nelson and Ron Bentley had been partners for years. Each had their particular style when interviewing suspects. Brian coaxed information out while Ron had a more hard-edged style. Between them, they'd already decided Danny would be the most likely to flip, so Brian took him, and Ron took Calvin. They expected Calvin to say nothing and "lawyer up" right away.

The detectives audio-taped and video recorded both interviews. Sheriff Nolan stood behind the two-way mirror, looking into the interview room with Calvin Hix. Ron Bentley entered the room and sat down in a chair across from Calvin. He took out a pad and pen. He asked Calvin for his full name and asked him to spell it for him. Calvin complied. Ron asked him about the horse stolen at the parade last weekend.

"I don't know nothin' about that." Calvin snarled.

"Well, we know you stole the horse, and you and your brother probably sold him for a few hundred bucks. Were you aware that particular horse is worth about 2.5 million dollars?" Ron asked. Calvin swallowed hard, and his eyes bugged out a bit at that, but he said nothing.

"If you just tell us what happened, tell us the truth, things will go easier on you," Ron told him. He looked directly into Calvin's eyes. "Right now, there are serious charges against you and Danny. Make it easy on yourself and tell me what happened."

"I want to talk to a lawyer first." Calvin spat, giving Ron an evil look. "I don't have to talk to you at all without my lawyer present, you know. I know my rights!"

Ron told Calvin his partner was talking with Danny at that very minute, and Danny was telling him everything.

"Danny's blaming you for this, you know. Are you sure you don't want to tell me the truth and make this a little easier on yourself?" Ron asked.

"Like I said, I ain't talkin' to you without my lawyer!" shouted Calvin.

He was sweating and tense, pulling on the chain holding his handcuffs to the table. He fidgeted in the chair, which made the ankle bracelets clank.

"Can I have something to drink?" he finally asked.

"Sure, be right back. Any preference? Coffee, Coke, Water?" asked Ron as he stood to leave the room.

"Coke's fine," Calvin answered, not looking at him.

Ron conferred with Sheriff Nolan in the corridor. That interview had gone as expected. Ron went to call the DA and arrange for a Public Defender for Calvin.

Detective Brian Nelson was having just the opposite situation in the interview room with Danny. Danny was scared out of his wits. And he wasn't the brightest bulb in the package either. Danny was spilling his guts.

He told Detective Nelson everything in great detail. Brian secretly thanked the department for the audio and videotape system. He couldn't scribble notes fast enough to keep up with Danny. Brian Nelson kept repeating questions, and Danny answered them the same way every time.

Brian felt Danny was truthful from how he acted, the ease of his delivery when questioned, and his body language. Brian knew the audiotapes and video would come into court if and when a trial was held. He wanted the story in detail, with everything repeated several times. He kept at it until he got what he thought they needed for a conviction in this case. It took a while.

He offered Danny something to eat or drink. Danny asked for a coke and a sandwich and aspirin for his headache. Brian stood and headed for the door, promising to be back with food and drink in a few minutes.

He met Sheriff Nolan in the corridor. Nolan watched the interview through the two-way mirror. He was pleased. Now all they had to do was pick up the horse where Danny said they'd left him and close the case.

CHAPTER THIRTY-SIX

B rian Nelson thought about what Danny said. Danny told him where he and Calvin took the horse. Brian knew that was in Los Angeles County. He knew a little about the area and thought either Acton or Palmdale Sheriff's offices would be where they could locate a deputy to take them to such a remote spot. Since Palmdale was urban, he thought Acton would probably have someone on their staff who knew the area.

He remembered the Station Fire of a few years ago. It burned almost 125,000 acres up there. It might be challenging to locate a small valley that hadn't burned. Maybe they should also get in touch with the Federal Fish and Wildlife people. They would know the area as well.

He talked to Sheriff Nolan. They reviewed the interview tapes. The Sheriff agreed with Brian. Sheriff Nolan stepped away to call the LA County Sheriff and enlist his support. He also called the Fish and Wildlife Department with a request for help on standby.

The LA County Sheriff confirmed Sheriff Nolan's and Detective Nelson's opinion. He had two officers in Acton with twenty years' experience there. They knew the area well. He set up a meeting for Detectives Nelson and Bentley to meet with them and one officer from Little Rock at 1:30 in the Acton substation.

Brian Nelson asked one of the staff to take a sandwich and coke into the interview room for Danny. He knew Becky Howard was fighting for her life in Mission Hospital right now. As far as Danny's headache was concerned, Brian wished he'd been the one to give it to him. Danny could forget his aspirin. Brian Nelson couldn't have cared less. He and Ron had to leave immediately to get to the meeting in Acton.

Nelson and Bentley hurried to their car and jumped on the freeway. They drove for miles to get to the meeting. They pulled off the highway and arrived at the LA County Sheriff's office in Acton with five minutes to spare.

Brian asked the officer at the front desk for coffee when they checked in. "Sure, we have a fresh pot brewing right now. It's hot and strong. The guys here chip in for Starbucks. Help yourselves. Let me buzz you in. Take this corridor to the first left. That'll be our lunchroom. The coffee and supplies are in there. I'll let the guys know you're here."

Four Deputies joined them in the lunchroom and poured coffee for themselves. They introduced themselves and asked why Nelson and Bentley were there. Brian told them. There wasn't a law enforcement officer in Southern California that hadn't heard about the horse theft at the Swallows Day Parade. They were all whistling at the value of the horse involved.

"How's that little girl doing?" one of them asked. Brian told them she was still in a coma. "She's from a very prominent family, and they are the nicest people you'd ever meet. It's so sad."

The men adjourned to a conference room. Detective Nelson and Bentley told them what they knew about where the horse went. They repeated directions Danny gave them to the LA County officers. They brought a copy of the interview tape between Brian Nelson and Danny Hix. They played that portion of the tape for the LA County Deputies.

Deputy Ramon Ramirez, from Little Rock, said, "I bet I know who you're talking about. That sounds like it could be Carl Nixon's place. I've never been there but have heard the stories. Carl's been up in the mountains for close to twenty years now. It's a real sad story. He used to have an excellent job at Lockheed in Palmdale, a wife, and a pretty 12-year-old daughter. The daughter had a thing for those Arab horses. His wife was driving her home from a riding lesson when some idiot got in a hurry to pass a truck out on the highway and took them out in a head-on crash. Both died instantly."

"Carl stuck around about two weeks after the funeral. He cleaned out his bank accounts, took his retirement savings, maybe sixty grand altogether, and just disappeared. The neighbors with a key checked on his house when nobody had seen him for a month, and they found the house empty but neat as a pin. Clothes still in closets and dressers. It looked like someone was coming home any minute."

"It was months before anyone saw him again. He showed up in Little Rock for supplies looking like a mountain man. Now he comes into town in an old rust bucket pick-up truck and buys supplies and hay for his horses every few weeks. He doesn't talk much. Says he does a little prospecting up there and brings a few flakes of gold to some pawnbroker over in Palmdale for cash to keep him going."

"You said he buys hay for his horses?" asked Brian Nelson.

"That's what I hear. The boy at the feed store says he doesn't say much. But I guess he keeps a couple of packhorses up at his place. The boy told me he bought grain and some brushes and curry combs this week. He thought that was strange. The old man doesn't buy things like that."

"Can you get us up there? We need to talk to Carl Nixon and see if he has the horse we're looking for." Ron Bentley asked.

"Look, you're probably driving a Crown Vic or a Taurus. That road is too rough for one of those. You'll break something and get yourself stranded on the mountain, and then we'll have to bring in search and rescue to find you. Why don't we take my four-wheel drive? That road ain't pretty." Deputy Ramirez chuckled.

"What are we waiting for?" asked Brian Nelson.

One of the Acton Deputies joined them. Ramirez drove them to Little Rock and turned off the main highway heading south into the mountains. They had paved roads for the first few miles and then dropped onto dirt roads. The ride was very uncomfortable. The tension built the closer they got. Nelson and Bentley hoped they would find Prince Ali and get that part of the case closed.

Carl Nixon's place was ten and a half miles off the pavement as the crow flies. But the road twisted and turned, sometimes meeting itself coming around a corner. Driving time was close to two hours. When they finally saw the little valley with the tumbledown shack and makeshift horse corral, they all breathed a sigh of relief. Deputy Ramirez stopped his vehicle in front of the cabin.

An old man who looked to be in his seventies came out of the cabin with a shotgun pointed toward the ground. The guys all got out of the four-wheel-drive vehicle and approached him.

"You guys here about a horse?" Carl Nixon asked. "If so, you're about a day late. The horse escaped last night. No telling where he's at now. He could be a meal for a cougar by this time if he were unlucky."

"You wouldn't be Carl Nixon, would you?" asked Deputy Ramirez. Carl nodded his head. "Mr. Nixon, would you mind telling us all about it?"

"Sure. And you can call me Carl." Carl said, walking back to the cabin and placing the shotgun just inside the door.

Carl filled them in on the Hix brothers' arrival at his place, wanting to sell him a two hundred dollar packhorse. When the horse came out of the trailer, he said he knew he wasn't a two hundred dollar packhorse. But he was the prettiest Arab horse he'd ever seen in his life. He told them his daughter had been partial to Arab horses.

He told them about the horse going after Danny. He'd assumed Danny had done something mean to him. He didn't know about Becky. Carl said he'd been rolling it around in his head for several days, wondering why such a nice horse was here for just a few hundred dollars. He had a suspicion the horse was stolen, or there was a lot more to the story than the Hix brothers told him.

Carl said he woke up Sunday convinced he needed to go to the Sheriff's Department in Little Rock and make inquiries, but the horse was gone when he went outside to feed. He told them how attached he'd gotten to the horse in such a short time. They noticed tears welling in his eyes as he spoke.

"I rode all over the area this morning looking for him and couldn't find a trace of him," Carl told them. "The only thing I did find is an old blue and white trailer. It looks like the one the guys that brought him used. It's about a mile and a half down the mountain in a thicket of trees. I'd be happy to show it to you. It wasn't there before they showed up with that horse, I'll guarantee it."

Despite his appearance, Carl Nixon was articulate and educated. And they could tell he was genuinely upset over losing the horse. Carl referred to him as "Buddy" when he spoke. And he was very concerned about Buddy's well-being.

The detectives filled Carl in on the horse and the little girl lying in a hospital bed. That really affected him. He broke down and choked back tears. It was too close to home for him. Only, his little girl didn't make it. He promised to keep searching for the horse and tell them if he spotted him, alive or dead. Then he drove them to the location he found the trailer parked.

Deputy Ramirez happened to have a hitch and ball on his four-wheel-drive vehicle that matched the hitch on the trailer. With Carl's help, they hooked it up. They thanked Carl for his help and cooperation and promised Deputy Ramirez would let him know if the horse turned up. Deputy Ramirez gave him his card and asked that Carl contact him if he found evidence of the horse on the mountain.

"I'll keep looking for him and hoping I never find what's left of him," Carl told them.

Detective Nelson told Carl his boss called the Department of Fish and Wildlife. They had people who worked in the area and knew it well, so they'd also be searching. Carl said he'd be on the lookout for them.

The officers left hauling the trailer to the substation as evidence. Now LA County had charges to pile on for the Hix brothers.

Detectives Nelson and Bentley finally got back in their car in Acton close to 8:00 that night and made the long trip home, missing dinner again.

Sheriffs Tishman and Nolan held a joint press conference and announced a break in the case of the injured girl and the stolen horse. They had two suspects in custody. They promised more details as they had them. They took few questions. They didn't have all the answers yet.

At 2:00 that afternoon, a representative of the Orange County Sheriff called Walter on his cell phone and told him about the arrest. He didn't have more information but promised to contact Walter when they knew more.

"Did they find our boy, Ali?" Walter wanted to know.

"I don't have that information yet. I know the Detectives are working on it. We'll call you when we have more information," the officer told him.

Walter told Caroline. They both made a flurry of phone calls. They started to have hope again. It was the first good news they'd had for days.

CHAPTER THIRTY-SEVEN

On their way from Acton to Orange County, Detective Brian Nelson called Walter Howard. He knew the Howards were anxious about Prince Ali.

"I've got some news for you." Detective Nelson said to Walter. "You knew we busted the guys that stole your horse? We chased down the leads we got from them and did get to talk to the old man who bought the horse from them. We're on our way back from there right now."

"You mean you found Ali?" Walter said hopefully.

"Well, not exactly. Let me give you the whole story. The old man who bought the horse from them is Carl Nixon. He prospects in the Angeles National Forest up by where the Station Fire was a couple of years back. He was looking for a packhorse. He contacted a horse broker about it."

"I see." Walter said.

"From what we learned, the horse broker was going to buy the horse from the thieves. But when he learned about your horse being stolen, he put two and two together and told the creeps no deal. Apparently, they were anxious to unload the horse, and he told them about Carl Nixon."

"The old prospector?" asked Walter.

"Yes. They took the horse to Nixon. Nixon bought the horse for about four hundred bucks. But he had a suspicion there was something wrong. The horse was too nice. That nagged at him for a few days. So he planned to go to the Sheriff's office in Little Rock to ask about it this morning. When he woke up and went out to feed his horses, Ali was missing. He said it looked like he forgot to latch the gate on their corral."

"So what you're telling me is Ali isn't there?" Walter asked.

"That's what I'm telling you. Ali walked away. He's somewhere up in the Angeles National Forest. I've notified the Federal Fish and Wildlife people. They are on the lookout for him. Carl Nixon does have another horse, and he's out looking for him too. I don't know what to tell you, Mr. Howard. There are mountain lions, bears, and many hazards for a horse like that up there. We're doing the best we can." Detective Nelson offered.

"Would it help if we put up reward money for him?" asked Walter.

"It wouldn't hurt. The area he walked away from is wilderness country. There aren't many people up there. I think Carl Nixon and the Fish and Wildlife people are our best hope. But a reward might bring in a few more eyes to look for him if he's still alive up there. I can certainly help you get the word out."

"Well, let's do it then. I'm willing to put up Fifty Thousand. Can you work that out for me and get the information to the media? My little girl is going to be devastated when she wakes up. I'd like to find him first, so I don't have to tell her he's gone. She loves that horse!"

"You bet, Mr. Howard. I'll call it in to my supervisor right now, and we'll get our Public Information Officer working with the media. How is your daughter today? Has she shown any improvement yet?" Detective Nelson asked.

"Not so far. Her vital signs are good, and she's off the critical list, but she's still in a coma. We're hanging in there and hoping for something soon," a dejected Walter Howard told the detective.

"Look, Detective Nelson, I don't know how I'm going to tell my wife about Ali, much less my daughter when she wakes up. If you think I need to make the reward higher, please let me know. Ali is very special to my family. We'd do just about anything to get him back. Let me know what we can do, will you?"

"We've got good people out looking for him. I promise you we'll do the best we can. Carl Nixon is very familiar with the area since he lives up there. He got pretty attached to the horse too. He's going to be out there looking for him until he finds something that tells him there's no reason to continue the search."

"Okay. I just feel so helpless here. There's not much I can do but wait and worry. That's not a very good feeling." Walter confessed.

"I know," Detective Nelson said. "But you are where you need to be right now. We'll do the best we can. We have the two creeps that did this in jail, and they will spend a long time there, I assure you. We're still figuring out their charges, and the DA is working on the case now. I know that doesn't bring back your horse or heal your daughter, but you will get justice for this."

"Justice feels pretty hollow right now. As you said, it won't bring back Ali or make Becky well again." Walter answered.

"I appreciate that. I don't know how I would feel. I have a 14-year-old daughter of my own. Just hang in there with us and let us do what we do. Think positive. Okay?"

"I'll try. We'll try. And thank you. We, Caroline and I, really do appreciate your work on this case."

"No thanks are necessary." Detective Nelson told him. "That's why I became a cop in the first place. I like helping people.

Carl Nixon saddled Max after the Deputies left his place. He took water and his shotgun with him and headed out in the forest. He thought he knew the approximate area the mountain lion called her territory. He was going to start there. He'd heard her several times that week, snarling in the night. He hoped he would find nothing of Ali.

When Carl got to the center of the lion's territory, he started circling. He looked for horse dung, hoof prints, piles of leaves that didn't belong, scratched-up soil, anything that looked a little out of place. For the longest time, he found nothing. Then he saw the bone.

He dismounted and walked over to a pile of leaves with disturbed earth in front of them. He could see the lion's claw prints. She'd obviously scratched the leaves into this pile to cover something up. Carl poked into the pile and then began to uncover it with a stick he found nearby. There was a carcass here. All that was left were white bones, mostly scattered and disjointed.

He finally found the skull. The bones all looked fairly small, and the skull confirmed his suspicion. This was a small deer. He breathed a sigh of relief. Not Ali. This was an old carcass. What the cat didn't consume, the other creatures of the forest had. When he backed up and looked around, he noticed bones had been dragged from under the leaf pile and scattered around for quite a ways.

He walked back to Max and mounted up, increasing his circle slightly. He spent the last hours of daylight searching the area. When he decided it was time to go back home, he left a pile of rocks where he ended his search. He would return in the morning and continue.

Carl spent Monday and Tuesday in his search. He covered the territory he thought was the mountain lion's and the black bear's, which overlapped slightly. He found several old carcasses in the lion's territory, none of which were large enough or new enough to be Ali. He found gnawed shoots, overturned deadfall where the bear clawed open the trees looking for worms and grubs, and he found a fawn that had been taken recently but nothing large enough to be a horse.

Every time he returned home unsuccessful, he thanked heaven. He really didn't want to find Ali's body up here. He hoped the horse was as smart as he looked and headed back to civilization where someone might recognize him and get him back to his owners.

While searching the edges of the mountain lion's territory, Carl ran into Randy of Fish and Wildlife. Randy was on horseback doing the same thing as Carl. They spoke briefly, and Carl showed him the territory he'd already covered.

"Heard the owners put up a fifty thousand dollar reward on the horse," Randy told him. "They must want the horse back pretty bad."

"He's a very nice horse. If he were mine, I'd probably do the same thing." Carl said. "Since we're both in the same area, why don't we split it up a little, so we don't cover the same ground. I'll head north along that ridge," pointing in the direction he meant to cover, "and why don't you try south."

"Sounds good to me. I'll be in touch with the Deputies down in Little Rock if I find anything. Where's your cabin? I can stop by and leave you a note if you're not there." Randy suggested.

Carl gave him directions, and they parted. Carl spotted horse dung along the rocky ridge that Ali climbed on his last day in the forest. He also found hoof prints of shod hooves. It looked like the horse was smart after all. He was heading over the ridge to the High Desert. Carl knew there were people there. He had higher hopes someone would find the horse. Carl turned Max around and went back to his cabin. He took care of Max, fed him some of the new grain he'd bought with a heavy flake of hay, checked his water, latched the corral gate, and left. He drove down the mountain to the sheriff's office and asked for Deputy Ramirez.

Carl told Deputy Ramirez what he'd found on the mountain and his suspicion that Ali was heading north and would be in the high desert by now. Deputy Ramirez thanked him for the information and told him he'd get the word out to the patrols so they could be on the watch. He said he would also call LA County Animal Control in Lancaster and San Bernardino County Animal Control, just in case they got calls about a stray horse in the area.

"Do me a favor, will you?" Carl asked the deputy. "If you find the horse, can you have someone let me know? I got pretty attached to him while he was at my place, and I'd just like to know he's okay."

Deputy Ramirez smiled at Carl and said, "Yes, I will handle that personally. If we hear anything about someone finding the horse, I'll drive up and let you know. If you're not at your cabin, I'll leave you a note. Thank you for helping with the search. I'll pass your concern on to the owners too."

"Thank you so much," Carl said as he left.

CHAPTER THIRTY-EIGHT

Sunday morning Ali saw the first rays of sun on the eastern horizon turning the black sky to coral, rose, and pink. There were a few clouds in the sky that glowed in deeper hues. As he watched, the light of the rising sun painted the bottoms of the clouds gold. The clouds lightened with time to white as the sky changed to blue.

He wasn't the only creature to notice the arrival of the new day. Birds began scratching in the soil for breakfast and flying from tree to tree. He could hear small creatures scurrying through the pine needles and dead leaves beneath shrubs and trees. None of these sounds gave him reason to pause. They were the usual sounds of early morning in the mountains. Most of the predators had long since sought shelter and were sleeping away the day.

Ali was stiff with cold. He moved forward slowly, working out the kinks. He had no idea where he was or how he would get back to his family and Becky. He'd been gone from his family for eight days.

He remembered the barren rocky hills to the west. He saw those through the windows of the trailer and knew he wouldn't find much to eat there. He started walking east. He was hungry. He walked into deeper woods looking for something to eat, picking at the few blades of new grass he saw poking up at the base of rocks and trees. The sunlight dappled his silver coat through the leaves of ancient oaks and tall pines.

He came upon a small meadow drenched in the early morning sunlight. There were several whitetail deer grazing there with their fawns. He hesitated before stepping into the light. The deer picked up their heads and stared at him. *"Is this a good place to get something to eat?"* he asked.

The lead doe hesitated then answered, *"Depends on what you eat."*

"Fresh grass is good," he told her.

"You're not a meat-eater, then?" she asked.

"Oh, no! Not at all. If you don't mind me asking, what are you? You are small but have four legs like me and sort of look similar." he asked the doe.

She visibly relaxed. *"We are the Inheritors of the Forest. We are called deer. We are grass eaters like yourself. We share with other grass eaters, so please eat in peace. And if you don't mind me asking, just exactly what are YOU?"* she asked him.

"Oh, you are deer. I've heard of deer but never saw one before. You are quite delicate and beautiful. Thanks for sharing your grass with me. I'm a horse," Ali answered.

He and the deer were hungry. Now that they understood he was harmless to them, they resumed eating. Five or six does, previously hidden in tickets around the meadow, seemed to appear from nowhere and joined the herd on the far side. He watched them for a few minutes and then joined them for a bit of breakfast.

Ali spent most of that day wandering, eating where he could, and drinking from small streams of snow meltwater. The water was cold and clear with an earthy taste. He skirted around several areas where the fire had scorched the earth and everything on it. Dead, blackened trees and shrubs raised twisted and gnarled branches toward the sky in those areas. Roots of some were starting to send out shoots of new green, proving they weren't dead, just burned above ground. Fresh green sprouts from seeds had started growing to replace foliage. There were blades of new grass poking through the black soil as well. Life was renewing itself.

As dusk crept up on Ali, he looked for a place to spend the night. He was out in the open for the second time in his life. There was nothing secure here. He finally found a small canyon, narrow and surrounded on three sides with granite boulders. He walked in and turned around. He thought the rocks might protect his hindquarters. He could watch the area in front of him because he saw pretty well in the dark.

He settled in for the night. The small canyon also offered him another benefit, shelter from the cold wind. Dead pine needles and dry leaves covered the ground, providing a soft place to lie down. For the first time in days, he did just that. It felt wonderful to get off his feet and give his legs a rest. He laid there for an hour, then stood and shook himself off. He dozed on and off through the night.

About dawn, Ali woke with a start. He heard rustling in the leaves. It took him a few seconds to locate the source of the sound. He saw a strange creature slowly moving on its belly through the leaves and pine needles several feet from him. He stared at it with intense curiosity. It had no legs! Its head was shaped like a triangle, and it blended perfectly into the surroundings by coloration and dark markings along its five-foot length.

Ali took one step in the creature's direction lowering his nose to see if he could catch any scent. The creature pulled itself into a coil in an instant lifting its head and the tip of its tail. The tail began to shake, making a dry rattling sound. Ali froze. Then the creature opened its mouth, showing long white fangs. Suddenly it struck, using its coiled body to propel it toward Ali.

It was too far away, and the strike missed Ali by two feet. In a flash, the creature resumed its coiled position, and the tail shook again. It was hissing at him. Ali decided to take no chances. He quickly moved away from the creature and left the small canyon.

He found a cold stream and drank his fill, then wandered through the woods, still in an easterly direction. What he didn't know was that he had now walked into the territory of the cougar. Ali looked for new blades of grass to nibble on as he moved along. These he found most often at the base of rocks where the water from winter rains and snowmelt ran down to the soil below and watered the seeds of last year's grasses that blew in there.

The she-lion lay at the top of a granite outcrop catching the morning sun on her tawny coat as she licked her sore paw. The outcrop was fifteen feet above the floor of the woods. She smelled and heard Ali before she saw him. She froze and watched as he came closer and closer. Ali spotted a patch of new grass at the edge of her granite post and walked toward it.

Cougars, also known as mountain lions, are ambush hunters. They watch and wait. In this case, the she-lion watched Ali coming closer and closer to her and tensed her muscles like coiled springs.

She noticed this creature was much larger than the white-tailed deer she usually preyed upon, but she was hungry, and this animal would feed her for more than a week. She decided to take a chance and try to bring it down.

She waited patiently for him to get close enough. Finally, he did. She leaped. Ali heard the scraping sounds from her paws on the top of the boulder he was standing next to and jumped forward.

The she-lion was a whisker late again. She aimed for Ali's neck so she could land her body on his back and grab hold, sinking her large fangs into his neck with a stranglehold that would cut off his air supply. With her sore paw and her belly full of kittens adding weight, she missed and landed on Ali's rear quarter, too far back to hold onto his neck.

Her sharp claws tried to gain purchase. They slipped and tore gouges down Ali's back and flanks. Blood streamed from the gouges making his hair and skin slippery. She kept trying to hold on. Every attempt made it worse. More bleeding. She bit Ali's back, sinking her teeth in deep. Ali reared, screaming in panic and pain.

The she-lion had not anticipated that. She slipped. Her hindquarters hung behind his tail. Ali felt the cougar slip. He used his shod hooves and kicked out at her. One of his rear feet connected. He kicked again. The second kick caught the she-lion in the rib cage. It knocked the air from her lungs. She tried to release her grip with fangs and claws. The next kick connected again, tossing her into the boulders. She crumpled into a pile at the base of the rocks and lay still. Ali took off like the wind, screaming in fear and pain.

The she-lion lay at the base of the rocks for a few minutes. Then she stood and shook herself. She limped back to her place on the outcrop, lay back down, and licked her sore paw. She'd try again when she had an opportunity. This time she'd misjudged the size and strength of her prey and could have been seriously injured herself. She wouldn't make that mistake again.

Ali ran as he'd never run before. Horses can see close to 360 degrees because of the placement of their eyes on the side of their heads. They have blind spots only directly in front of their nose and directly behind their tail. For that reason, he only saw the she-lion as she landed on his backside and saw her fangs sink into his flesh. He was bleeding from bite marks and long deep scratches from the cougar's claws.

Because she jumped on him from above where he didn't expect it, he hadn't seen the attack coming. He was lucky he heard the cat before she landed on him. He was terrified, and he was feeling the pain. He ran and ran and ran until he couldn't run any further.

CHAPTER THIRTY-NINE

Ali stopped in the middle of a small meadow, dropped his head, and began taking in great gulps of air. His heart was racing from the exercise and the fear. He trembled. He stood there for a while until his heart slowed down and his senses returned. The pain remained along his flanks, hips, and back, but the she-lion had not inflicted severe damage. Fresh blood oozed and dripped from the deep scratches and bite marks.

Ali heard a great splashing not far from the meadow and knew it could only be water. He had a tremendous thirst. He walked toward the sound. A small waterfall tumbled over a dark rocky ridge into a shallow pool.

He drank from the edge of the pool and then tested the pool with one hoof. It wasn't too deep or too slippery. He needed something to cool the burning along his backside. His feet found purchase on small stones lining the pool.

Slowly he moved deeper into the pool and turned his backside toward the falling water. He backed up until the cold water fell across his back and cooled the burning there. He stood there until the cold began to penetrate his bones. He slowly walked out of the pool and stood with a drooping head for a few minutes.

Ali began to wonder if he'd made the right decision. "*What am I doing here?*" he thought. "*I don't know if I can find my way back to the old man's place now. This wilderness stuff is crazy scary! Maybe Max was right after all."*

He took a few steps and stretched himself. The cold water temporarily eased the pain in his back from the bites and clawing of the big cat. It washed away most of the blood. The ache left behind got worse by the minute. Ali closed his eyes. Suddenly he had a vision of Becky's face. She was only eight years old and pressed her face to the back window of her parents' truck as Mom and Dad drove off and left Ali at his new "school" in Colorado. Tears streaked her face. He'd never seen her look that sad before. He knew she loved him. How sad would she be if he never got back home to her? Suddenly his resolve came back to him with power and strength. He lifted his head. He shook himself. He would get home! He had to get back to Becky! He survived that horrible attack. What could be worse than that? *"Becky, I'm coming! Wait for me! I'll be there as soon as I can."*

Then he knew which way to go. He had been looking at the high desert plateau for a week. He knew there were people there. He'd seen and heard their vehicles from the corral at Carl Nixon's place. He saw the lights. That's where he needed to go. In his experience, where there were people, there would be food and water. He began walking north. There were too many scary creatures in the woods, and he didn't feel safe at all.

He walked slowly and began his descent from the mountains. He had several hills to climb and valleys to get through, but he avoided rocky outcrops. He didn't stop to eat, just continued on his way. He did take water whenever he found a running stream but only stopped for a few minutes each time.

As dusk fell across the woods, Ali found a place in the open for the night. He no longer felt secure near rocks. He spent another cold, shivering night with no protection from the wind. He ate some grass in the middle of the clearing, carefully avoiding the edges and the darkness there.

At first light, Ali turned his head north and continued his journey. If he'd had any experience, he'd have noticed the scent markings and scat marking the edges of territory claimed by the she-bear. He crossed the barrier.

The California Black Bear's diet is about eighty percent vegetation; however, they will eat carrion when available and are just big enough and tough enough to drive other animals off their prey and take it over. They can also run very fast.

This she-bear loved the taste of fresh kill. The bear was perpetually hungry from feeding her two cubs. She was out early looking for food when she smelled the blood. She sniffed the air, coughed, and decided to investigate. She might get lucky and find the remains of a mountain lion kill. She ambled in Ali's direction and spotted him slowly walking through a clearing.

This was not a dead animal, but she could see the cuts on his flank and back, and she smelled the blood. It might be crippled enough for her to finish it off.

She attacked suddenly. She ran toward Ali with her jaws wide open, snarling viciously. She moved much quicker than one would think. Ali smelled her, heard her, and saw her coming. He screamed and took off, running as fast as he could through trees and shrubs, around boulders, his shoes clanking on rocks. He quickly outdistanced the bear. She wasn't going to waste a whole lot of energy on something that large that could move that fast. She stopped short and went back to digging for grubs in an old stump she came across.

Ali ran until he could run no more. He was sick with this crazy place and couldn't wait to get away from it. Ali finally stopped running and stood on shaky legs gulping in the air, trying to calm himself. He was in an open area where he could see all around him, and there was no other creature in sight.

To the north was a steep, rocky hillside. He thought about trying it but decided to move along the base and look for an area a little less steep to climb. He continued east until he found a good place; less steep, more grass and trees. He began his climb. Once he got to the top, he could see the plateau below him. This was the final hill. He began to descend.

By this time, dusk was settling over the plateau and the mountains. The setting sun painted the sky in the west with shades of coral to purple. His night vision was excellent, so he had no trouble picking his way. He did step into an area of loose shale and slipped a few feet but caught himself. The only damage was one of his back shoes came off. The shoes protected his hoof wall. Losing the shoe tore a small chunk from his hoof wall where the nails clinched on and held the shoe in place. It created a tender spot.

As he came out of the trees that ringed the top of the hill, the area below the crest had only low juniper trees and scrub. Little else grew there. He had reduced his elevation from over seven thousand five hundred feet above sea level to about five thousand feet. The air was a little warmer here, but not enough for him to notice the difference.

Ali continued his descent by dark until he was too tired to continue. He looked for a good place in the open to stop for the night. Ali spent another cold and miserable night without shelter from the wind and little or nothing to eat. He was also very thirsty, but there was no water on the surface here that he could find.

As dawn broke in the eastern sky, Ali began again. He began looking in earnest for water. He finally found a small stream tumbling down the mountain about two miles from where he spent the night. He drank his fill and moved on.

Off in the distance, he saw a couple of things that caught his interest. One was a large patch of deep green. The other was a small home with three horses in an area beside the house. They were both miles away, and there was one significant obstacle between him and them.

He watched traffic speeding by on a two-lane highway. There were numerous large trucks and many smaller trucks and cars speeding east and west. He wasn't sure how to get over or around the highway. He'd never seen one when he wasn't in a trailer. And the trailer always moved with the traffic, not across it.

He approached the highway with trepidation. As he climbed a slight rise above the highway, a semi-truck driver spotted him and blasted his air-horn. The loud sound scared him. He spun and ran the other way for a distance. He continued traveling east for a while and tried it again. This time he approached the highway from a level spot. He looked to the east and saw large trucks coming. He looked west and saw cars speeding toward that spot. He decided he wouldn't have time to cross before they caught up to him, so he walked back a distance and continued east.

After a while, the traffic subsided on the highway, and he approached it again. This time he watched as a large truck heading west passed. Cars were coming from the east but far off in the distance. He took a chance and ran across the road. He slipped on the final step on asphalt and skidded into a ditch on the other side of the road. He pulled a muscle in his stifle or knee joint on a rear leg but walked away with only a slight limp. He headed in the direction of the horses he'd seen from above.

The distance can be deceiving in the vastness of a desert. From Ali's higher vantage point, it didn't look to be all that far from him. But as he reached the plateau, he walked and walked and walked before he noticed the house getting any closer. He reached the property around noon. He was very thirsty and had not seen water for hours. He was also famished. There wasn't much to eat here. He'd tried nibbling on a few things but found some plants had hairy spines on the leaves, and they tasted terrible. He was traveling on his reserves.

The property was fenced. He couldn't get to the horses from the front, so he walked along the side. There were no openings along the side either. He tried the back of the property and found a hole in the fence large enough to walk through. Someone had left the back gate open.

He walked through the hole and looked for the horses he'd seen. They were standing in metal corrals with three-sided shelters munching on leftover hay from their breakfast. They called to him. He called back and galloped to their corral. He noticed large tubs of water just on the other side of the corral fencing.

The metal bars on the fencing were spaced widely enough to stick his head through and take a drink. The water was none too clear, but it was wet. He drank his fill and began to look around for something to eat. He found small chunks of hay that dropped from the owner's hands as he fed the horses that morning. Ali grabbed the hay eagerly and started to eat.

Just then, the little dog guarding the property saw him. The dog came running at him from the back porch of the house where he'd been sleeping. He barked furiously. Ali backed up and looked for the hole in the fence he'd come through.

The little dog showed no fear of Ali's size and came at him, snapping and biting his ankles. Ali kicked out and began to run, kicking as he went to keep the little dog from biting him. The dog chased him off the property and for nearly a half-mile beyond before giving up and heading back to his porch and shade.

Ali ran into a short cholla or jumping cactus bush in his haste to get away from the nasty little creature. Spines from pieces that broke off the bush embedded themselves in his chest, right front leg, and right side. They burned like fire. He attempted to pull one of the pieces from his right foreleg and got spines stuck in his lip for his effort.

He walked on, limping now on his left rear leg and his right front leg. He headed in the general direction of the vivid green patch he'd seen from the higher elevation. He was ravenous. The dog prevented him from eating more than a mouthful at the ranch. Fortunately, he'd gotten water.

Ali walked slowly but steadily through the rest of the afternoon and finally reached the green patch. It was an irrigated field of alfalfa. He could smell it long before he reached it, and it quickened his pace.

He looked out over the field and saw a large mechanical device spreading water on the growing crop. There were giant wheels attached to long arms crossing the field, spraying water. The wheels turned very slowly as the arms sprayed the crop and made little noise.

Ali watched it for a while and decided it would do him no harm. He took a tentative step into the field. It was muddy from the water, but that didn't bother him. He carefully took a bite of the fresh alfalfa, trying to avoid disturbing the cholla spines on the right side of his lip. It was fresh, damp, and delicious. He began munching in earnest, cropping the plants off above the ground.

One of the men who worked the field drove his truck back to this field to turn the water off for the night and spotted a horse standing in his field eating the alfalfa. He stopped his vehicle, leaving the engine running, and took a jacket from the front seat. He ran at the horse, waving the jacket in his hand and screaming at Ali.

Ali spooked and started to run, slipping and sliding in the mud. He changed his gait to his high floating trot. This worked. He quickened his pace, flipped his tail over his back, arched his neck, and snorted as he went.

The man stopped in his tracks and caught his breath. He stared slack-jawed at the horse, his arm holding the coat dropping to his side. The skinny, lame, dirty horse transformed into a magical creature that floated on air in a second.

The itinerant worker wondered if he should tell his Patron about the magic horse. He decided not. El Patron would think he'd gone loco. He needed this job. He would tell no one.

As soon as Ali noticed the soil change to dry, he changed gears to a gallop and ran until the man could no longer see him, just a plume of dust showing where he'd been. The man walked out into the field looking for hoof prints to be sure he'd seen a real horse. He found Ali's tracks and stood looking in the distance at the dust plume in wonder. He wondered if this was an omen. He might talk to the priest after mass.

Ali stopped running as soon as he thought he was far enough away to be safe again. He walked east, slowly. There was no place out here that looked safe to spend the night, so he kept on walking. About 11:00 that night, the wind kicked up. The gusts blew across the desert at fifty miles per hour, with some even stronger. It blew dust and sand everywhere.

There was no shelter here and no place to get out of the wind. The tallest tree in the area was about four and a half feet high, stunted by the heat of summer and lack of water. Ali wandered around for a while and then finally did as horses have done for thousands of years. He turned his butt to the wind and waited it out.

The wind hard blew all through the night. Ali was miserable. His hips and back hurt from deep scratches and bite marks, his front leg and chest hurt from the cholla, his right rear foot was sore from losing his shoe. His stifle was sore from the pulled muscle. He was cold and thirsty and hungry.

Dawn came with no let-up in the wind. Ali was reluctant to move. The sand blew so much it was difficult for him to see. Dust and sand filled his nostrils so that he couldn't smell much either. He remained right where he was with his butt to the wind.

Ali slipped into daydreams. He remembered all the times he and Becky were at various showgrounds when Chris was showing him. Becky was always there to help get him ready for his classes, and she was always in the stands or on the sidelines cheering him on. After his classes, she insisted on walking him to cool him out. They walked around the grounds with her proudly holding his win ribbons. Todd walked with them most of the time. It was hard to tell which of the two youngsters were most proud of Ali's accomplishments.

The terrible wind continued throughout the day and the entire following night. Ali stood in one place, locked three of his hocks or knees at a time so the fourth could rest, and stayed where he was. He had no shelter, no food, and no water. The cholla spines burned constantly. The wounds in his back and flank area seeped blood. His only movement was to switch which leg rested periodically.

CHAPTER FORTY

The wind finally stopped abruptly about 11:00 that morning. Ali shook himself to throw off some of the sand and dust coating his body and began to walk east again. The shaking hurt the wounds on his back, chest, and legs. His body ached, his thirst was terrible, and his stomach growled from hunger. He began thinking he would never make it after all. Max was right. He was an inexperienced youngster out of his element. Maybe he should just lie down and let nature take its course.

Just about then, Ali remembered watching Becky slam into the building head first and tumble into a heap, not moving. He couldn't give up now. Ali had to get back to her. He had to protect her. *"Becky, I'm coming home! I don't know how, but I'm not giving up yet. Hold on and wait for me!"*

He limped along until after 2:00 p.m. In the distance, he saw a ranch. He saw animals in pens near the back of the property. He wasn't sure what kind of animals they were, but he kept walking toward them. Where there were animals in pens, there would be food and water!

As he got closer, he noticed a single horse in a pen by himself. The closer Ali got, the more familiar the horse looked. Finally, it dawned on him the horse looked a lot like his older brother. Excitement gripped him. He had no idea how his brother would get here, and he was too tired, sore, thirsty, and hungry to care. He hurried his steps and limped faster.

The other horse noticed Ali and called to him. Ali called back and began to gallop. He came to a slide stop at the fence near the other horse. The horse looked just like his brother, but suddenly Ali knew it wasn't him. Disappointment crashed in.

Ali saw the rear gate to the ranch was open. He knew there was food and water here, which he desperately needed. Ali hurried to the gate and began searching. He'd gone about halfway to the ranch house on the 70-acre ranch, still not finding a source of food or water outside of the animal pens when a large black dog charged him from behind. The dog barked loud and excitedly, bounding toward him. Ali didn't have the energy to run but put on a good fast trot. The dog outdistanced him and came around in front of him. Suddenly the dog stopped and whined.

Clyde recognized this horse! He knew his scent. Clyde couldn't place him, but he definitely wasn't a stranger. He smelled the blood on him and saw the cholla stuck to his chest and leg. Clyde got into cholla once and knew what that meant. This horse needed help. Clyde approached Ali, who'd stopped when the dog did.

"Hey, I know you! I've seen you before. Where did you come from?" Clyde asked him, wagging his tail.

Ali was standing with his head down, too tired to move anymore. Clyde sniffed Ali and Ali sniffed Clyde. Ali recognized Clyde's scent too. *"You seem familiar to me too,"* Ali said to the dog. He didn't remember where he knew him from but knew he was friendly.

"You smell just like a horse my owner lady takes me to see sometimes in the truck. Do you know a young girl with golden hair?" Clyde remembered going with Ginny to a ranch far away where she worked with this horse and a little girl.

"Yes! Becky! How do you know Becky, and can you help me find her?" Ali asked him eagerly.

"It was a long ride in the truck to the place where I saw you and the girl," Clyde told him. *"You sure don't look the same. What happened to you?"*

Ali was too tired to tell the whole story. He was very thirsty and starving. He barely had the strength left to stand on his four legs.

"*It's a long story. Can you help me?*" he finally asked the dog. "*I need food and water.*"

Without another word, Clyde spun around and ran toward the house. He dove through the doggie door on the back porch and disappeared inside. Ali stood there with his head hanging. He had no more energy.

Clyde ran for Brody's room. Brody was doing his homework and left his bedroom door open. Clyde ran in and put his paw on Brody's leg, then barked at him. Brody pushed Clyde's leg off and told him to shush. Clyde whined and then barked again.

Brody looked up from the book he was studying. Clyde was doing circles on the hardwood floor and kept looking at him, whining.

"Okay, Clyde," Brody said as he stroked the dog. "Show me what's up." Brody followed the dog to the back door. Brody opened the door while Clyde jumped through the doggie door. Clyde turned and whined again, then turned back to the ranch leading Brody.

Brody spotted the horse and saw his general condition from a hundred yards away. Passing one of the corrals near the house, he grabbed a halter and lead rope and followed Clyde. Clyde went directly to the horse and sat down in front of Ali, whining.

The closer Brody got, the worse the horse looked. He slowly walked up to the horse, talking to him as he approached.

"Good boy, I'm not going to hurt you. Yes, please be a good boy." Brody carefully put the halter and lead rope on the horse and gently led him to the barn. He slid open one of the empty stalls and led the horse inside.

He noticed the horse was limping, and he saw the cholla. He also noticed the seeping blood on his back and down his rear legs. Brody stroked the horse's neck, unbuckled the halter, and backed out of the stall, closing the door. He dropped the halter and lead rope in the barn aisle and sprinted to the west side pens where his Uncle Mike was working horses.

"Uncle Mike!" Brody shouted. "Uncle Mike, you gotta come to the barn. A horse just showed up here, and he's hurt. We gotta help him!"

Mike rode his horse to the rail and stopped. "Say that again?"

Brody was excited and talked fast. "Uncle Mike, Clyde came into my bedroom and made me follow him outside. A horse was standing there, and he's in pretty bad shape. He has cholla stuck all over, he's skinny, and he has blood all over his back and legs. He's been hurt and needs our help."

Mike got off the horse and tossed the reins to Brody. "Put this guy up, will you. I'll go check the horse out and see what we can do with him. Meet me in the barn."

Mike strode to the barn and found Ali standing in the stall with his head down, trembling. He cautiously entered the stall and looked him over. Mike saw the cholla Brody mentioned and worked his way back to the horse's back and flank area, crossed behind the horse, and came up the other side. He stopped at Ali's shoulder and put his hand on Ali's neck, sliding down to his withers. He scratched the itchy place. Ali moaned and sighed.

Brody put Mike's training horse up and ran back to the barn. He stopped at the doorway and walked in like he'd been trained to do. No sense in spooking any of the horses inside by running down the aisle. He walked to the stall with Ali and Mike.

"What do you think, Uncle Mike? Can we help him? What can I do?"

"Well, he's pretty sucked up in the flank, so he's probably not had water for a while. Why don't you get two buckets of fresh water and hang them in here? Then get me a pair of pliers and some iodine. We have to get the cholla out of him first. Then we'll take a look at wounds on his back and flanks. One more thing you can do is make him a warm bran mash. Put a cup of mineral oil in it. I don't know when the last time he ate was, but we don't want him to colic on top of everything else."

Brody hurried out to get the buckets of water. He brought the first one in and hung it up in the stall. Ali stuck his muzzle in the bucket before Brody could get it on the hook. Brody stepped out to get the other bucket and hang it. Ali didn't take his muzzle out of the first bucket until it was half empty. He stood there catching his breath and dripping water into the wood shavings they used to bed the stall. He took a few long breaths and dropped his muzzle back into the bucket for more water.

"Jeez, Uncle Mike, he was thirsty!" Brody exclaimed. "Should I get the pliers now and hold him for you, or should I make the mash?"

"Get the pliers. We need to get the cholla spines out of him. He'll be much more comfortable. Then we may need to ice him down. Do you remember how the cholla spines make the horses' legs swell? Get me the ice packs from the barn freezer."

"Okay. Here's the halter and lead rope I used to catch him. Be right back." Brody told his uncle.

Brody got several ice packs, and a couple of pairs of leg wraps, then stopped in the tack room for the tool kit. He pulled a pair of pliers out and hurried back to the stall. He put the wraps and ice packs in the corner feeder in the stall and handed his uncle the pliers. Brody took the lead rope from Mike and talked to the horse as Mike pulled chunks of cholla and spines out of the horse's skin. Carefully Mike put the cholla and spines in the feeder's bottom so he could collect them later.

When Mike pulled the first piece of cholla off him, Ali squealed and backed up a step. He knew the two people were helping, and it felt good to get rid of that pokey stuff, so he stood very still as the rest of them came out. Mike washed the area with diluted iodine solution and then wrapped Ali's leg with ice packs using leg wraps to hold them in place.

As the cholla spines came out, the swelling began and became more pronounced as Mike worked. There wasn't much he could do with the chest and side of the horse, but the leg wraps would reduce swelling in his leg. Mike found the three spines in Ali's lip and pulled them out as well. Ali was so relieved.

Mike sent Brody to make the mash. He worked with gentle hands and an antibacterial cleanser to clean the deep scratches and bite marks on Ali's hips, flanks, and back. They were packed with sand and dirt from the wind storm the night before and had to be cleaned out to prevent infection.

Ali flinched when the pain was terrible, but other than that, he didn't move a muscle while Mike worked on him. When he had the wounds all cleaned out, Mike found a salve in the medicine area of the tack room. He gently smoothed it into the wounds to draw out any infection that may have already started there. The salve soothed the burning caused by the cleansing. Mike checked his stock of injectable medications in the barn refrigerator and found a tetanus shot. He carefully injected the medicine into Ali.

Brody came back with a warm bran mash and held the bucket under Ali's nose. Ali immediately dived into it. Brody added maple syrup to the mix to make it taste better.

"We'd better give Doc Martin a call in the morning. This fellow may need stitches in those deeper scratches. He has bite marks too. It looks like he was attacked by something pretty big, a mountain lion or a bear, probably a single one, or he wouldn't have gotten away. I wonder if he's been up in the mountains. There aren't too many mountain lions or bears down here. Too bad he can't talk. Let's give him a small flake of hay for tonight. We have to go easy on the feed until he gets used to it again."

Brody cleaned up the cholla and supplies they'd left in the feeder and brought Ali a small flake of alfalfa hay. He went into the stall and stroked the horse's neck and talked to him for a while in soothing tones.

Ali laid his head on Brody's shoulder. Ali was so grateful to feel safe again. Brody threw his two arms around Ali's neck and hugged him back. "You'll be okay, boy. Wait and see." Brody told him.

Brody topped off the water buckets, removed the ice wraps which had done their job, closed the stall door, and left for the night, closing the main barn doors on his way out. The wind was back and howled outside, but Ali was safe and warm inside this time. He slept peacefully for the first time in two weeks.

Mike called Doc Martin first thing in the morning. He had vet calls to make in the area anyway and stopped by Mike's ranch first. Mike took the horse out of the stall so the vet could have a good look at him.

Ali limped slightly on his left leg from the muscle pull in his knee. He was a little tender on the right rear, where he'd lost a shoe. The swelling from the cholla was gone, and there didn't appear to be any further tenderness in that area. His ribs showed all down his barrel, and his hip and backbones protruded. He was several hundred pounds underweight. And he was dirty. His former silver coat was the color of the sand that coated him from nose to tail.

The wounds on his back and flanks were another story. They were days old and starting to heal from the bottom. Mike told the vet he'd given the horse a tetanus shot the night before, so that didn't need to be done again. The vet was worried about infection, so he left Mike and Brody antibiotics to give the horse twice a day for the next five days.

"This boy has missed a few meals," the vet said when he finished his exam. "I'd feed him small flakes of hay three times a day for the next few days. It would help if you gave him a bucket of soaked hay pellets and beet pulp too. It gives his system a chance to get used to food again. He needs groceries. Other than that, there's nothing time, and a good farrier won't fix. I looked at the other shoes he's got on. Top-notch work there. But your farrier can fix him up. I'd have all four feet done, so they match. He's worn those shoes down. One of the other's about ready to go as well. Do you have any idea where he came from?"

"Looks like he walked in the back gate. I leave it open until I close the ranch down at the end of the day. He probably came in looking for food and water. Too bad he doesn't talk. For an *Arabian* stallion, he's pretty well behaved. He must belong to someone." Mike said. "I'll be putting out flyers at the local feed stores around and see if we can find the owner. My guess is he's pretty high-strung when he's fit. He probably got away from someone, and they're looking for him."

"Uncle Mike, don't you let Aunt Ginny hear you talk like that," Brody remarked. "She loves her Arabian horses and would smack you upside the head if she heard you." He laughed. "Besides, this boy hasn't given you a lick of trouble. Remember how good he was while you pulled cholla stickers out of his hide? He squealed one time then stood like a statue."

"I know," said Uncle Mike. "Now don't you go tellin' your Aunt Ginny I said bad things about her *Arabian* horses, or I'll have to git on you and give you extra chores." He pulled his hat brim down and grinned at Brody.

"Okay, Uncle Mike," Brody said with a grin. "I promise not to tell."

CHAPTER FORTY-ONE

The week Ali wandered in the wilderness, Becky remained still and silent in her bed in the Intensive Care Unit. She did not move on her own at all. She made no sound. Caroline stayed with her most of the time.

Becky spent most of the time in the fog. Occasionally she would find herself dreaming or remembering things she did with Ali. She could hear Mom and Dad and others talking in her room, but they remained far away, and she could never hear what they were saying.

She found herself getting up before the sun to help get Ali ready for his first class in Scottsdale, Arizona. She helped wash him. He used his upper lip to scrub the top of her head while she squatted down to scrub the shampoo into the front of his forelegs. She was in the grandstands next to Todd when Chris asked Ali to trot into the arena. When the crowd in the stands first noticed him, he noticed them and started putting on his best trot. The crowd began cheering. That encouraged Ali to trot higher and higher until he reached his signature high floating trot. It was so exciting to see. Ali won his first class. She was bursting with pride. Becky slipped back into the fog with the sound of crowd cheering ringing in her ears.

Another day she rose from the fog to find herself at Maverick Stadium in Denver, Colorado. She and Todd stood at the Mavericks Players tunnel watching Ali charge down the sideline behind the players' bench as the announcer introduced him. Ali cantered out and stepped into his high floating trot. Seventy thousand fans in the stadium cheered him on. He stopped and reared on command at mid-field and screamed his stallion challenge. The fans went wild. Someone started chanting "Ah-li! Ah-li! Ah-li!" and the others picked it up. The encouragement led Ali to higher and higher levels. He looked like he floated above the ground! The game was over, and the Mavericks won. Players celebrated on the field. One rushed into the tunnel and asked Ali to join them. Ali head and shoulder bumped three hundred pound linemen, and nose to fist-bumped the running back that scored the winning touchdown. It was all so exciting, but the sound receded as she slipped back into the fog.

Hours or days later, she had no sense of time, she was on an airplane with Mom and Dad, Sharon and Todd O'Neal on their way to Paris, France. She walked into the famous Salon de Cheval to watch Ali compete in the World Championships. He made the top ten! She noticed how nice she was dressed for the finals on Sunday afternoon. Around her, everyone dressed in formal clothes. Men wore tuxedos. Women wore gowns and dripped in jewels. It was the most beautiful sight. Chris trotted Ali into the judging ring. The judges called the winners, starting with tenth place. Ali won! Chris ran his hardest to keep up with Ali on his victory pass. Ali tossed his head and snorted and blew as he floated above the ground. The cheering receded as she slipped back into blackness.

Becky noticed her parents' voices were getting closer. She could almost hear their words. She hoped she could reach them soon. The blackness wasn't so dense.

***

Walter returned to his office Monday that week to handle several large projects coming due. Those projects required his signature. He spent no more than four hours at the office and returned to the hospital so Caroline could leave to shower and change. The two of them took turns sleeping on the cot in Becky's room in the ICU each night.

Walter broke down and told Caroline what Detective Nelson said about Ali. They worried about him. Ali was a pampered show-horse. Nothing prepared him for life in the wild. He was intelligent and courageous, but he was a prey animal.

At Caroline's urging, Walter called Detective Nelson and increased the reward for information about Ali to a hundred thousand dollars. Brian Nelson told him the Fish and Wildlife Inspector was in the area on horseback looking for signs of Ali. The inspector ran into Carl Nixon doing the same thing. There were two people on horseback searching, and both of them were very familiar with the area. Brian Nelson hoped one of the two men would find signs of Ali and maybe enough to track him.

"That old man, Nixon, really has a soft spot for your horse," Brian told Walter. "He was broken up about horse getting away. He told us he planned to go to the Sheriff's Department that morning to find out what he could about the horse, but discovered he was gone when he went to feed him. He told us he had been concerned he might have purchased a stolen horse when he bought him. Nixon lives up there in the mountains with no radio or TV. He didn't hear the news broadcasts, and he doesn't get the newspaper."

"That's the old guy who bought him for four hundred dollars?" Walter asked.

"Yeah. Nixon told us he called a horse broker looking for a two hundred dollar packhorse. Our suspects showed up with your horse in their trailer. Nixon told us one look at that horse brought his daughter to mind, and he couldn't pass him up. He said it was like having a piece of his daughter back. Nixon told us he paid twice what he expected and would have paid more, but the two creeps took his offer. He had no idea about the situation at the parade. By that time, it was all over the news. Nixon had no way to know about that."

"Do you think the reward is high enough now? Do you think it will help to get him back?" asked Walter.

"There are people out there that would turn their mother in for fifty bucks. Yes, I think the reward is high enough. We'll probably get lots of calls about loose horses. Let's hope one of them is the right horse if the horse gets down to the desert from where he was. Nixon told the Fish and

Wildlife Inspector he was circling the territory of a mountain lion to see if the cat had taken the horse. He hadn't found anything. The inspector told me there are also a few black bears up there in the same area."

"Please don't say anything to Caroline about that. She's worried enough about Becky, and she knows the horse was last seen in the mountains. I won't tell her he could be walking into a mountain lion. Like I told you before, that horse is like a son to her." Walter said. "Let's keep that between us, please?"

"You got it," Brian replied. "I've got some leads to run down right now, so I have to go. I will call you if I hear anything else. If you need anything, please call me. And let me know how Becky is doing if anything changes, will you?"

"We sure will. And thank you again for all you are doing to help us on this."

"One thing before I go, Calvin and Danny Hix were arraigned yesterday in San Diego Superior Court. The San Diego DA has them for multiple charges on the bust we did last Sunday. The Orange County DA is charging them with Attempted Murder, Great Bodily Injury in the Commission of a Crime, Grand Theft, and several other things in connection with our case. I don't think either of them will ever see the light of day again."

"That's good to hear," Walter answered. "I hope they throw the book at them. Do you think you have enough evidence to get convictions?"

"We got 'em cold. We have fingerprints, DNA, and a good solid witness that will ID 'em. Nixon picked them out of a photo lineup. We have the horse trailer they used. We can probably get DNA from the horse out of that, but we need the horse to compare it to. They won't be walking away from this." Brian told him. "You can take that to the bank."

Walter relayed parts of his conversation with Brian Nelson to Caroline after they'd hung up. He looked at her. She had blue circles under her eyes, and she'd lost weight. She had a perpetual worried look on her face. And there was a sadness that seemed to overwhelm her. It was hard. He was worried too. He hoped they'd get through all this.

CHAPTER FORTY-TWO

M ike asked Brody to put together a flyer on the stray horse. Brody was better on the computer than Mike was. Brody asked Maryann Wilcox for help. Maryann was a young volunteer who was working off her riding lessons with Aunt Ginny. Normally she scrubbed water buckets, mucked stalls, and cleaned tack. She went to school with Brody, and he knew she was better with artwork than he was. They put a flyer together, including a photo Brody took of Ali with his cell phone. It wasn't the best picture, but the horse didn't look very good anyway.

Mike had one of his guys make copies and drop them off at the local feed stores. Mike fully expected to hear from some idiot who had no business owning a stallion with a silly story about how the horse got away from him.

Mike put Brody in charge of Ali. He was taking care of the rest of the ranch with Ginny gone. Brody was a big help, and he was happy to take over Ali's care. He and Maryann spent time with Ali before and after school and weekend days. They washed and put new ointment in the wounds on Ali's back and flanks, fed the horse three times a day, and brushed the knots out of his mane and tail.

He and Maryann brushed the rest of Ali, except for the area with wounds taking care to miss the sore spots where the cholla stickers had been. They re-iced Ali's leg to keep the swelling down and called the farrier out to replace Ali's shoes. Brody and Maryann kept Ali's stall clean and his water buckets full. They spent time with Ali just talking to him. Ali looked and felt better by the day.

Clyde had the run of the ranch every day. He stopped in to talk with Ali when no one else was around.

"You never did tell me what happened to you," Clyde said.

"It's a long story. The last thing I remember was Becky leading me back to our horse trailer after the parade and two guys walking up on me while Becky was in the trailer changing clothes. One of them stuck me with a needle. I saw Becky fall but couldn't help her. I woke up in a stinky horse trailer on my way up to the mountains."

"Wow. What happened next?" the dog asked.

"The two guys dropped me off in the mountains with an old man and another horse. He forgot to latch the corral gate a week later, and I walked out. I have to find my family!" Ali explained. *"I know you've been there. Do you know how I can get home?"*

"Sure wish I could help you," Clyde said. *"I rode in the truck, so I don't know the way. Maybe when Ginny comes home, she will recognize you and help you get home."*

"That's the most hopeful thing I've heard. Thank you. Do you know when she's coming back?"

"Naw, I just hear bits and pieces of conversation when Mike, he's the big guy, talks to her. I'm an old dog these days and go to sleep early, so I don't hear much of what he says to her when she calls home at night. What I meant to ask you was how you got those wounds."

"I was in the forest trying to figure out which way to go and looking for something to eat at the same time. All of a sudden, a huge monster jumped on me. It had the biggest teeth I've ever seen and huge paws full of long, sharp claws. I'm sure it was trying to kill me. It used those huge teeth to hang on when I reared and tried to run away. I saw it slipping behind me, so I used every ounce of strength I had to kick it off and get away. I was scared to death!"

"Really? How big was that thing?" Clyde asked with eyes open wide.

"Bigger than you! It was at least twice your size and then some. It looked a little like one of the barn cats we have at our barn, just huge."

"Oh, that will give me nightmares. Some of the barn cats here don't like me much as it is. I can't imagine one of them that size."

"You wouldn't have liked the other monster that chased me either then. That thing was huge and brown and hairy. It came at me with its mouth wide open full of sharp teeth. Its paws were gigantic and ended in long claws. That thing sure moved fast for as big as it was. I'm just lucky I'm a horse and could outrun it." Ali told him.

"Wow. I'm kinda sorry I asked you. Now I will have nightmares for sure." Clyde admitted.

Ali looked forward to Brody's and Maryann's visits to the barn. The wounds on his backside burned a lot less with the ointment and the cleaning. He ate good feed and drank fresh, clean water. They kept the stall deeply bedded so Ali could lie down and take the pressure off his feet for a few hours each day. He felt safe here and enjoyed the companionship of Clyde, Maryann, and Brody.

Ginny called Mike every night to report on her day and how Becky was doing. They talked briefly. Mike wasn't a big talker in the first place. Mike just gave her a running summary of daily activities at the ranch, which wasn't all that much.

Ginny explained there had been no changes with Becky and that she and Sharon O'Neil worked with the Howard horses, helped Fernando maintain the ranch, and told him what delightful meal Esperanza prepared for dinner that night. She usually called home after Brody had gone to bed, so she didn't have a chance to talk to him.

Friday night, Ginny told Mike that Becky finally had some movement, and the nurses told Caroline she might be waking up. There wasn't much change to report on Saturday, Sunday, or Monday nights.

For whatever reason, Ginny called around 8:00 p.m. on Tuesday. Brody answered the phone this time. She hadn't talked to him in over a week. She was delighted.

"How are you doing, kiddo? How's school? What have you been up to?" Ginny wanted to know.

"Did Uncle Mike tell you about the horse that strayed onto our property last Friday?" Brody asked her.

"What horse?" Ginny asked him.

"Well, I was doing my homework, and Clyde came into my room and got me. He let me know he wanted me to follow him, and we went out back. There was this poor horse just standing there. He's skinny, he's dirty, he was covered in cholla, he'd lost a back shoe, and he was bleeding. Poor guy had blood all over him."

"No, Uncle Mike didn't tell me a thing about it. You know your uncle, a man of few words. Guess he forgot. Tell me more about this horse." Ginny said.

"Well, I thought Uncle Mike would've told you since he's one of those, as he calls them, "*Arabian*" horses. We put flyers up at the feed stores, but nobody's called us yet. This poor horse looked pretty sad. Me and Maryann have been taking care of him, so Uncle Mike can get the other stuff done, with you gone and all."

"An Arabian, you said?" Ginny asked.

"Yup. He looks like a purebred to me. He's really pretty, and he's getting better since we've been working with him and feeding him. He must've gone without food for a while. He's not so sucked up now as he was when he got here. Oh, did I tell you he is a stallion? But he's really well behaved too."

A light bulb went off in Ginny's head like a bomb. Walter told her the creeps that stole Ali took him up in the Angeles National Forest and sold him for four hundred bucks. He escaped from there, and nobody could find him. Could this be him? How far would that be? She couldn't fathom. It was quite a distance as the crow flies, but there's a three or four-thousand-foot elevation change and so many obstacles Ali would have encountered.

"What color is this horse?" Ginny asked and then held her breath.

"Aunt Ginny, I thought I told you. He's gray!" Brody answered.

"Oh, my Dear God!" Ginny said. "Find Uncle Mike and get him on the phone, will you?"

Brody laid the phone down on the kitchen counter and went looking for his uncle. "Uncle Mike, Aunt Ginny's on the phone for you! It sounds important!" he shouted.

Mike picked up the phone. "Hey sweetheart, how're things down south?"

"Why didn't you tell me about the stray horse?" she asked.

"Oh, gosh, I forgot. I miss you and just wanted to talk about the ranch stuff when we get to talk. You know how busy it is around here. Brody's been taking care of him, and it just slipped my mind."

"Didn't I tell you Ali was loose in the Angeles National Forest? They've been up there on horseback looking for him for days now. Maybe he made his way down out of the mountains. Maybe that's the horse you have there. Brody told me he was a gray Arabian stallion. That could be the horse everybody and their pet duck have been looking for."

"Oh, my gosh! Do you think it's possible that horse made it all the way here?" Mike asked her. "That poor horse was attacked by something big. He has deep scratches on his flanks and back, and bite marks from something that looks like it could've been a mountain lion or a bear. Maybe you'd better come up here and take a look. We put flyers at the feed stores, and nobody's called us."

"I'm on my way!" Ginny said. "See you in an hour and a half. I'll bring Sharon O'Neil with me."

Ginny closed her phone and ran to the back patio where she'd seen Sharon last.

"We gotta go!" she said to Sharon. "Brody just told me they have a stray horse at our ranch. He showed up late Friday. He's a *Gray Arabian Stallion*! Brody told me he's skinny and dirty but pretty. He and Mike told me a mountain lion might have attacked the horse."

Sharon jumped up and ran to her room to grab her shoes and purse. She met Ginny outside, and they climbed into Ginny's truck. Ginny had already told Esperanza they'd be gone for a while. Sharon grabbed her cell phone and started to call Walter and Caroline at the hospital.

"Let's wait before we call them," Ginny said. "Let's make sure it's Ali first. We know how worried they've been. Can you imagine! That horse walking onto my ranch of all places? God, please let it be him! But, let's be sure before we celebrate."

"You're right!" Sharon agreed and put her cell phone back in her purse. She didn't want to get anyone's hopes up and then find out it wasn't Ali.

Ginny drove straight to the ranch and, as she put it, didn't spare the horses. They made the hundred miles in about an hour and fifteen minutes. As soon as they drove up, Mike opened the back door. He, Brody, and Clyde came out and walked with them to the barn.

Ginny and Sharon looked into the stall. Ali was standing with his head down. Sharon spoke first. "Ali, is that you?"

The horse snapped his head up at the familiar voice. He stared through the bars in his stall and nickered a greeting to her. He walked over and poked his head out of the stall, and began nuzzling Sharon.

"This is Prince Ali!" Sharon shouted with tears welling up in her eyes. "I'd know him anywhere, anytime, anyplace! Boy, is this going to make a bunch of people happy!"

Ginny pulled out her cell phone and made the call to Caroline. Sharon pulled her cell phone out and made the call to Chris. They danced in the barn like a pair of lunatics.

CHAPTER FORTY-THREE

The same Friday Ali walked onto the Hartley Ranch in the High Desert, Becky felt herself moving out of the fog and into a brighter world. She could hear her mother singing one of the lullabies she sang to her when she was very little. Becky could hear the words clearly for the first time. She struggled to move. She could move her eyelids just a tiny bit at first. Her mother didn't notice it the first time or two. She was holding Becky's hand in hers. She felt the first movement when Becky tried to squeeze her hand. Caroline shot out of the chair and stood over Becky. "Becky, can you hear me? Becky, if you can hear me, can you open your eyes? Can you squeeze my hand?"

Becky felt everything all at once, but she was so tired by the effort she drifted off again. When Mom saw no movement and got no response from Becky, she hurried out of the room to the nurses' station looking for Becky's day nurse.

"I think she's trying to wake up!" she told her. "I'm sure I saw her eyelids move a little, and I'm very sure she was trying to squeeze my hand." Tears welled up in her eyes.

The nurse rushed to Becky's room with Caroline right behind her. She checked Becky's vital signs – all good. Becky appeared to be sleeping. The nurse shook Becky's shoulder firmly. "Becky, are you there? Can you open your eyes?" Nothing. She shook her more firmly a second time. "Becky, can you hear me? Can you open your eyes?"

Becky felt like someone was trying to shake her out of a deep sleep. It irritated her. She wanted to sleep. She squeezed her eyes shut and turned her head away from the person shaking her.

"Did you see that?" Caroline almost whispered.

"Yes, I sure did. I think she may be coming around. It might take a while. She's been out for almost two weeks. Give her some more time but keep talking to her. She hears you now. Her brain is processing information," the nurse told Caroline. "I'll be right outside if you need me."

Caroline called Walter on his cell phone. Walter was in the shower and covered with soap when his phone rang. He opened the shower door reaching for the phone, and almost dropped it from his slippery palm. He gripped it and pulled it to his ear. "Yes?"

"Honey, she is waking up. She tried to squeeze my hand. The nurse shook her, and she squeezed her eyes shut and turned her head. You have to come back here now!" Caroline told him.

"Be there in ten minutes!" he shouted and ended the call. He rinsed off, dressed, and ran out the door. He drove to the hospital, not running red lights but ignoring speed limits all the way. He ran through the hospital lobby and pressed the elevator button. "Why, oh why, are elevators so slow when you need one?" On the floor for the ICU, Walter sprinted to the entry door and picked up the phone to the nurses' station to give him access. When the door cracked open, he shoved it out of his way and sprinted to Becky's room.

"What's going on?" he asked Caroline. She was sitting next to Becky's bed, holding her hand.

"I've seen her eyes flutter a couple of times. She squeezed them shut when the nurse shook her, so I closed the blinds in here. Maybe the light was too strong for her just yet?"

"Has she said anything?"

"Not yet, but she seems to come and go. She's squeezed my hand a couple of times. I think it tires her out, and she drifts off again. Why don't you sit here for a few minutes and just watch her, see what you think?"

Caroline gave the chair to Walter and sat down on the cot alongside the wall. She was exhausted. She didn't sleep well, and she wasn't eating well either. Two weeks of this, and she was running on fumes. She lay down on the cot to rest a few minutes. She drifted off too.

Walter sat in the chair and stared intently at his daughter's face for at least thirty minutes before anything changed. He noticed her eyelids flutter a tiny bit. Then he felt the pressure of her hand in his squeezing a little bit. He began to talk to her. He told her how much he and her mother loved her and wanted her back. He told her how her friends at school missed her. Her teachers missed her too. Espie sent her love and many hugs. Fernando sent her a kiss on the forehead.

Becky heard every word! She didn't understand what all the fuss was. She was just sleeping, after all.

Becky came and went over the next five days. There were times her parents were sure she would open her eyes and times when they were sure she was trying to speak to them. Becky squeezed their hands with more force. She moved her legs and feet, tiny movements at first, but more and more purposefully. The struggle to move, speak, and open her eyes exhausted her, and Becky fell back asleep, but it was sleep now, not the deep fog and blackness it had been. She heard most of the conversation in the room now and understood the words spoken.

Tuesday night, Caroline's cell phone rang. Caroline answered, "Hello." She remained silent and just listened. Suddenly her shoulders began to shake, and tears streamed from her eyes. She couldn't speak.

Walter took the phone from her, "Who is this?" Ginny told him everything. "Oh, my Dear God, Thank you! Our prayers have been answered." was about all he could say. He cleared his throat, "Thank you, Ginny. Will you please tell Mike and Brody how much we appreciate what you've done. Caroline and I will see you here in the lobby when you get here."

Caroline stood up and threw her arms around him, and cried silently for a while. He comforted her and stroked her back until she regained control of herself.

"Oh, I'm so relieved," she told him. "He's okay and coming home soon. In the meantime, he's in the best place possible."

"I agree with you. We'll talk to Ginny when she and Sharon get here." Walter held her close.

"Mom? Dad?" Becky spoke for the first time in weeks. The words were clear as day and stopped her parents in their tracks.

Caroline and Walter spun around dumbfounded, split, and went to each side of the bed, reaching through the side rails to hold her hands. As they stared at her face, her blue eyes shined at them. She smiled.

"Mom, is Ali okay?"

"Yes, dear. Ali is fine. He is waiting for you!"

Becky sighed, closed her eyes, and fell back into a peaceful sleep.

CHAPTER FORTY-FOUR

G inny and Sharon arrived at the hospital two and a half hours after the call to Caroline. They called upstairs and waited in the lobby for the Howards.

When Caroline and Walter stepped out of the elevator, Ginny and Sharon rushed to hug them. They were all in a celebratory mood.

"I have something else to tell you guys," Caroline said. "Right after we got your call, we were standing at the foot of Becky's bed. I was crying happy tears because of your phone call. Walter was holding me. All of a sudden, we heard Becky say, "Mom? Dad?" out loud and clear as a bell. We rushed to her bed, and her eyes were open, looking at us. She asked me if Ali was all right. I told her, "Yes, and he's waiting for you!" I know she heard me. She smiled and went back to sleep. But this time, it really is just sleep. She'd been trying to wake up since last Friday. Wasn't that the day Ali walked onto your ranch? Well, anyway, I think she's just tired out from trying to wake up, but how great can this be? We find Ali, and Becky is waking up at the same time!"

Everyone was thrilled. Walter called Brian Nelson to give him the news about Ali and Becky in the middle of the night. Brian didn't mind one bit. He was happy to get that kind of good news.

The following morning, Brian let his boss know about the developments of the previous evening, including the current location of the horse. Calls went out fast and furiously once again.

The news media was alerted by the Sheriff's Public Information Officer. Hartley Ranch was mobbed by print and TV reporters, as was the hospital. Brian Nelson called Deputy Ramirez in Little Rock to let him know.

Deputy Ramirez got in his four-wheel-drive patrol car and drove up the mountain to Carl Nixon's cabin. Carl was just saddling Max for another day of searching.

"You can stop searching for Buddy now," Deputy Ramirez told him. "He's okay, and he's on a ranch about seventy miles from here in Pinon Hills."

"Oh, thank goodness," Carl said. "Can I go see him?"

"I have a better idea. I'll take you there myself. I know my car will make it. I'm not sure your truck can get that far," Ramirez chuckled. Deputy Ramirez saw the changes in Carl Nixon right away. He wore a new pair of jeans, boots, a clean shirt, and a new cowboy hat. Ramirez looked around. He noticed the trash scattered about was missing. He saw trash bags stacked alongside the cabin and filling the bed of Carl's old truck. Carl's hair was clean and clipped, as was his beard. He didn't have to stand 10 feet away because of Carl's body odor. Did that horse make such a change in the old hermit?

The Deputy had two good reasons to make sure Carl Nixon saw the horse at the Hartley Ranch. It was necessary that Carl positively identify the horse as the one sold to him by the Hix brothers. The second reason was more personal. Ramirez knew Carl had spent every daylight hour over the past week or so looking for that horse and hoping he wouldn't find his remains. He knew Carl would want to see him personally and know he was in good hands.

Carl put Max in his corral, fed him some extra grain, and topped off his water. The two men climbed into the patrol car and made the trip to the Hartley Ranch. They arrived to find a mob of news media people clambering for specific details.

Detective Ramirez talked to Mike privately, away from the reporters, to explain the reason for his visit. After their conversation, they took Carl Nixon to the barn. When they got to Ali's stall, Deputy Ramirez asked Carl if Ali was the horse he bought from the two men.

"Can I go in the stall?" Carl asked.

"Sure, go ahead," Mike told him.

Carl slid the stall door open and slowly walked inside. "Hey, Buddy! How are you?" he asked Ali. Ali lifted his head, dropped it over Carl's shoulder, and nuzzled him. Carl reached out and scratched his withers. He turned his head and told Deputy Ramirez, "This is the horse I bought from those two guys for sure."

Carl spent a few minutes scratching Ali and looked him over. "He's lost some weight and needs a bath. Those wounds were probably from the she-lion that lives near my cabin. If the bear had gotten to him, I don't think he would have survived. He's lucky the cat didn't finish him off."

Carl patted Ali's shoulder affectionately before leaving the stall. "I'm one hundred percent sure this is my Buddy." He stood for several minutes just looking at Ali. His lip trembled a bit once or twice. "So this is what a two and a half million dollar stallion looks like?" he asked.

Mike nodded his head in the affirmative. "Yup, he's the one. My wife is in San Juan Capistrano with the family. Becky is doing much better. Looks like she's going to make it too."

Carl wiped his eyes quickly and looked away. "He's probably worth more than that!"

On the way back to Carl's cabin, Deputy Ramirez handed his business card to Carl. "If you ever need anything, please call me. I will get the name and phone number of the owners for you. I'm sure they would love to hear from you when this all settles down. I heard they were very grateful for the way you treated their horse."

In Orange County, Brian Nelson and Ron Bentley met in the Sheriff's office for the final update in the case of the Million Dollar horse. They briefed the Sheriff personally on the entire matter, from beginning to end, and gave him the location of the horse trailer and the horse. They listed all witnesses in the case for him in their case book. The Sheriff was pleased he could close the book on this one at last. All the missing pieces were in place, and the case now proceeded to the District Attorney's Office for prosecution.

Newspapers and TV stations across the country carried the news of Ali's discovery. Photos of him and Nan carrying the red, white, and blue banner for the Colorado Mavericks were on the front pages of the papers.

Becky woke up the next day. Mom and Dad filled her in on the travels of Prince Ali in bits and pieces, not too much at a time, over the next few days. Dr. Spencer moved her out of the ICU and into a regular hospital room on Thursday. Becky was scanned, x-rayed, poked and prodded, blood tested and examined by several specialists at the hospital. They found her to be healthy in general, no mental deficits presented themselves, and she was ready to be sent home four days later – with restrictions. Dr. Spencer was very clear with her parents and Becky about what she was allowed to do and not allowed to do. Unfortunately, riding a horse was on the No list. Becky was most upset about that particular restriction and told Dr. Spencer. She and Ali spent hours and hours getting ready for the Youth National Championships in July. It was now late March. She couldn't put off riding for long and still be able to compete.

Dr. Spencer said, "I'm sorry about the no riding restriction, but we do need to enforce that right now. I will see you in a month, and we can take new x-rays then. I will let you ride again when your body heals enough, but never, under any circumstances, are you to ride without a helmet!"

Becky reluctantly agreed to comply with the restrictions. She knew her Mom would enforce them anyway, so there was no arguing her way out of them. She promised Dr. Spencer she would follow his orders to the letter.

Becky had her cell phone back and called Brody at the Hartley ranch for daily updates on Ali. She knew Brody but hadn't spent much time with him in the past. They got to know each other very well, sharing information about Ali. Brody also told Becky about Maryann and how Maryann helped with Ali.

Becky called Todd in Colorado after she talked with Brody to give him the daily updates. They had been close friends for a long time, and Todd loved Ali almost as much as Becky did.

Ali had his own form of medical poking and prodding. Before Ginny left her ranch the night they confirmed his identity, she had a list as long as her arm for their vet to do. Ali was not a stray horse. He was a Million Dollar horse. She wanted him checked out thoroughly. She told Mike to have the vet pull x-rays on the tender back foot and the sore stifle for sure. She suggested he do blood tests to make sure Ali hadn't picked up something during his travels. She wanted to make sure he was getting the very best medical care. All the x-rays came back normal. So did the blood work, which the vet personally ran to the lab. He was fit as a fiddle but needed to heal some, gain weight, and get back in shape.

There was one other matter Walter Howard wanted to address. He spoke with his wife first and got her agreement. That was the matter of the one hundred thousand dollar reward for information to locate Ali. Their first thought was Carl Nixon, who had been so kind to Ali. Carl flat refused the money. He didn't need it or want it. "I never did get down to the Sheriff's station to report him anyway. I was going to, but Ali escaped. And I wouldn't take it if I had gotten down the mountain and reported him."

The Howards settled on someone else. Brody Hartley had taken care of Ali since he wandered onto the Hartley Ranch. They talked it over with Mike and Ginny. They set up a scholarship fund for his college education with the reward money. With what that fund would grow into in the next five years, Brody would be able to go to any college he wanted to.

Becky's release date came. Mom and Dad checked her out of the hospital and brought her home. Espie met her at the front door. She cried when she saw her. "I have your very favorites for dinner tonight," she told her. "You look like you lost some weight like your mother. We need to fatten you both up a little."

Becky stood in the open doorway to her room. "It's wonderful to be home again," she told Mom. After putting her things away, Becky walked out to the barn and stood in front of Ali's empty stall. She just stood there with tears running down her face. Caroline came up behind her and put her arms around her. "Mom, I miss him so much. When can I see him?"

"How about tomorrow? We will hook up the trailer and drive up to Ginny's place and bring him home."

The following morning Walter hooked up the horse trailer early. Caroline and Becky had breakfast with her dad and Espie and walked out to the driveway. "Is Aunt Ginny sure he's ready to come home?" Becky asked Mom.

"Absolutely. Now let's go get him!" They climbed into the truck for the drive. They pulled their rig onto the main driveway at the Hartley Ranch. Becky jumped out of the truck before her parents could open their doors. Becky saw Brody and Clyde walking toward the main barn and ran to catch up with them.

"Where is he?" she asked Brody. Brody showed her Ali's stall. Becky slid the door open and walked in, interrupting Ali's breakfast. Ali squealed. Becky squealed in return and threw her arms around his neck, hugging him for dear life. That's how Mom and Dad found them a few minutes later. Becky had both arms around Ali's neck, pressing her tear-stained cheeks into his silken coat. Ali's eyes were closed, and he had his neck turned to hold her close to him. Ali had her ponytail in his mouth.

www.ingramcontent.com/pod-product-compliance
Lightning Source LLC
Chambersburg PA
CBHW051636260626
47170CB00004B/1200